Chris Lane has lived and worked in Cumbria for fifty years. He founded two Lake District Mining Museums and has an in depth knowledge of Industrial History. For three years he moved his family to Bermuda to take up a teaching post. Recently he has worked on filming the mining heritage of the Lake District, above and below ground as a record for future generations and Television. He has a PhD. In Mineralogy and Physical Geography, having been employed as a consultant by The National Trust, The Lancaster University Archaeological Unit, Forest Enterprise, The National Park Authority and the Outward Bound Trust. He served as Show Director on The Grasmere Sports Committee for twenty years and as Chair of the Claife Parish Council. For many years Chris was an active member of both the Mountain and Mine Recue. During his lifetime he has amassed an extensive and important collection of local minerals. He and Liz, his wife, were married in Brathay Church, Ambleside, in 1969 and they have two daughters both living locally and six grandchildren.

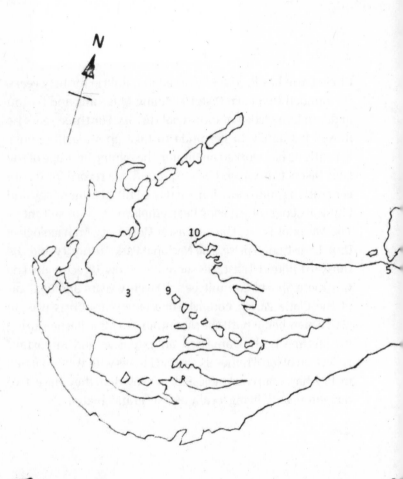

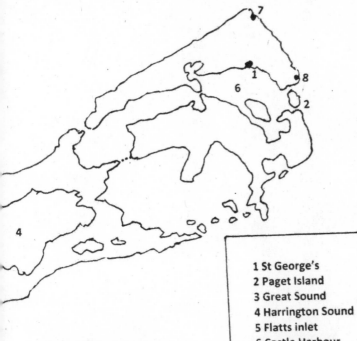

BERMUDA

1 St George's
2 Paget Island
3 Great Sound
4 Harrington Sound
5 Flatts inlet
6 Castle Harbour
7 Fort St Catherine
8 Gates' Fort
9 Pearl Island
10 Spanish Point

C.L.2021

JOHN
'MOSES'
RIGG

A sweeping eighteenth century tale of love, loss and betrayal from the Lake District to Bermuda and back.

Chris Lane

ISBN, paperback: 978-1-80227-181-2
ISBN, ebook: 978-1-80227-182-9

This book is typeset in Nueva Std

On the high fells of the Lake District there are several tracks, 'trods', named after an historical figure, 'Moses' of whom little else is known other than he was a smuggler.

In recent years a number of stashes of best quality 'wad' or Graphite have been discovered in remote Cumbrian valleys, hidden and never recovered by the person who stole it.

For Lizzie

CONTENTS

ACKNOWLEDGMENTS

Firstly my wife Liz for her encouragement, support and enthusiasm over fifty two years. Our daughters Hannah and Sophie who put up with the cold and wet on expeditions underground in ore mines across the north of England. The grandchildren who have accompanied me in recent years into the depths of Coniston Copper mine.

My companions investigating and exploring the many Lake District mines. In particular Roy Garner, David Briggs and Peter Barton. The members of the Shropshire Mining Club, Mike James, Mike Summerfield and the others who showed me the importance of industrial history. The Lakeland Mines and Quarries Trust for bringing the story of the Borrowdale wad mine to life.

And last but by no means least Jane Renouf for her hard work proof reading and correcting the manuscript.

INTRODUCTION

My name is John Rigg, I was born in High Wray which is part of Lancashire beyond the sands in seventeen thirty eight. My parents' home was Old Hall the biggest house among a small group of farms at the place where the road from Hawkshead to Ambleside meets Old Hall Lane. An important route along the shore of Windermere to the Claife ferry.

My father Isaac, was the land agent for Sir Richard le Fleming whose family held large estates in Furness and Westmorland. Coniston Copper Mine was also owned by the le Flemings' and my father was responsible for the ore shipments from the port of Greenodd. In seventeen forty two, while engaged in this task an accident occurred which took his life. My mother died soon after and at six years of age I was an orphan.

Shortly afterwards I was sent to Ambleside into the care of relatives before I went to live in Hawkshead to attend the Grammar school there.

The sudden early death of my father left many debts, to keep the house and estate at the age of fourteen, I joined a gang of smugglers stealing valuable wad from the mines near Keswick, my companions called me 'Moses'.

I will now relate the memoirs of my extraordinary life.

CHAPTER ONE

*T*he sharp, cold mountain air caused me to huddle into my Herdwick cloak, pulling it close around me. My pony, sturdy and willing carried me steadily up Far Easegill. Grasmere lay well behind, soon I would be moving off Greenup Edge and down into Stonethwaite.

I revisited the events of the past weeks but it was yesterday and Elicia that returned to banish all other thoughts. We loved each other and had since we first met. Yet I had lied and avoided being honest with her. Even worse I had abused her disgracefully.

The night was frosty and still. I eased myself into a sheltered hollow to rest while my pony nibbled softly at the wiry grass. It snuffled loudly, in a companionable and comforting way. I could sense the dark bulk of the Fells around me and just make out the violet velvet of High Raise, snow clad on my left. I was king of this secret and lonely mountain land. I, John 'Moses' Rigg, smuggler of 'wad', plumbago, the finest graphite in all of England. During In the year of grace 1762.

By ten of the clock, next day, on a fine February morning, I was crossing Stonethwaite Bridge. One of Daniel Bragg's lads answered my hail and led my pony off to the stables. Maggie Bragg herself came out to greet me. A fine woman, a typical daughter of a yeoman farmer hereabouts, sturdy and down to earth, comforting and dependable. Her ruddy face broke into a wide smile of welcome when she saw me.

"Why, John Rigg, 'tis a grand day to be on the trod. Get yourself in, Daniel will be along soon enough."

She ushered me into the low ceilinged, parlour-kitchen. It was filled with simple oak furniture and warm, musky, lingering scents. Dominant above all was the mutton stew that half-filled an iron pot suspended from a hook above the open fire. I sat down on the settle taking off my damp cloak and riding boots. Maggie bustled around, filling a large bowl from the iron pot. She handed me a wooden trencher full of fresh baked bread as an accompaniment. I wriggled my toes and leaned back into the settle. Now that the journey was over, I had begun to relax and drifted in a drowsy, half waking daze. The warm stew in my belly added to a sense of ease. I dozed quietly while the household sounds around me, blurred and faded.

The excited barking of several dogs woke me. The early afternoon sun streamed through the open shutters. I heard Daniel laugh at some little incident in the yard. Then he was in the doorway. His stolid, swarthy figure radiated strength and vitality. The latest in a long line of Statesmen farmers, his forebears had settled this corner of Westmorland back in the mists of time. He stood taller than most, his face strong yet kindly, dark brown eyes and curly hair.

"Ye are truly welcome John. I was in the intakes with gimmer lambs an did not rightly know ye were come."

He sat down next to me pulling off his clogs. Maggie bustled in and once more ladled stew from the black iron pot over the fire.

"Well man, tonight's the night!" he said.

"Aye, if all is well, we shall be several hundred pounds the richer by the morrow," I replied.

"We must take care not to be caught as the 'Act' means a whipping, hard labour or gone away, deported!"

"Indeed, we will be cautious, 'tis our last run even so. Parliament is too eager to ensure a safe supply of wad for the King."

In Keswick town, the sale of the stolen graphite was spoken of as the 'Black Market', it was a rich one indeed!

"The boys will be on the fell atop of mine by nine o' the clock to night."

"How many guards. Have you been able to find out?"

"None but t' mine steward and five others."

I pondered this information. The house occupied by the guards, stood upon the northern bank of the infant river Derwent, slightly to the north of Sour Milk Gill. It was a strong, low, three roomed building, designed with an eye to defence rather than comfort. With 'wad' fetching three guineas for the little a man could hide in his mouth; it was no wonder. A mouthful could be equal to wages for a full years work. I knew many of the mine lads who had, in the past, managed pretty well from the small scraps smuggled out in this way. As I saw it, any guardhouse constructed to defend something was not worth an assault. However, Daniel had convinced me that a sled full of burning wood and hay set alight in front of such a building would imprison anyone defending its contents for long enough.

Talk of the night to come slowly petered out, Daniel went off to settle his day's affairs on the steading. Left to myself my thoughts again turned towards Elicia and my untypical brutality to her ours had been a shy and pure love until yesterday. We had promised ourselves to each other after 'Charlie' was trounced in the 'Forty Five.' I had served with the County Militia as a drummer boy and the experience had helped me grow up fast. Though I had not lacked female companions wanting to warm my bed, I had remained constant to Elicia in my heart.

My feelings for her were different somehow. Lord, how I was changing, growing older maybe? I should be settling into my own steading, to bring up a brood and drift out the years. No one was more surprised than I to have survived the '45 rebellion unscathed. A deep feeling of gloom settled over me, had I destroyed our love? What sort of life could I now expect? Would I live to set things right between Elicia and me? To know her as my wife would be ample reward for all that I had hoped for. Elicia, my Elicia, she had always been. Not any more I thought grimly, my mad actions had seen to that! The previous day was dreamlike and unreal and I felt disconnected from what had occurred. Sitting with a foolish but sad smile upon my face, staring into the fire, I threw more peat into its bright mouth. Tiny sparks flared and scattered upward. Like my life, a brief yellow flame burned brightly and was gone. Melancholy enfolded me. Once again, thankfully, my thoughts slipped away in sleep.

CHAPTER TWO

*D*aniel and I set off from Stonethwaite at seven o'
the clock that evening. Leading our string of eight
pack ponies we moved at a steady walk, reaching
Seatoller by a quarter to eight with deep shadows of night
well upon us. The trod took us alongside the river Derwent,
keeping a sharp look out for any other travellers. Having met
no other soul, we reached the bridge, crossed the beck and
headed up to Seathwaite. Turning off we followed the river
around to the Borrowdale Yews.

By nine we were within pistol shot of the guard house
below the mine and the 'wad' washing shed beyond. I could
just make out the stepping stones in the ford. We pulled the
ponies back into the cover of the trees and waited. Our fellow
conspirators had seen us and within a few minutes a lantern
flashed briefly up on the side of the fell. Daniel answered with
our own covered lantern, followed by silence for perhaps
three minutes or so. The rattle of small stones and rustle of
dry bracken warned of the approach of the others, taking no
chances, we separated, with pistols cocked, to await events.

Shortly, two shadows appeared moving swiftly down the slope towards us in the gleam of a pale moon.

A soft whistle broke the stillness. Davey Dixon and Rob Benson moved stealthily into our clearing. Daniel and I rose to greet them.

"Grand night, lads" whispered Daniel. "Have ye got sledge and horse, with combustibles?"

"Nay, I had to yoke up the long horned ox, t' horse is fair knackered!" answered Rob in a breathless whisper.

"Ye daft bugger!" muttered Daniel under his breath, further invective failing him.

I was concerned. The ox would be of no use for what I had in mind and I had no desire to use the ponies, for we would need them later.

"Where's the sledge?" I asked.

"On the fell, back of the washing shed" replied Rob.

"Right then, it's up to us" I said. "We shall have to do the job, instead of the ponies".

We tethered the ponies and worked our way around to the sledge. It was piled high with combustible material, tied down with lengths of hempen rope. A barrel was perched insecurely on the top of it all.

"In God's name what's that?" I said.

"That's black powder", replied Davey proudly, "Ah brought it!"

"Ye darned mindless bugger!" Daniel muttered behind me.

For the second time this night, I silently agreed with him.

"Bring the sledge but leave the powder" I said, silencing Davey's objections by turning away to pick up the traces of the sledge.

We all set to with a will. The ground was rough but downhill so that the sledge moved easily on the short grass. Drawing near to the guardhouse, we glimpsed faint chinks of light and could hear murmured voices inside. The last yards were agonisingly slow, with the constant need to stop and listen. All remained peaceful as we finally reached the door. It offered the only point of entry and exit and raising a fire here would be most effective in keeping the occupants confined. The windows, having been built as narrow slits for both light and defence made any exit through them nigh on impossible. We quietly stacked as much material as possible against the iron clad, wooden door and using a lantern, set it afire.

Daniel and I went back to collect the ponies and lead them up the track to the lowest mine entrance. Rob and Davey climbed directly up the steep slope from the guardhouse. Looking back, I could see that our 'gift' was well alight. It would not be long before those inside realised that their door was on fire.

Reaching the clear space outside the entrance to the mine, we were greeted by Rob and Davey with the other four members of our band; who had already silenced the remaining guards, binding and gagging them The glow from the burning sledge now cast a bright light throughout the dale. Shouts and sounds from Seathwaite Farm meant that others had also been roused by the distant flames. I walked towards the ore bins, when suddenly the whole valley was lit by a bright yellow flash that was gone in an instant. It was followed by a roar and crash like thunder. The sound echoed and rolled around us. I turned, in time to see what remained of the guardhouse, falling back into the same flames that had launched it heavenwards. Embers of burning straw rained down around us, singeing our clothing.

"Christ in heaven, what was that?"

"The other powder" answered Davey.

"What other powder, man?"

"Second keg, on t' sledge."

Daniel sprang into life, gripping Davey by the throat.

"Have ye nowt in thy head?" "By all that's holy I should strike ye down now! You've made murderers of us all."

I shouldered my way between them.

"Forget that, we have to get what we came for"

Daniel struck Davey soundly at the side of the head, knocking him to his knees. He glared down at him for a moment, then turning on his heels, strode across to the ore bins.

We loaded the ponies with sixteen casks of best quality wad. Worth one hundred and thirty guineas gold, in value for each cask. Some would say that we had had a good night.

Each man took charge of a pack animal with its precious load and we headed up to the brow of Seatoller Common.

As the night proceeded, we passed down Brandreth and around the foot of Gable Crag. It was about then that we became aware of a party in pursuit, some way behind us. We urged the ponies on but even at a trot we could not hope to out distance a group of fast moving men on foot and to do so might risk an accidental slip down the steep slopes of the fell. Calling a halt, we all strained to catch any sound that might give some indication of the size of the following party.

How many times before had I lived through the possibility of failure in my mind? The life we led was precarious in many ways, not least the risk of capture and even death. The Parliamentary Act of 1752 had made the manner by in which I 'mined' the black wad a felony. It could bring the whole weight of His Majesty's Government, in the shape of the army, down on our necks.

"Moses!"

The hoarse whisper interrupted my thoughts.

"Moses!"

It was Tickle Blencarn, leading the rear pony in our string.

"What is it?" I asked in a low voice, several possibilities flashing through my mind.

"Summat up there!"

Tickle pointed to the barren slopes above and to our left.

I strained to hear the indistinct sounds made by men moving over the rocky mountainside. Yes, very slight but undeniable, a group of four or more were trying to work around our flank. By such means, they wished to delay our progress long enough for the main group behind to catch up. I felt sure that it must be possible to escape the trap being prepared for us, before it was sprung.

Without warning, musket fire was directed down towards us, a ball struck a large rock away to my left. I scrabbled further down the slope, away from the edge of the trod we had been following. We kept our heads and waited for the erratic, un-aimed fire to cease. After some few minutes the shooting died away and we could hear men moving off to our left.

Following a short lull it started up again, the best part of a thousand yards away. The pursuers were clearly unsure of our whereabouts, hoping for a lucky hit. I concentrated my mind to create a map of the surrounding fell tops.

"Daniel, do you think that we could turn about and follow Lingmell Beck? We can reach Wasdale Head by the other side of the crag".

"Ah don't know for sure John." He replied. "Ye must ask yourself if we have time enough before dawn".

"We have no choice. We can't stand and fight with the

ponies fully laden. I, for one, want to see this cargo safely home".

"There's nought to worry with the lads, fight or flee they'll follow thy lead," He reassured me.

"I don't doubt that, but this could lead to the gallows for us all." I warned him.

"Enough said, we should be on our way."

"By God! We'll be cursed if we don't try!"

The string of ponies was turned about. Tickle took the lead and we started off following the line of the fell around to the head of the valley. Painfully slowly and with great care, we crossed the beck and climbed towards Lingmell Crag. Every little stone dislodged, sounded to our straining ears like an avalanche, and each soft snort from the unsettled ponies was loud as thunder. The animals had been made more nervous by the noise of musket fire. Using the faint light of a dark lantern, I opened my timepiece.

"God's blood, it is nigh on seven, daylight will be with us within the hour".

"Don't worry yourself John, to get down just follow the gill to Hall Farm. We'll be in a fold. They canna spy us there." said Daniel.

He stood with his back to the lightening sky, gazing down towards Wasdale Head, exuding a stolid confidence, like a faithful hound. Daniel was indeed a very old and valued friend. We met during happy schooldays spent at Hawkshead

Grammar School. He was almost as dear to me as my Elicia and just the very thought of her aroused my guilt for what had so recently passed between us.

The looming bulk of Scafell Pikes deepened as the sky gained colour. The first rays caressed the highest fell tops, theatrical in their striking beauty. Now the hue and cry was up, a chance sighting by some solitary shepherd, able to pinpoint our whereabouts, all would be lost.

"We will have to scatter, dump the wad, leaving it to heaven or to hell," I said to no one on particular, although most heard me. With each of our companions concentrating on the rock strewn path they had no time to reply, or think even.

On starting down we followed a rocky gorge, carved out by the Beck in its headlong rush to join Wastwater far below. No one spoke. The mountains and gullies were still darkly shadowed. Keeping well below the brow of every ridge so our movement remained secret, the party made steady progress. Only the ravens witnessed our passage as they launched themselves from the crags in readiness for the dawning day.

I began to plan ahead, "Daniel, I wonder if our 'Dutch' friends will still be impatiently waiting for us and our load of wad. If not, we will have to cast about, looking for a deep and secret valley as a place for a stash".

A temporary hiding place could do for us, in an extremity. However, I need not have feared, fortune smiled, we reached

Hall Farm at eight o' the clock, without further incident. The sun was beginning to shine wanly on Wastwater. The looming bulk of fells behind us glowed bright and clear in the crystal hush of the morning. Even the sheep in the stone walled intakes had not yet risen, to nibble the close cropped sward.

Thankfully we clattered into the yard and coaxed our tired ponies into the many outbuildings. Not until the cargo was safely stowed and ponies settled, did I feel relaxed enough to take some ale and a bowl of coarse porridge. We had, by some miracle, eluded our pursuers thus far.

The lads lay around, each huddled in his heavy cloak. Exhaustion and strain from the night's work showed on every face, even in repose. I had found a cosy nook in the back kitchen, and was still there when Daniel stumped in, his clogs rapping on the slate flagged floor.

"There ye are John, good enough, all is away tight. I'm out to see the Dutchman."

It never ceased to surprise me that all foreigners, even Lancastrians, were 'Dutchmen', to Daniel, whether male or female, European, African or Chinese.

"Will you not stop man? Rest a while."

"Nay, don't bother yourself, the work needs doing, and the sooner the better."

"I'll come with you."

I made as to rise. Daniel's big rough hand came down to gently push me back onto the bench.

"Nay lad, thee's fair winded. With your brains here, there's nowt to worry on."

Had I only known then how this parting was to affect my life? Thanks be, that we cannot see our future, for if so, I would have thrown my arms around my dear friend and said many more meaningful things. Instead, I bade him farewell:

"Right Daniel, take care, I shall meet you on Lingmell bridge in three hours' time."

Daniel nodded, warmed me with one of his rare smiles and was gone.

I heard his clogs clattering in the cobbled yard as some of the lads shouted,

"Tek care - good luck".

It was in this simple way that Daniel Bragg, the finest, truest friend that I had ever known, walked out of my life.

CHAPTER THREE

*T*hirty minutes past twelve of the clock, found me standing on Lingmell Bridge, trying not to attract attention. Leaning on the moss covered parapet watching the busy stream, drops of water dancing like diamonds in the sunlight. Scafell Pike, with its scree covered slopes, filled my vision. It did not look possible to climb its bulk, yet even now that appearance was belied by the many groups of figures, descending the main trod over Lingmell. Ponies pulling sleds, pack ponies and laden humans, all with goods to carry to Wasdale Head, Ravensglass and beyond. Yet still there was no sign of those who had pursued us during the night. They must have lost our trail where we had veered away from the main trod.

Above me, high in the silent vault of heaven, a buzzard sailed in slow circles. I watched it until my neck ached, when suddenly a loud discharge echoed from the Fell to my left. Another ragged series of shots rang out as I peered intently at the brightly lit slopes, and again, faint puffs of smoke followed by the crackle of musket fire. Small specks of scarlet betrayed the progress of a line of soldiers moving rapidly across the flank of the fell. I was just able to perceive that they were in pursuit of something or someone. Yes! There! Some three hundred paces in front, a small figure dodged and weaved. *Dear God no!* I almost screamed out in my horror. *It was Daniel!*

I watched, mesmerised by the dreadful game being played out before me. Another volley rent the stillness. The tell-tale powder smoke, to be followed, as if from another direction, by the sound of the discharge. The leaping quarry stopped and hung for an instant, as if time itself had ceased, before falling prostrate. Too soon, the figure was surrounded by a mass of scarlet and I saw Daniel no more. I turned away with fierce frustrated anger. Cries of grief caught in my throat and threatened to choke me. I walked away as quickly as possible while trying not to run, making my way back to Hall Farm, I urgently needed to warn the rest of our men, who were sheltering there.

I stumbled into the house, still shaken by shock and grief. It was only a moment's work to relate to those who awaited me the drama that I had witnessed. All stood dumbstruck, hardly a movement broke the stillness as each man contemplated this shocking news. Somewhere on Greenhow, a lone sheep bleated, the haunting sound like a final lament.

My mind began to race as I struggled to throw off the images seared on my brain. Maggie Bragg burst into the kitchen, her usually rosy face, pale and frightened. One look at us told her everything. A soft cry formed in her throat and rose to a steady wail. Trying to comfort her was in vain. I most urgently needed to make plans for our immediate escape. I hustled the men outside to gather the wad from numerous hiding places. Each one of us toiled steadily, secreting wad in the gullies and gills that slashed the fell with ragged courses above and behind the farm.

This done we removed all trace of our stay, both inside the house and in the yard. It had been hectic, unhappy work. When finally finished, nigh on two or more hours had gone by since the death of Daniel. We gathered together in the big barn while Daniel's two boys kept watch outside. I have never been a good speech maker, though I felt the need to express in words, what it was that we all felt for our fallen companion.

"Well Lads, a black day for us all. Soon we must separate and make our own ways home. In that, I wish you good luck and Godspeed. Daniel Bragg will not be coming home. There's none here who can say that he did not spend some nights running the Black Wad. Even so, I for one, know that he was a good and a Christian man. He loved this high country as he loved Maggie, his dear lass. Wherever he is, I hope it is on the top of the fells, with the sun, the wind and freedom as his friends. May God rest his pure soul."

"Aye, amen to that," echoed around in the shadows.

Silently and with bowed heads the first of them began to leave for their own hearths. Maggie stood in the doorway of the house, red eyed and weeping. Each man took off his hat and with head bowed squeezed Maggie's hand, or touched her shoulder gently, before passing out into the daylight and over the bright green intakes, walled about in grey stone. No words were exchanged, indeed there was no need, for our sorrow was shared by us all.

I waited until Tickle Blencarn, the last to leave, was across the nearest intake and had vaulted the wall to disappear beyond, leaving me alone. Searching for Maggie, I discovered her slumped on the settle, beside the large old kitchen table.

"Maggie, I hate to leave you like this, but I need to be away with all haste."

"Daniel?"

I shook my head and turned away as she rocked back and forth weeping quietly. The two boys came in, young men now but still they threw themselves down to clasp their mother in a tight embrace, the three of them weeping openly.

"I will come back as soon as it is safe," I promised.

She nodded absently, as though I had already left her. As I gently stroked her hair, the sobs increased. Reluctantly, I went to the door, looked back at them briefly and stepped through into the sunlight.

The whole dale was softened by the approach of evening. Even now, longer shadows were starting to fill the gullies and hollows. I paused once more, to take in the majestic sweep of the landscape. After a moment's hesitation I turned my pony towards the stiff climb that awaited us up Lingmell.

Topping Scafell Pike and around onto Esk Hause, the rising moon filled the vale with velvet blackness. By midnight I was descending into Great Langdale, only eight miles more, to Ambleside and finally, Elicia. God knows what kind of reception awaited me.

The miles lay behind me in a blur of dozing, while the pony carried me home. Dawn had come, yet I hardly noticed. My exhausted mind and body refused to work anymore. It was with an intense feeling of relief that I reached Ambleside and saw the old low house that I knew so well. What sort of welcome might I reasonably expect? I had much to mend.

Reining in my tired pony, I dismounted and with my stiff joints easing, led him to the water trough at the corner of the front porch.

The door flew open violently and Elicia was framed against the dark space inside. I stepped towards her reaching out my hands. The greeting froze in my throat. Elicia had been crying and was much distressed.

"Run John, run, I…"

Her words were cut short by a scarlet clad arm that reached from behind, a hand clamped over her mouth, Elicia fell backwards into the house. *Soldiers!* I turned to run, crashing into the arms of three burly fellows who had come up, undetected, behind me. I struggled with a fierce determination, but briefly. The musket butt which struck me on the back of the head drove me to my knees.

I was hauled towards the house, semi-conscious and limp. Elicia was pushed, struggling, out of the doorway by a heavily whiskered Sergeant. An officer appeared behind him.

"John Rigg, otherwise known as Moses, smuggler of black wad, I arrest you in the King's name!"

CHAPTER FOUR

*O*f the dismal and painful journey to Carlisle gaol, I can recall little. I only remember the sharp pangs that pulled at my emotions as we left the shadow of the fells. Our party travelled northwards at a steady rate and I watched with despair as the familiar peaks sank out of view behind me.

My greatest regret was having been unable to set things right with Elicia. Would I ever again have a chance to say the things needed to mend our relationship? My whole being was weighed down with guilt at the way I had treated her.

As if to underline my utter reversal of fortune, the weather broke and continuous torrential rain soaked my body linen and skin. Tied to the saddle of my horse, there was little that I could do to protect myself, without even a hat to wear upon my head.

We arrived at the gates of the Citadel late the next night, in the never-ending rain. Feeling totally miserable, without food, drink or bedding I was thrown into a dark stone cell. For two days I saw none but the gaoler who delivered a weak but hot broth about mid noon each day. My damp clothes refused to dry completely and as the single narrow window, high up in one wall was without casement, I was never warm. Suffering attacks of fever, I did not care what fate awaited me. Alternating between waking and dreaming, inhabiting an unreal world of half seen shadows, *Elicia, Daniel, Soldiers!*

A further four days passed timelessly. On the sixth day I was transferred to Carlisle Castle to await nightfall, thence by open cart to the port of Whitehaven. It became evident that I was to be given no trial and I guessed that deportation was to be my punishment, but to where?

My escort handed me over to the Captain of the 'Sally', a three masted Brig belonging to the Carlisle Shipping Company. Hastily bundled below decks, my hands were chained at the wrist and secured on either side of a thick oak stanchion. Left to my own company, I fell into a deep sleep, overcome by the totality of exhaustion.

The sickening and unpleasant round of weeks that made up the journey that followed swirled through my dazed mind, yet I clung to flashes of sanity through mists of fever. Hours spent in the slime and stench of the small dark space in the very bowels of the ship gave me plenty of time to consider my fate, for I had lost everything of value in my life.

Chained in a close embrace with an oak pillar left little room to move. Squatting in my own filth, I grew stiff, aching unbearably in every joint. A few brief minutes were allowed on deck when a bucket of saltwater was sloshed over me, before I was speedily returned to darkness and silence. There was nothing, other than the slap of waves against the hull a few feet away, as the brig ploughed its way across the ocean. No man aboard the vessel would hold converse with me nor say where we were bound. I held my own counsel, determined not to break down and plead for mercy, although every particle of my being wished that I should.

Elicia, what was to become of her? I woke sweating and unsettled from frequent dreams in which I vainly pursued her distant figure. Losing all notion of the days and weeks, they passed by unobserved. The gradual increase in temperature did, however, suggest that we were travelling south, but wither east or west, I knew not.

So it was that the lowest and most miserable time in my life, passed slowly, moment by moment away, until eventually, the final day at sea dawned.

CHAPTER FIVE

he spice laden scent of land close by woke me, even in my stinking hell hole, it was so strong. The cool pre- heat of an early dawn refreshed me, as I was hustled up onto the deck for the last time. Blinking my eyes I was momentarily blinded in the tropical sunlight. The sea around the ship was a clear turquoise. Purple and dark blue showed through the sparkling surface. Away in front of us, a line of lazily rolling breakers, marked the presence of an underwater reef. Beyond, in the crisp, clear light lay a lush and golden island, displayed like a basket of beautiful fruits. I stared in wonder at this unreal vision, in extreme contrast to the miserable plight of my recent weeks.

Dark trees spread inland, fringed by tall palms along the shoreline. A rough shove from behind brought me back to reality. I stumbled awkwardly and fell against a hatchway, hitting the deck heavily. I lay there dazed and sore. A bucketful of cool sea water sluiced over me, followed by the foot of the bearer. He kicked me hard in the ribs and leered towards me.

"Welcome to the Bermuda's lad!"

Laughing evilly, he turned and strode away.

Bermuda! I knew little of the place. Pulling myself up, I hobbled over to the rail, leaning out with the fascination of a child, watching the ship edge her way through the breakers.

A trickle of blood ran down my face, I wiped it away with irritation, my wounds were of no consequence. The ship's crew scrambled to reduce sail, marking our arrival in a fine and sweeping natural harbour. We passed a small fort flying the Union flag to join the throng of shipping gathered in the bay. Clustered below a hill, a town spread down the slope ending at a stone built quay. All the roofs shone white, above walls painted in pastel colours. The 'Sally' docked at a small island, close by and opposite the town's main square. On a carved stone flanked by two ancient cannon a sign declared this as 'St George's'.

Two men came aboard to drag me ashore by my shackled wrists. Walking was made difficult by the iron shackles still attached to my ankles. I had been locked into them in Carlisle, they had not been removed since. My ankles were bloody and raw from their constant rubbing. The escorts passed me into the care of four Red Coats and a Sergeant. Without speaking they led me across a stone bridge into the main square. Few of the traders and others busy about their business took note of us. The air was full of the fragrance of cedar wood. Entering a maze of narrow alleyways, we headed towards the largest, most impressive of the buildings I could see in front. It was tall and square, simple yet with a crude elegance.

"What is that building?" I asked of my escort, between gasps, as I attempted to breathe and talk, while being moved briskly along.

"The State House," was the gruff reply from the sergeant.

The morning was already well advanced, the temperature had begun to rise steeply. Thankfully we entered the shade that the State House offered. The transition from the bright street left me struggling to clear my sight. A voice boomed out of the gloom and I strained to see the person it belonged to. A large desk stood in front of me, behind which a very corpulent individual sat on a tall stool.

"John Rigg, you are transported here to Bermuda. To remain so at the pleasure of His Majesty King George the Second for a minimum twenty five years"

I was shocked and surprised, I had been guessing all along that this was to be my fate but for *twenty five long years!* How terrible to hear it pronounced in such an unemotional, matter of fact, way.

"You will be marked as a felon and set to hard labour upon the King's works."

Marked as a felon', what did that mean in God's name?

I was soon to discover. Being branded on the left shoulder with the mark of a circle containing a crown at its centre. Sweet Jesus! The pain was bad but the stink of burning flesh even worse.

I tried to flinch away from the hot iron but was held firmly by the soldiers, being forced to bear it. A short cry escaped my lips. It was impossible to prevent. The shame and helplessness in the face of this indignity brought tears to my eyes. With no further discourse, I was manhandled once more and pushed out into the street. My shackles tripped me into falling clumsily down the steps. Although I was dazed and confused the escort hurried along, until the houses were left behind. We climbed a steep track along the cliffs. On the right-hand side, the whole extent of the bay was apparent. Many ships rode at anchor, with smaller craft darting 'to and fro' amongst them. Further out, a sea of almost impossible, brilliant blue washed the darkly wooded land with a line of sparkling wavelets. Richly coloured flowers grew along the roadside verges. I felt uplifted by the pure beauty of the scene, despite the tiredness and physical agony.

Our route descended in a series of twists and turns, until we were once more, almost at sea level. In front, amongst a group of palm trees, I could see the squat form of a stone-built blockhouse. A Union flag caught in the breeze, flying proudly from a pole on the roof. 'Gates Fort' announced the carved stone next to the entrance. Several soldiers and civilians lounged about in the shade. After a short exchange my escort handed me over to a Red Coat Captain, who led me through the gateway and into the fort. I found myself on a low gun platform, set on a rock shelf, some fifteen feet above the sea.

The internal dimensions were extremely small. I recognised it as the fort we had sailed past, when entering the harbour, earlier that morning.

Five twelve pounder cannon, on wooden carriages, covered the channel through the reef. The squat, solidly built tower rose twenty or so feet to a battlemented parapet lined with musket loops. More soldiers sat about in the shade, while a healthy-looking Negro was making repairs to the door into the tower.

The Captain ordered me to wait in the yard while he disappeared inside the tower. I could feel the heat of the sun drying my skin and re-burning the fresh brand on my shoulder. I felt dizzy and lightheaded. I had drunk no liquid since leaving the ship. As a consequence, I was now fiercely thirsty. After a short time, the Captain reappeared and beckoned to me from the doorway. I shuffled inside. The whole of the ground floor was one dark, cool room. A wooden stair rose from one corner to the fighting platform. I could hear footsteps and murmured conversation from above. The rafters creaked every time anyone on the roof moved. Around the walls stood a varied collection of furniture and from its fragrant scent, all appeared to be made from cedar wood. In the centre, behind a heavy and wide desk, was a strongly built man, a little above sixty years of age, with a large flowing wig, slightly awry, on his head. He wore the uniform of a Colonel in the King's army.

I waited while he looked me over in silence. It seemed that he liked what he saw for he grunted with satisfaction and waved the Captain from the room. Pulling out a white kerchief and raising the wig, he wiped his bald pate. I waited, expecting the worst.

"John Rigg, you are undoubtedly a felon but maybe you can be of use to me. Are you able read and write?"

"Yes sir, I was educated in the Classics, Geography the Sciences at Hawkshead Grammar School. Spelling, reading and writing were an everyday part of our schooling, as was Mathematics".

"Here! Write your name on this."

He pushed a sheet of paper and a pencil across the desk. I regarded the pencil with surprise, it was clearly marked as a product of the Keswick wad workshops. I wrote my name as well as was possible, with the weight of heavy manacles on my wrists. Passing the paper back across the desk, he studied it and bellowed with laughter. This startled me, did he consider my effort to be poor indeed? Continuing, his words were spoken with a distinct local burr.

"Well, John Rigg, this will do very well. Hard labour would be waste of such an obvious talent."

I was taken aback at this statement, *what was to happen now?*

"My name is Colonel Thomas Tucker, Military Commander of these islands."

He rose to face me, banging loudly on the desk with a paperweight.

"Sergeant!"

A soldier entered, and saluted.

"Take this man to the smithy and have his chains removed."

I was led outside once more, rather more gently this time. We crossed the yard to a small lean to containing a forge. The blacksmith lost no time in breaking open my bonds and freeing the limbs so long confined. Re-entering the tower, I stood before Colonel Tucker once more.

"We are lacking in educated men to undertake the administrative work that is required to keep our island running efficiently. Yellow Fever always takes those most difficult to replace. Will you give me your word, not to try to escape if I grant you a limited freedom, working in my employ?"

I could hardly believe my good fortune. There was a better future before me than any that I could have expected possible, only moments previously.

"Gladly, I give you my solemn undertaking as a Gentleman, to do nothing that would break this agreement".

"Excellent! Now let us see to your wounds, Sarah!"

A young Negro woman entered, bearing a bowl of warm water and towels. A chair was pulled forward, for me to sit on while she carefully bathed my bloody wrists and ankles. The sores stung but the water was soothing. I began to feel less like a wild beast caught in some freak show. When she had finished, as well she could, the Colonel came around the desk and clasped my hand.

"Welcome, John Rigg, if you serve me truly and diligently, I think, in time, we may become acquainted, even as friends". He poured a tankard of beer and pushed it towards me.

"Drink! Drink as much as you wish, you have a short journey to make on foot"

With that, he raised me from the chair and ushered me to the door. A soldier stepped forward to take my arm and he was instructed to deliver me to the Colonel's own house, with all speed.

The remainder of that day went by in a muddled blur of images. I hardly noticed the scenery that we passed, nor noted much once we arrived at our destination, such was my state of exhaustion. I was given food and another drink, while two Negro matrons bathed and shaved me, washing the accumulated grime from my battered body. They giggled and talked loudly in an unfamiliar version of English while they worked.

My tiredness overtook me and when led to a bedchamber, semi-conscious, I was quickly fast asleep. No dreams disturbed my repose. How long I had been thus, I knew not. I was woken by the sound of household activity downstairs.

I lay, slowly returning to reality, musing on the remarkable events of the previous day. The bed was a wide, canopied, four poster, set in the centre of a plainly whitewashed room. A couple of primitive seascapes adorned the walls, a large wardrobe and chest of drawers stood either side of the door. The wooden floor was covered in part, by a fine oriental rug. The shuttered window let in small shards of light, showing the day outside to be sunny and somewhat advanced. Upon investigation, I discovered in the chest, a set of clean, pressed linen, while in the wardrobe, several waistcoats and breeches were neatly folded on the shelves. Making a selection, I dressed, revelling in the touch of clean clothing against my skin.

Opening the shutters, a delightful view was revealed. Green lawns either side of a driveway, lined by an avenue of tall palm trees ended at a pair of iron gates, set in a high stone wall. Flowers of many colours grew in profusion. Stepping out of my room I found myself in a corridor with several doors leading off it, to left and right. A long oriental runner was laid on the cedar boards. Noises came from below and following the sounds led me to a landing, above a wide sweeping staircase. On reaching the bottom, I was greeted by a smiling Negro servant who indicated, with a wave of his hand, a doorway on the left. Moving ahead of him I entered a large room, lit by three tall glazed windows. A long table with a place set for one, stood in the centre.

Conducting me to a seat he left with a polite bow, reappearing moments later, carrying an assortment of silver tureens. Setting them down before me and lifting each lid, I exclaimed aloud at what was revealed therein. A wonderful assortment of fish, cold meats, cheese and fruits prettily arranged on each. A jug of ale placed at my elbow. Leaving me to savour this most memorable of repasts, in my own company, I attempted to do justice to the feast. Replete and contented, with little other than my sore limbs and shoulder to remind me of my situation, I went out to explore my prison.

And what a prison it was! A two storeyed house, green painted shutters at each window, white walls and roof, a porch in the centre of the façade completed the elegant and fashionable design. The whitewashed stone roof was 'crow stepped' making the whole structure look solid and strong. Strolling in the grounds, I marvelled at the variety of colourful flowers filling the air with such a rich scent. The birds too, were many coloured, blue, red, yellow; their calls provided a cheerful accompaniment to the buzz of a myriad insects.

The shade offered by the trees was a welcome relief in the intense heat of the sun. What appeared to be green lawns were in fact something else, dotted with purple flowers, not grass at all. This was a beautiful, magical place indeed, perhaps I might find happiness here? Hearing my name being called I returned to the house where Colonel Tucker stood on the porch, waiting for me.

"Good afternoon John, are you well rested?"

"Thank you, Sir, I am indeed".

"Then you may rest, recover from the journey for another week, take time to find your way around, learn our ways. Once done, I will set you to the tasks that await". Before I could answer, he had turned abruptly, retreating into the house.

The next seven days proved to be exciting and fascinating. The sights, smells and sounds of my new home were constantly changing. Seeing little of the Colonel, I took the opportunity to explore as much of the islands as possible. The main island is about twenty miles long yet only one or two across. The coast is broken into a series of excellent bays and harbours, particularly in the south east.

In all, more than forty islands and others too small to be called such, are scattered within the protection of encircling reefs. The local shipping is most distinctive, being sloops, with sails arranged in a triangular fashion, I was told when I enquired of a local man. Configured in this way, a boat could be sailed upwind, even in a gusty sea. He assured me that there was a great advantage in being this nimble, when faced with a larger, more powerful enemy at sea.

The coast and harbours were protected by a number of stone built forts, the largest of which was Fort St. Catherine. Occupying a headland, beyond St. George's, it faces and defends the one navigable channel through the reef. It is strong and well designed and I spent half a day investigating its defences and accommodation.

The week passed quickly, my physical wounds were healing. The shackle scars faded, but the emotional wounds around the loss of Elicia and Daniel proved more difficult to erase. So much so, even as the old John Rigg confidence returned, my heart remained an empty vessel, bleak and cold.

All in all, I had been very lucky, very lucky indeed. The servants, mainly Negro, had nothing but praise for Colonel Tucker. He was a kind, considerate, enlightened employer who did not countenance slavery in any form. His extensive estates were run as a co-operative. This attitude was unusual for most of the sugar plantations had been worked by slave labour, although sugar had been less successful in Bermuda than on others of the West Indies islands.

I was intrigued to discover that Colonel Tucker was a member of The Society of Friends, a Quaker, freeing any slave he acquired and adding them to his extended family. Consequently, the slaves became house servants, builders or trustworthy sailors, independent and free.

With the failure of sugar, the population turned to farming and onions were grown and exported in large numbers. Salt was produced for home use and export, on Turks Island, almost one thousand miles to the south. The soft limestone of the island can be cut with a handsaw when first dug, yet hardens when exposed to the air. It was then cut into blocks and carried as ballast, and traded as a building material to the Bahamas and West Indies. I learnt much during my exploration of the islands in the first week.

Following my change in fortune, I wrote a letter to Elicia begging her forgiveness for my wanton behaviour, which I have no heart to reveal as yet, being so filled with shame. The letter was dispatched by the next fast packet ship to leave for England.

CHAPTER
SIX

*O*n a clear sunny day in late August 1762, I was summoned to a meeting with the Colonel. He sat in the corner of his study, relaxed in a comfortable chair, with papers scattered on the small table next to him. He was smoking, a long clay pipe in one hand, and the other holding spectacles steady on the end of his nose. Putting the paper that he was reading, aside when I entered, he said:

"John, I hear that you have made good use of your time over the last few days"

He proceeded to amaze me, with a detailed report of my every move. He knew exactly who I had spoken to and what about and the places I had visited including how long I had stayed there. It was obvious that the Colonel had an extensive and effective way of knowing the business of all who served him.

"How have you come to regard us and our ways?"

"I have been mightily impressed with all that I have seen. Bermuda is truly a remarkable place," I said. "Tell me, what was your favourite, of things seen and done?"

"Where to begin?" I pondered. "Perhaps it is the natural richness and extensive sea trade that has been developed."

"Yes, indeed, and it is my job to defend it all. We are troubled greatly by pirates. I must ensure the fortifications are strong enough to repel attackers and protect what we have."

"I thought Fort St. Catherine well defended."

"It is strong but not strong enough, we need more. To that end I have arranged for a further shipload of convicts to be transported here in order to speed our progress."

I started at the mention of convicts, fearing I was to be included, returning to my original status as one of them. If this was the Colonel's intention…?

"I have resolved to have you become my Clerk of Works. It will be your task to set about the design and construction of new defences, of whatever kind may be appropriate."

God's wounds, I had not expected that outcome! I said; "I will do my utmost to achieve whatever it is you desire of me, although I am no architect, military or otherwise."

"Good that is settled, you can train as you learn. Now for a glass of wine to seal the agreement."

The Colonel reached down beside his chair pulling out a bottle and glasses I had not noticed earlier. He poured two full measures, handing one to me. We drank to the success of the future. Handing me a pile of papers and maps, with the exhortation to study them in detail, to form a plan with all speed, we parted.

Due to the vagaries of the weather and sea conditions the next three months were those when an attack by Frenchmen, Spaniards or Pirates was usually, more than likely.

I set to with vigour and enthusiasm. At last I had a task to stretch me and give me back my self-esteem. My resolve was to undertake a close examination of the places most likely to support a clandestine landing by an enemy force. I was cordially received wherever I went, the letters of commendation that I carried from the Colonel opened every door. By visiting all of the existing forts and batteries distributed around the coast, from St. George's to Southampton at the other end of the island, I was very quickly coming to realise that the first lines of defence ought to be where the surrounding reef was most easily penetrated. The many scattered islands offered good forward positions that, until now, were but lightly defended. It was to see this for myself that I crossed St. George's harbour to visit Paget Island where a rudimentary gun battery had been built some fifty years earlier. I had landed for barely two hours, before a fierce wind from the north and made my return trip across the harbour more perilous than any boatman was prepared to consider. Therefore, I needed to seek lodging for the coming night.

The small settlement that had grown up around the fort catered for the garrison, being served by several bawdy houses and Inns, none of which promised a night of peaceful repose. Upon enquiry, I was directed to follow a rough track beside the shore leading to a few scattered houses further out. Passing a dozen or so rather mean buildings with packs of dogs and semi-naked children playing in the yards, I did not stop. Determining to find better, I could see a neat, stone built house, with a well-tended garden, set back on rocks above the sea.

By this time, the storm had gained strength and stinging rain was being blown horizontally in my face in great gusts. To add to my discomfort, the light was fading, it would be quite dark very shortly. Crossing the little garden and knocking on the door resulted in it being opened only wide enough for a boy, of no more than eight years, to peer through the gap. He looked at me, his eyes wide with fear. Greeting him, I said; "Good day, I have been directed hence in the expectation that you can furnish me with a night's lodging?"

After regarding me for a few moments he did not reply and slammed the door shut, leaving me to consider returning whence I had come. I decided to try again and banged on the stout planks with rather more urgency than before. This time the door was opened by a woman, obviously of some mixed race descent, even so, a great beauty. She frowned and looked beyond me as though expecting others.

"Yes sir?"

"I am sorry to have caused you any distress. I am seeking a nights lodging, having been stranded by the storm."

"Well…?"

She seemed uncertain so I said; "I will willingly pay for my board if that is your concern?"

"How much?"

"Whatever you may deem to be fair for such an arrangement."

"Four pennies".

"Pardon?"

I thought this rather high for a night's rough accommodation.

"Four pennies, Four pennies, in advance!"

I searched my purse for the required coins which I placed in her outstretched hand, noticing the roughness of the palm.

"Come in Sir, take off your wet cloak".

I stepped inside, grateful to be out of the worsening weather. I was in a room, cosy with a good fire burning in the grate. A settle was pulled close on one side with a stool on the other. Something aromatic was cooking in a pot hung over the fire. The table was set for two, clearly a meal was in preparation. The woman took my cloak and hat, hanging them near to the fire, where they soon started to steam. She and the child stood looking at me expectantly.

"Let me introduce myself, my name is John Rigg".

"I am called Arabella, Arabella Tucker, this is Thomas, my son."

"Tucker? Coincidentally my patron and employer is a Tucker, Colonel Tucker."

"Well John Rigg, will you take supper with us? We were about to sit down to our meal when you knocked at the door."

"That would be most welcome indeed, it has been some time since I last ate."

I sat on the settle while Arabella busied herself, laying an extra place and serving a rich fish chowder with chunks of coarse bread. It was really good, warming me from head to toe.

Thomas did not speak but watched me intently, Arabella spoke little and the atmosphere around the table felt awkward. I caught her looking at me with curiosity whenever I glanced in her direction. She was a very handsome woman, clear deep brown eyes that held a depth of sadness. Her skin was the colour of burnished copper, it glowed in the firelight. I was strangely drawn to her.

We finished the meal and Arabella indicated that I return to the settle while she disappeared into the next room. Thomas cleared the table without a word, then he came to sit on the stool opposite.

"Thomas, what do you want to do when you are grown?"

He continued to search my face with serious eyes, whatever he may have replied remained unspoken. I made another attempt.

"What does your father do, is he out in this storm?"

"He is mute and has been so since he was born, we first thought him deaf but it must be some other malady!"

I had not noticed Arabella's return from the next room, she had appeared quietly behind me.

"He is my greatest joy and comfort, we can communicate, words from me and writing and hand gestures from him."

Thomas moved to sit on the floor in front of the fire while Arabella sat on the stool he had vacated. She remained looking into the fire, deep in thought. I chose not to interrupt her, giving me time to admire her profile against the fire's glow.

Perhaps ten minutes passed, I was beginning to doze off in the warm glow, Arabella suddenly spoke, bringing me back to the present.

"John Rigg, you are a gentleman I think. If you have no objection, I will acquaint you with the coincidence of my name being Tucker."

I woke then, fully alert, she was intriguing, I was keen to hear what she had to relate.

"I will begin by appraising you of the circumstances of my birth."

I waited expectantly not daring to speak less I dissuade her from her story.

"I was born to a servant woman working in the household of Colonel Tucker."

I took a deep breath in my surprise.

"The same who is your patron. She and the Colonel had in their youth been caring of each other in a way that eventually became a mutual love. The Colonel would have married my mother had it been considered to be socially acceptable. European Bermudan society was opposed to it. They continued their romance in secret. That is, until my mother was carrying me, her first child. It was not something that could be kept from the other servants in my father's house. So it was, he had this house built here, that she might live and give birth in peace."

All the while Arabella spoke softly, her head bowed, looking up towards Thomas, occasionally, to see if he to, was paying attention to the story she was relating.

"The Colonel and my mother stayed true to each other, he supported us in every way. Later he married a girl from the Americas. It was social convention forced him do so. His position would not allow that he remain unmarried while gaining further promotions. My mother died ten years after, of a broken heart. I was just fifteen years of age and very ignorant of the world and its ways, having been brought up here in relative isolation.

"The Colonel carried on supporting me and saw to my schooling by sending a tutor, who visited once a week, weather permitting. Three years later he arranged for me to wed another of his servants, Portuguese, older than I but kind and gentle, nevertheless. We were happy in some sort for twelve months, before he travelled to Turks Island to serve at the Colonel's salt works. He never came back, dying of Yellow

Fever shortly after he arrived. My dear Thomas was born six months later."

The child, tiring of the conversation had fallen asleep, head on his mother's lap. Arabella paused, absentmindedly stroking his curly head. I waited patiently, after sighing deeply she resumed.

"The Colonel had sired three children with his new wife. He found some happiness in them, the youngest, a boy, in particular. After my man died, I was engaged to act as Governess to the children, to live with my Thomas, under the same roof. Two years later, the Colonel had cause to travel south to Turks Island, in order to check on his business interests there. While he was absent, the whole of the Bermuda's, were ravaged by a severe outbreak of Yellow Fever. Every one of the Colonel's children and his wife were taken, I nursed them as best I could but to no avail, they all died within one week. On his return the Colonel banished me once more to this island, he could not bear to see us. We have lived here quietly these two years since."

"You have not seen him at all, how do you live?"

"True to his word he has continued to support us with a monthly allowance, we grow whatever else we need."

I was overcome, so much sadness, so much loss. I looked again at this beautiful woman and my heart filled with compassion. She had suffered too much to bear for one so young. I felt I was coming to know the Colonel better, his kindness went deeper than I had realised. Arabella sighed again and rising to her feet, laid Thomas in front of the fire. She looked down at me for a heartbeat and then, as though making up her mind said:

"Come Master Rigg, I will conduct you to your bed chamber."

I followed her into the next room where a solid looking four poster bed dominated the one or two smaller pieces of furniture ranged against the walls. The bed had been made up with clean linen. Seeing it, I was suddenly overcome with a great weariness. The comfort it offered brought an overwhelming desire to yawn, stretch and retire as soon as possible. I sat down on the edge of the bed, beginning to unbutton my shirt. It was an obvious hint to my hostess that I wished to retire. She hesitated, unsure how to react.

With some embarrassment, Arabella backed towards the doorway, hesitated again, wanting to leave. Finally, wishing me a good night, she closed the door quietly behind her and left. Without further delay I stripped off all that I was wearing and without caring, let it fall to the floor where it may. Climbing into the bed, after pondering her story for a little while I drifted into a deep, dreamless sleep.

Sunlight streaming through the shutters, slowly roused me. I could hear movement from beyond the door, obviously the household had risen already. I rose and on opening the shutters I looked out at a sea that was still in violent motion.

Yet the wind had abated, the sky was cloudless. Looking for my clothes, I discovered they had been taken, dried and returned, neatly folded, while I had slept. Dressing in the shafts of sunlight slanting through the window, I basked in that luxurious state somewhere between waking and sleeping.

Opening the chamber door, I entered the room that had appeared cosy and dark last night and I was struck by the now bright, airy space that greeted me. Arabella was busy at the fireside making oatcakes on a griddle. I noted a pile of rumpled bedding on the floor in front of the fire, of course, in my tired state the previous evening; I had not paused to consider whose bed I would occupy. Through the wide-open door, Thomas was at play in the heat of the early morning sun. Arabella nodded in my direction and returned to her tasks. Stepping outside I sat quietly watching Thomas for some time. This really was a most beautiful place, the builder had taken advantage of the flat rocks to raise the house above the sea giving it, an extensive view across St. George's Bay to the ocean beyond.

On hearing our names called from within, we returned to a room filled with the enticing smell of fresh oatcakes. Arabella had set our places at the table coming to sit down with us, she smiled. The change the smile brought to her face was arresting. Her eyes sparkled as I had not seen before and her beauty shone, I was utterly entranced. A flash of guilt

71

brought a vision of Elicia briefly to mind, but it quickly faded, Arabella asked:

"When do you leave?"

"As soon as it is safe to make the crossing."

"It will soon be so, the sea is calming as we speak," she said.

"As I have observed," I replied. Summoning up my courage, I continued: "Arabella, a strange request after so brief an acquaintance. Would you permit me to visit you on some future occasion?"

I barely had time to think of the boldness of my request. I expected her to refuse and waited, strangely excited, for the answer. After an exchange of glances with Thomas, she smiled again and looking down at her lap, demurely and in almost a whisper, she said:

"Yes John, we would both like that."

"Good! I will return before the next moon, I promise."

After collecting together all of my gear, I left them, standing side by side, in the doorway. They watched me, until I had rounded a bend in the track and passed out of sight. My thoughts were full of everything that had happened. The words spoken yesterday evening, were reviewed in every detail. I was curious to know more, to befriend them both. The deeply felt sorrow, her beauty and vulnerability, the mute child, had touched me. I wished to show my deep respect for all females and to prove that I was a gentleman at heart, despite my uncharacteristic treatment of Elicia.

CHAPTER SEVEN

I worked with frantic energy on the task that Colonel Tucker had set me. Whenever he was home it had become his habit to summon me to join him in his study of an evening. He listened with keen interest to my reports, while we enjoyed a convivial glass or two of imported wine. I did not speak of Arabella, although I had numerous opportunities to do so.

The Colonel was always interested in my stories of smuggling wad and of the lakes and fells of my homeland. He had not experienced winter snow and was fascinated by my descriptions. In his turn he related stories of his youth, travels to the Americas, of trade and sometimes, the loss of his family. Of the relationship with Arabella's mother and indeed of Arabella herself, he never spoke. There was a sadness in him that became most apparent after wine, during our evenings spent together.

The next few weeks brought the anticipated raid on the islands. Two Spanish men of war cruised outside the reef and in the course of one week they were able to sink or capture any boat or ship that ventured out of the harbour. Unable however to inflict any damage on the town of St. George's itself, they had sufficient range to reach Gates Fort where there was some limited damage. The soldiers manning the Fort's cannon replied with enthusiasm but little hope of a hit. Fort St. Catherine was better placed, with heavy ordinance and succeeded in driving the Spaniards further out to sea. They were finally beaten off by a combined fleet of Bermudian, Dutch, English and Privateer Ships.

I travelled over to Fort St. Catherine in order to watch from the safety of the upper casements but it was hardly a battle, rather a skirmish. The highly manoeuvrable Bermudan sloops were more than a match for the better armed but unwieldy galleons. The sloops were built as "Privateers," licenced by the English crown and able to attack any enemy vessel. This, I thought, was very near to piracy though it did bring a great deal of extra wealth into the islands. It was surprising to discover that Colonel Tucker had built and fitted out two Privateers of his own.

The extent of the Colonel's interests constantly amazed me. The raid did motivate me to greater effort in drawing up the plans for batteries and forts, better sited to defend the main towns and harbours. I needed the promised convict labour to arrive so that work could be commenced with all haste.

While waiting, I resolved to pay another visit to Arabella. The opportunity arose at the start of the following week.

I set out across the harbour, excited and cautious in equal measure. Would she welcome my visit, would she even still be there?

Upon landing, I made my way along the familiar track, until rounding the bend, the neat little house came into view, looking as I had remembered. It seemed as a dream in my memory, making me question whether or not it had really existed. But there it truly was, the door wide open with a small figure playing outside the gate. Looking up, Thomas saw me, hesitating for a moment, unsure whether to greet me or to go indoors to let his mother know I was coming. He chose the latter course of action and disappeared into the house. Moments later Arabella appeared on the threshold and wiping her hands on her apron she gave an embarrassed little wave. As I reached the gate Thomas appeared at her side and she greeted me:

"Master John Rigg, I thought perhaps, never to see you here again?"

"I promised you that I would return, here I am, as you can plainly see."

She smiled, "You are no ghost out in the morning sun, that's for sure."

We stood looking at each other, the silence between us became awkward so I looked down and around at the little vegetable plot. It was Arabella who broke the spell, she turned and pushed Thomas before her into the house.

Following her inside, the room was much as I remembered, paper and pen were laid out on the table. A fire burned in the grate, despite the increasing warmth of the day. Glancing at the paper I saw that a writing exercise had been completed. Arabella had written out some lines, Thomas had copied them in a clear round hand. Arabella noticed me looking.

"He is an intelligent boy, very accomplished in all things but speech."

"And his mother is a talented tutor." I said admiring the fine penmanship on the pages.

"He is an eager student, always ready to learn, I sometimes wonder if he might be better off in a school among his peers. The lack of speech will make him a target, bullies will hurt him and I cannot, will not, countenance that."

"Perhaps you will permit me to undertake some activities with him, does he like to go fishing?"

Thomas looked up from where he was sat at the table, nodding furiously. His mother smiled and said; "There is your confirmation."

"Wait while I return to the fort, it will take only a matter of minutes for me to obtain the equipment needed for a fishing expedition."

Thomas was dancing around excitedly, clapping his hands.

Whilst walking to the fort I began to question my motives. Was my attraction to this woman making me untrue to

Elicia? She and I had first met twenty years before, in the December of 1742, I an orphan child of six years, had been sent to celebrate Christmas at her father's house, a distant relative of my mother's. Elicia Salkeld was then three years my junior. We had begun a friendship that had never faltered with the passing years. Captivating me with her pretty ways, quick mind and charming smile, inevitably she stole my heart. Kisses and a childish promise of betrothal we had exchanged, nothing more. I owed it to Elicia to resist Arabella's charms. The thought that I had behaved so abominably towards her and now was tempted to turn to Arabella was disgusting.. A wave of self-loathing overwhelmed me for the remainder of that afternoon.

Within half of the hour, I had returned having acquired line, hooks and bait from a helpful fisherman. Arabella admonished Thomas that he be careful, to follow my instructions. Taking his hand, we climbed the rocks behind the house to a place where they overhang a deeper part of the ocean. I showed Thomas how to bait a hook, also how to cast a line to the most promising spot. He entered into the sport with great enthusiasm, frowning with disappointment when our bait was taken by the little, yellow and black striped Sergeant fish or the larger, brightly coloured Parrot fish.

After around two hours had passed most pleasantly, Thomas leapt up as the line uncoiled violently, he had caught something big! With some difficulty, I managed to grab the line and halt the rapid unwinding. A sharp jerk driving the hook home while wrestling with the monster strained every sinew. Thomas moved over to stand beside me, helping in the struggle to haul up onto the rocks, what proved to be a small shark. The thrashing and snapping caused us both to step nimbly back out of danger. Keeping a tight grip of the line I shouted Thomas to find the biggest rock that he could carry to bring to me. He quickly returned, to my great relief, with two rocks and we both set to with a will, beating the shark until it thrashed about no more.

We bore home the prize, with great pride. When Arabella saw us, she ran out to help carry it into the house to lay on the table. It was nearly four feet long from snout to tail, with skin as rough as sandpaper. Arabella's eyes shone with joy, smiling broadly.

"Oh John, what a splendid catch, this will last us for many days, you are both so clever." She hugged Thomas to her and swung him around. "I will get knives and bowls right away." I could hear her humming as she went about her work, gutting and filleting. The fish was soon cut up into steaks and salted.

Arabella placed the liver into a pot which she hung over the fire. Thomas and I stood at the table, watching her work, every now and again flashing a happy smile in our direction. When all was done, Arabella hugged us both, then slightly embarrassed, stepped back, looking into my eyes. Without warning, she leaned forward and kissed me on the cheek, I went to respond but she turned shyly, avoiding my mouth. I remained looking at her as she moved away, turning her head to smile over her shoulder. I was strangely elated; the kiss had been unexpected though not unwelcome. I had given a great deal of thought to Arabella and Thomas over the past weeks. The idea of a more intimate relationship caused my heart to beat faster. Such a fine, beautiful, intelligent woman did not deserve what fate had dealt her. Could I help her and lay the ghost of Elicia that stood between us, could we remain as acquaintances, nothing more?

The hour was getting late, the boatman arrived in anticipation of my return Taking my leave, Arabella touched my hands lightly as we parted, not offering another kiss. Thomas hugged my legs; it was with some difficulty and not a little laughter, I managed to extricate myself setting off down the track to the harbour, with one last wave, rounding the bend to pass out of sight.

CHAPTER EIGHT

*T*he following week pirates attacked the unmanned redoubt on a small island at the entrance to Flatts Inlet. They tipped the three, ancient cannon into the sea and advanced on the undefended settlement situated on the banks of the narrow channel leading into Harrington Sound. A serious amount of damage was done to several buildings, a great deal of property and valuables stolen. Thankfully there was no loss of life, the residents, having had some warning by the initial attack on the redoubt had scattered, to hide in the many local caves.

I visited Paget Island four times more, managing to spend many happy hours in company with Arabella. We talked, she of her past and I of mine, omitting the parts that shamed me regarding Elicia.

We became close, a deep understanding, respect and regard developed between us.

The forts at Pembroke, Southampton and Devonshire all required urgent attention. The moats and ditches were cleared and deepened, while Charles Fort and Kings Castle had the garrisons doubled. All of this kept me fully occupied for almost two months. Having thrown myself into my task in the previous days, it was Arabella who had filled my night-time thoughts and dreams. I still cared deeply for Elicia, yet found it increasingly difficult to recall the exact line of her face. Guilty memories often overcame me, I tried to persuade myself to cease visiting Arabella. My weakness revolted me yet I was bewitched and unable to resist.

Women there were a-plenty on the islands, three to every man or so I had heard tell. Why then was I so taken with this widow, living in exile with her mute son? Her voice, fine looks and natural grace, it was these that stole my affection and bade me thirst for more. I could not help my heart. So it proved, when I found myself crossing to Paget, eager to see Arabella once more. Excusing the action to my conscience, telling myself that Elicia had not answered my letter nor I suspected, had forgiven me and yet, I knew for certain that she could not have received it or been able to reply already. What poor fools we are to knowingly convince ourselves of something we wish to believe, yet know not if it is the truth.

I hurried past the fort and along the now familiar track in the pale wash of dawn, pausing to compose myself before entering the neat little garden. The house was quiet, all the windows were close shuttered. It was early but I had expected, wanted, to see them at the door. Had they gone? I became irrational in my disappointment. Hastening up to the plain wood door, I tried the handle, it was bolted. In anger and frustration, I kicked the stout boards. Suddenly the bolts were withdrawn. The door opened a crack to reveal Arabella's pale face, her eyes wide with concern.

"John !?"

"Arabella, I thought..was afraid…oh Arabella!"

"John, John."

She opened the door, her light nightshift showing she was fresh from her bed. Stepping towards me she held my face in her cool hands. She searched my eyes for a moment. Without another word she drew my lips to hers, in a brief brush of a kiss. Leaning back, she regarded me with such a serious expression, I feared that I was about to be scolded for my uncivil arrival. The silence between us was full of unuttered thoughts and desires. In a moment, she had reached out her hand to hold mine, drawing me gently into the house.

After no more than a single heartbeat, with one glance towards Thomas, asleep by the fire,

she led me through to a familiar room, her bed chamber. I stood on the threshold, it was as I remembered from my first visit, which now seemed so long ago. The covers were in disarray from where Arabella had suddenly risen to answer the noise at her door. I remained, paralysed, struggling to catch the breath locked in my throat. Leading me, unresisting, trancelike, to the bed she began to slowly strip off my garments. Her lips fluttered over each piece of flesh as it was revealed.

Finally, I was naked with Arabella running her hands over my body, lightly tracing the brand on my shoulder. Kneeling, her tongue flicked over, around the tip of my erection. The trance that until now had held me captive, fell away and I responded to her touch. Reaching down I grasped the linen of her shift, pulling it up over her head in one swift movement. My breath quickened at the sight of her body, unclothed for the first time. Her skin glowed in the dim light of the still shuttered room. I raised her, holding her close, delighting in the warm, and soft touch of skin on skin. Her velvet cheek snuggled the hair on my chest. A great sigh of contentment escaped my lips.

Sunlight caressed the shutters, piercing the room with stabbing shafts of gold, each one alive with a myriad dancing dust motes. She moved to sit on the bed lying back, parted her thighs, unfolding the black curls between. I knelt over her sucking and nibbling at the dark nipples. My tongue traced her navel, on down the curve of her stomach to the delights below. Gentle probing my fingers found the entrance between her legs, silk soft lips. I entered her slowly and gently, revelling in the warm, wet closeness. Arabella moaned, arching her back, drawing me in deeper. I lay unmoving, tightly embedded in her body. Then, drawing back and returning in a rhythmic motion, soon becoming more frantic. We abandoned ourselves to the thrashing urgency of lust. My seed erupted, the subsequent wild convolutions racked us both. Our individuality gone, utterly lost in the moment, we lay together, pearls of sweat glistening on our bodies.

How long we remained thus, I know not but eventually consciousness returned and I became aware once more of the room around us. Arabella lay next to me bathed in bright strips of light; her dark hair spread wildly across the bolster. My whole being ached with the intensity of love. I lay on my side, the better to admire every curve and line of her glorious body. The lashes, long, lustrous, lying on her golden cheek, eyes shut in repose.

Rising, I rolled out of bed to throw back the shutters, revealing the amazingly blue sea, where sparkling waves broke languorously on a pure white, coral sand beach.

Returning to Arabella, I caressed her eyelids, murmuring, "I love you".

She stirred, lifting my hand to her lips, "I love you too, John, with all my heart!"

Thomas was barely stirring when we had dressed and returned to the next room. Following my previous visit, I had asked Joseph, the carpenter on Colonel Tucker's estate, to make a model schooner, for me to present to Thomas. It was fully rigged with canvas sails. Joseph had lavished so much care on the detail, it was as grand a little craft as any I had seen.

Thomas yawned and stretched, sitting up in the tangle of his rough bedding. I placed my present into his lap. He gave a squeal of delight, jumping to his feet, waving the boat for his mother to see. Arabella glanced at me, smiling warmly. Taking the little craft from Thomas, she admired its lines. I was pleased that my gift had been so well received. Thomas came to hug me, he was joined by Arabella, we all three held each other, secure in a shared affection.

Over breakfast, I decided to open my heart to speak, the so far unspoken thoughts that had filled my mind every day and night since my last visit. Memories of Elicia that I had attempted to submerge and blot out now came to upbraid me. The guilt that I still carried made me hesitate as I struggled to compromise the two things pulling me apart.

Taking her hand, I said: "I have not yet spoken about us to the Colonel, but I must. Arabella, could we be wed, would you wish to marry me?"

She pulled herself free saying:

"John, do you know what you ask? It will ruin you. My father will not allow it. He will cast you from him as he did me!"

Fear, also anger, flashed in her eyes, she paced about the room, much agitated.

"Don't be afraid, I will bide my time and choose the right moment with care."

"John, I wish with all my heart to spend the rest of my life with you, but the Colonel…"

"Shush now my love I whispered. Let us enjoy our short day together, we can talk of this further, once we have had more time to think. For the present it is enough to know that my love for you is requited".

Elicia still held a keen presence in my heart, yet distance made her more of a life lost in the distant past, somehow never to be recovered.

Thomas looked from one to the other, searching our faces, unsure of what we really held in our hearts. To reassure him and change the sombre mode, I said; "Come Thomas, let us take this fine craft to the harbour, we will find out how seaworthy it is."

CHAPTER
NINE

*O*ver the following months, I sought for an opportunity to talk to the Colonel about Arabella, to share my feelings for her. That chance came, one April evening, in the year of our Lord 1764. The day had been fine and warm. I had spent three days attending to the Colonel's business in Smiths Parish, riding home along the coast, taking ferries from one island to another. The farmers were tending their fields and the labourers sang as they worked in the crisp clear light. Houses clung to the hills, in scattered little blocks of white and viewed from a distance they looked like a flock of sheep on the Westmorland fells, raising brief pangs of home sickness that quickly passed when observing the boundless beauty of Bermudian scenery.

The bays and inlets sparkled with little wavelets on a quiet sea. I felt cleaner, more refreshed and happier than I had for the past year. Optimism was the cause of this burst of euphoria. There did seem to be more to the future than I had thought possible before.

I could not help but recall the angry words exchanged with Elicia at our last meeting. The image of her stood in front of me, hands on hips, her beautiful blue-grey eyes sparkling in the sunlight reflected from the yard outside.

"Why can you not stay here with me, what is so important, more important than me?" she had demanded.

Looking down at my feet, I shook my head, yet did not answer her.

"Come John, tell me this!"

"I cannot, my sweet, it is better that you do not know," I said.

"Huh, I know everything about you, there are *no* secrets between us."

"But there are, this is one that must remain so," I replied.

"Is it that you no longer love me?" she asked, the sarcasm clear in her voice.

I reached for her hand, only to find it snatched away.

"No my dearest, I have not lost my love for you."

She raised a hand to brush away stray tresses of golden hair, fallen across her pale face.

"What is it that you do in such secret John am I not worthy of your trust?"

Fierce eyes bored into mine, her eyebrows raised in query. I dared not tell her that I was to smuggle wad the next night.

But time and circumstances had moved forward since that fateful day and Arabella on the other hand, was here now and I did most truly love her. My heart was no longer the desperate, empty husk that it had become. The speed with which Arabella and Thomas had captured my heart was scarcely believable. The liaison with this woman and her unspeaking child was everything to me. I desperately needed Arabella to fill the void created by the break with Elicia. To share, to love, to live life to the full together. Hence, on my return to Colonel Tucker's house, my mind was set, ready to take issue with a future, if any, that Arabella Tucker and John Rigg might aspire to.

After a hearty dinner of fresh crawfish, the Colonel invited me to join him on the veranda. We sat at ease, facing the sea, drinking a pot of the locally brewed, sweet, heavy ale, discussing business, the weather and politics. The Colonel had a mind to build another Privateer to send against the increasing number of enemy shipping prowling Bermudan waters.

I enquired of him, what made a man a Privateer? He told me:

"Your true Privateer, is a unique creature half man and half shark. He is quick to take and slow to forget, being independent of both thought and honour, he rides the waves with a belly full of gunpowder. Such a man is to be admired both as a seaman and as a devilish rascal."

I was nonplussed, they were licenced pirates, nothing more and nothing less.

The Colonel continued; "Commissioning privateers to raid enemy shipping is good for profit, John, surely you can see the advantage in that?"

The light softened, fading into night and the lanterns were lit as we both became mellower in our cups. I encouraged the Colonel's conversation, turning to memories of lost family and lost loves.

"Sometimes John, I wonder what all of this is for, I have no heir to inherit my fortune and estate. Perhaps one day," he pondered.

The silence was warm and comfortable. Here was the chance I had been waiting for.

"Do you have no relations at all, sir?"

"I have relations. There are many who bear the Tucker name, but none I should wish as heir. The Tucker's were among the first to make a home on these islands in 1609. The ship carrying supplies to the English settlement in Jamestown was shipwrecked here and my ancestors chose to stay. They have prospered since."

"I have heard tell there is a daughter from a time before your marriage?"

He regarded me thoughtfully for a moment, sank lower into his chair and said, in no more than a whisper; "Yes…yes…"

"Do you not know her, see her?"

"No…" He paused, melancholy in his voice. "No, I have not seen her for these six years."

"But I do not understand," I ventured.

"Pain, too great a pain," he said with anguish. "Once it was easier not to see her, now it is impossible to bridge the distance between us."

I sat up and leaned toward him, sunken in his chair, looking somehow much older. His face was turned from the lantern, in shadow. I perceived tears glistening in his eyes.

"She has a child, you know, a boy. I send them money for support but do not have any direct contact. Once, three years ago, I went to the place where she is living. Alas, I lacked the courage to go to the door. Me thought I spied the boy in the garden, yet the fifty paces from whence I stood, might as well have been fifty miles. I could go no closer, having never dared, nor found the determination to return."

"She is beautiful, intelligent, as gentle a woman as any I have known. As for the boy he is named after you," I told him.

"What? I know the boy has my name. How do you come to know this of him?" he asked.

"Eighteen months ago, do you remember the night when a storm stranded me on Paget Island?"

"Paget Island? I do but you told me naught of this other."

"Indeed, I did not. Arabella begged me not to speak of her, although she had a thirst for knowledge of you."

"Tell me John, what of the boy, is he a good lad, does he speak of me?" he asked with genuine curiosity.

"He is a good and handsome boy, but he does not speak of you."

Sadness and disappointment settled on the colonel as he dropped back in his chair.

"Oh. He remains mute, after all this time?"

93

"Yes, but he is a happy child, serious, sharp in his wits," I reassured him.

"How can you say so, after such a brief meeting?"

"I have come to know him and his mother well, after many more meetings," I admitted.

"Many more meetings?"

"Yes, indeed, I have revisited many times, since the storm drove me to her door, seeking shelter."

"Come John, I must insist, you acquaint me in full."

My secret was out. It was time to reveal my secret love affair, thus it was the middle hour of the night, before I ended my story and had answered the Colonel's many questions. He was sat very still, looking out into the night, where a pale moon reflected on the sea like a silver ribbon, reaching to where we sat.

"Are you displeased with me sir?" I asked.

"Not in any way that may be regarded as wrong. In some regards I am grateful to have gained so much news of my daughter and grandson. Do you carry any feelings for Arabella?"

Relieved to have been asked the question, I poured all the pent-up emotion into my answer.

"Oh yes sir, most sincerely!"

"Then, much as it pains me, I must forbid you to have any further contact with her."

I sprang to my feet, my mind caught in a desperate cloud

of nervous dread at his words. A physical stabbing pain caused me to gasp for air, I reached for the chair back to steady the whirling nausea threatening to overcome me.

"No! Surely not, you cannot mean this, in all faith."

"But I do John, I am completely unable to countenance any courtship you may wish to pursue with my daughter."

"Why sir, why for God's sake!"

"John, I need hardly remind you of the circumstances that brought you to these shores," he said sternly.

"I am not…," I began.

"Nor the relationship that has formed our acquaintance, informal or not."

"Sir, I beg you…"

"Allow me finish Sir! I hold you in the highest regard, as a gentleman, a partner and most importantly, as a friend," he intoned.

I sat down again and sank into myself. Misery, utter and unbelievable misery swamped anything further that I could think or say.

"Over the past year, you have become important to me. However, that said, for many more years, you will continue to be a felon in the eyes of the law. I am your patron it is true, but I am also your bailsman. Ask yourself, how a relationship with a daughter of mine would be viewed by the King's Bench in London?" he demanded of me.

"Will they ever know, does it matter?" I muttered.

"Yes! It does matter. I am wealthy and influential; I hold a high office from the Crown. The Tuckers are a much-respected family; descended from the very first who settled this place one hundred and fifty years ago. Yet, I also have enemies, those who are jealous of me. They would delight in taking advantage of anything that might cause me harm."

I answered petulantly,

"Is it you frown upon my relationship with Arabella, or just the trouble that it will create for *you*?"

"God knows John, both you and Arabella deserve better. She is most dear to me; I cannot wish for more than to see her happy. You and she could be united perhaps, but not here, not now."

I did not answer, a mood of deep, dark despair, filled me with gloom.

"I must ask you to respect my wishes in this. The hour is late, I am most fatigued. We shall sleep on it and talk further, come morning.

Retiring to my bed, sleep eluded me. Once again, hopes, plans, love, all were lost in a river of sadness. I was angry for my circumstances, at the mercy of every ill wind, quite unable to control my destiny. For the first time in many years, I sought comfort in prayer.

CHAPTER
TEN

*T*he following morning, the Colonel did not take his breakfast with me, as was his custom. Upon enquiry, I discovered that he had breakfasted privately in his bedchamber, with strict instructions that he not be disturbed.

I drifted around the house, unable to settle or concentrate on anything other than the Colonel, Arabella or Thomas. Was I now to be expelled from this house and returned to the life of a convict, bound to years of hard labour? I made a nuisance of myself with the servants, who, tiring of me under their feet, chased me from the kitchens. I walked down through the gardens to the shore to sit on the rocks by the aquamarine sea. Should I make a break for freedom and run away? It was not worth the time wasted thinking of it, the islands were so small, I would soon be captured and then what treatment could I expect?

With the heat of the sun beating on my bare head, I moved to sit in the shade of a small grove of coconut palms and was lost in reverie. Eventually, I calmed my fears, resolving to accept whatever the future might be. I was called back to the house by a young negro house boy.

"Master John, the Colonel wishes to speak with you."

Jumping up, I ran all the way back to the house. So eager was I to learn my fate the boy could not keep up, trailing far behind. On the steps, pausing to compose myself and tidy my collar, the boy caught up, flustered and sweating. He gave me a look of astonishment and entered the house ahead of me.

The Colonel was in his large, airy study on the first floor. The shutters were closed to keep out the heat, and in the semidarkness, I did not first see him.

"Come in Master Rigg and sit yourself down."

It was a more hopeful greeting than any I had imagined earlier, although more formal than I had expected. I saw him then, sat at a bureau set against one wall. Picking up a handful of papers, he swung around to face me. I held my breath and waited, my mind in turmoil. He looked old and tired, more so than I had noticed before. My heart went out to him then, I regretted my resentful thoughts; this kind, honest man, filled with his own personal sorrow.

"John, I have given the matter between us, a great deal of thought. This is what I have decided to do, in such difficult circumstances."

I opened my mouth to speak, he held up his hand to stop me, so I settled back into my chair.

"I intend to ask Arabella and Thomas to come to this my house, to live with me for the rest of my days. Do you think she will find that to be agreeable?"

My heart leapt in my chest, I thought it would burst out, his words were not at all what I had expected!

"Yes Colonel, I am certain that nothing will be closer to her most earnest desire."

"I believe, with all of you in my house, under my protection, there will be less of a risk for any of us. I would hope to gain some little joy in my later years, from the company of my grandson, who, God willing, may one day succeed me in my various business endeavours."

I stood up, unable to speak being full of gratitude that my kind patron had so selflessly released within my breast. I went to him and clasped his hand warmly in both of my own.

Unable to let go and elated beyond words, finally I said:

"Thank you, Sir, I thank you with all my heart. I am forever in your debt."

The nights following our discussion were full of excited dreams. Often I lay awake wondering what possibilities the future might hold.

Two days later, on a clear, sunny morning, I was seated in the stern of one of the Colonel's fast cutters. He was standing at the bow, looking eagerly ahead, with a stiff breeze speeding us across the bay from St Georges to Paget Island. As we drew close to the jetty, I sighted a small figure on the distant shore, up to his knees in the surf, chasing a model schooner. Reaching forward, touching the Colonel's arm, I said, "See, your grandson yonder."

He gazed landward, pride and excitement shone in his eyes.

"Thomas, Thomas Tucker." I shouted.

The lad looked up. "Thomas." I shouted again frantically waving my arms.

Waving back, he gathered up his boat and scrambled barefoot over sand and rocks towards the house set on its low hill. We lost further sight of him and his progress as we reached the jetty. Quickly disembarking, leaving the crew to secure the craft, we hurried inland.

"Go on John, prepare the way," the Colonel said. "I know my heart will break, should Arabella refuse my purpose now."

I strode ahead. Before reaching the garden gate, Thomas burst out of the house followed by Arabella, still pinning up her hair. Thomas reached me first, picking him up I swung him onto my shoulders pig-a-back, his hands clasped around my neck. Arabella ran up smiling, flinging her arms about me and we embraced. I gently eased her away, lifting my finger to my lips and turned to look over my shoulder. Arabella followed my gaze, seeing who stood behind me. She stepped away, as if to flee back to the house. I restrained her softly, shaking my head.

"John, what is this?" she asked in a shocked voice.

"Arabella, daughter," the Colonel said hoarsely.

"Father?"

"I would deem it a great joy should you and Thomas agree to return home with me," Colonel Tucker said.

"Father, oh father" Her eyes brimming with tears.

"I love you my child, I cannot bear to be parted any longer."

Arabella fell upon the Colonel sobbing, her head on his breast.

"What do you say?" the Colonel asked. "Agree to come with us now to share my home, your home. Fill it once again with laughter and love."

"I will, oh I will, most gladly," Arabella cried.

I thought my yearning heart to burst. At last a woman who loved me, despite all the self-loathing that rose like bile in my chest without warning.

I lifted Thomas down and the Colonel, tousling his hair, turned to me. Taking my hand, he brought Arabella to me and placed her hand in mine, saying:

"My dear children, my everlasting blessing on your love. Now I hope that I too may share it with you."

The following year passed in a blaze of warmth and happiness. Never before had I felt so very complete, so very satisfied with my life. Arabella and Thomas quickly settled into the household, taking on their roles of Mistress and young heir respectively. For me the joy of their constant companionship gave new purpose to every thought and action. The Colonel was raised in spirit from his previous lonely sadness to that of doting parent and grandfather. For my part, I continued to court Arabella in private, revelling in our secret love. We did not repeat our lovemaking as at the Paget house, holding hands and stealing kisses was enough for now. Only the Colonel and Thomas shared our moments together.

The shipment of convicts eventually arrived and they were set to work immediately, updating and improving the islands' defences. I was a little disappointed, though not surprised, that no letter from Elicia, was delivered with them. How could I blame her for not writing? I had hoped that she would forgive me and tell me how she fared without me. Our childish promises of betrothal meant little except in our own hearts, yet a vow was a vow, however innocent it may seem.

CHAPTER ELEVEN

So it was that in September of the year of our Lord 1765, Colonel Tucker, called me once again to his study. I doubted not that it was to place some new commission on me, perhaps something pertaining to one of the Colonel's many and far reaching business commitments.

"Ah, John my dear boy, I have news of great import that I would share with you," he said.

I sat down opposite the Colonel and waited dutifully.

"I am growing older and feel these winter chills in my bones, more with each year that passes. It is my intention, that you will oversee my business concerns on Turks Island. The journeys hence are becoming more tiresome for me every year."

I was pleased for this position would enable me to travel freely to new shores. In addition, I would have the power to use my own initiative, to develop my own ideas. Turks Island was only three to four days 'sailing from Bermuda. Equally, I would not be parted from Arabella for more than a few weeks at a time, except perhaps in the summer, when the salt trade was at its height, and the island busied itself with the shipments to be sent out.

"There is a problem though, John," the Colonel paused. "I would have you understand that your status as a convicted felon will not allow you to travel from this island unaccompanied."

I looked down at the floor, my mind confused. Eventually I said:

"I have given you my word. You know that all I have or want is here with you. Surely I have your absolute trust?" I asked.

"I have shown you that already, many times. Your honesty is not in question, it is a matter of the law itself," the Colonel said gravely.

Frustration with my convict status which dogged me still left me speechless.

"It is in view of these matters John, that I have talked with Arabella, who I should mention, has pleaded eloquently on your behalf. As a consequence, I am resolved to put up the cash bail, in order to purchase your freedom," he said.

My jaw dropped and staring wide eyed, I was rooted to the spot. This was the very last thing that I could have possibly imagined.

"I trust this will not give you cause to take the first passage back to England?" the Colonel continued.

With these words he took from his desk a large sealed document, handing it to me. I held it in my hands, too bemused even to open it. I stroked the large seal, imprinted with the same image that scarred my shoulder. Neatly lettered on the outer vellum were the words; 'John Rigg, Gentleman, Royal Pardon and Release'. The Colonel held out his hand;

" Welcome to my house, Mr. Rigg. I am delighted to make your acquaintance."

We shook hands solemnly. Still in a dreamlike daze, I replied;

"Thank you sir, I shall never betray this most generous gesture."

The Colonel clapped me on the shoulder saying, "Come now John, this day will be celebrated with a glass of good French wine."

He rang the hand bell on his desk, immediately the door opened to reveal Arabella and Thomas on the threshold bearing a decanter and glasses. Arabella brushed my cheek with her lips, whispering her congratulations. Thomas, with all due formality shook my hand. Once the four glasses had been charged, the Colonel raised his:

"To us all, a long life, good health and happiness."

We each of us repeated his words, toasting each other, before drinking the rich red liquid.

At last, my heart's desire was within reach, yet at the back of my mind was the thought that I was unworthy of such good fortune!

CHAPTER
TWELVE

The following April I set off on my first voyage to Turks Island. It was wonderful being, once again a free man.

In 1668, a few adventurous Bermuda seafarers sailed south almost a thousand miles, to a small island of rocks and glistening sand. They went ashore only to find it uninhabited. They named it 'Turks Island', after discovering a cactus that looked like the head of a Turkish man wearing a fez.

The salt works the first settlers founded consisted of a series of shallow rock cut basins, called pans. The dammed lagoons and water channels linking them together guided sea water into the pans. Once there, it was allowed to evaporate under the natural heat of the sun. The remaining salt crystals were raked into piles, then transported to the beach where it was graded and sorted. A low range of buildings had been erected to provide shelter for the labourers, convicts and overseers, who undertook the hard, demanding work. Some salt was loaded into sacks as it was, but not all. The remainder was added to rainwater and collected in a series of stone cisterns then boiled in large copper vats to produce better quality salt for the table. This was used both within the islands and sent in shipment not only to the Americas but to England as well. The poorer quality salt, direct from the beach, was used throughout the archipelago to cure and preserve pork and more importantly, fish. This was a highly remunerative trade and one in which Colonel Tucker was the principal shareholder.

A large stone breakwater protected the beach forming a sheltered harbour, which was at this time, filled daily with many craft. April to June was the busiest time for transporting salt as late summer was often ravaged by severe storms and the chance to work the salt then was not so favourable or reliable.

My first two days were fully occupied, inspecting and familiarising myself with every aspect of the process. I also endeavoured to develop a working relationship with the overseers. Most were native Bermudians who represented and looked after the interests of a particular family or shareholder.

Finding great pleasure in the fresh sense of purpose that my freedom had brought, I entered into the daily round with enthusiasm.

After three days we departed, our vessel fully laden with salt for the return journey to St. George's. I made two further visits in the following months, before the August storms made further travel hazardous.

CHAPTER THIRTEEN

*O*ne evening around the middle of August, I retired to bed later than usual. After a good supper, feeling rather too full, I took a twilight stroll with Arabella and Thomas. On returning to the house, we found that the Colonel had already retired to his chamber.

Bidding Arabella and Thomas good night, I went to the Colonel's study to balance the accounts, due from salt sales to Bristol merchants. It was well past midnight when I finally climbed into bed. Sleep evaded me for some time, though eventually, despite the heat, I drifted into a dream filled state, only half-way to being fully unconscious. I dreamt a dog was barking and went in search of it, without success. Becoming more distressed, I awoke indeed to a hear dog barking nearby. A howl of pain, followed by brooding silence.

I strained my ears for any sound, all was deathly quiet. A barking dog was not unusual at night, such a howl of pain was. I lay there thinking I should seek out the sound but sleep began to drift me away. Suddenly roused again this time with eyes wide open to hear a shattering crash. I held my breath, trying to catch every little sound.

The household around me had not stirred so perhaps I was mistaken and there might be a simple explanation. Something or someone stepped on a fallen palm frond, it was dry and crunched underfoot. Fully awake now, I crossed silently to the un-shuttered window. The garden was in shadow, the sea beyond the palms was light enough to be seen between their trunks. All appeared normal until a slight movement, caught out of the corner of my eye, made me peer more intently. Yes, there it was, a dark shape moving between the trees, then, several more treading stealthily along the shore. A dull glint on metal, weapons! I gathered up my sword and pistols, donned a pair of soft slippers and as quietly as possible, left my room, tip toeing downstairs.

The rest of the house remained peaceful. In my anticipation I was shivering with excitement. God in heaven, it had been some time since I felt this level of nervous energy. Drawing the bolts as carefully as possible, easing the door slightly ajar, I looked out into the garden. There was no obvious threat to be seen, I stepped out onto the veranda. Sensing rather than seeing, I wheeled around in time to deflect a cutlass blow aimed at my head. I fired a pistol at the dark shape as it lunged at me again, the loud report echoed in the confined space, bringing sounds of alarm from within the house. As my assailant was down and not moving, I ran around the corner of the veranda to reach the large brass bell hanging on the wall. Grabbing the rope, I pulled on it frantically. The Colonel appeared in his nightshirt at the open door, a blunderbuss held aggressively in both hands.

"John, is that you making such a commotion, what is going on?"

He must then have seen the prostrate body at his feet.

"God's blood, what is this?"

"We are under attack!" I shouted, pointing into the darkness.

The Colonel following my sign, fired randomly into the trees.

Candles were being lit, the house servants, armed with an assortment of kitchen cutlery arrived on the veranda. The Colonel was struggling to reload the blunderbuss and shouting instructions to the servants.

"Keep a sharp look out. One of you, go to my daughter and grandson, lock yourself in the room with them, do not come out until I say."

A volley of shots came from the trees, the balls smashed glass and peppered the side of the house. Apart from a graze to the Colonel's arm, causing him to bellow in anger and pain, we escaped further injury.

I made up my mind to take the fight to our attackers and followed by a motley group of servants we rushed toward from where the last volley had come. As we got nearer it was apparent that whoever had attacked us was now attempting to reach the sea and embark in a longboat, pulled up on the small beach. We were shouting and roaring so loudly that we must have seemed a greater number than we were racing to the attack. I could see that a signal beacon had been lit on the roof of the State House, the general alarm had been raised. It would not be long ere the garrison at Gates Fort joined the fray. Reaching the beach, a shot brought down one of the men attempting to push the longboat out into deeper water.

As I moved to restrain him, a pistol ball fired from the boat struck, knocking me backwards into the shallow surf. Several hands held me, dragging me out of the water, on to the beach. They carried me back to the house, to be laid flat on the porch, where I began to revive.

"Thanks be, John, I was afraid that you might be dead."

It was the Colonel who stood over me still gripping the blunderbuss, looking very warlike in the candlelight.

Arabella rushed from the house, only to cry out when she saw me on the floor. Kneeling beside me with tears running down her cheeks, she wiped away the blood that oozed through my hair.

I was recovered well enough in the morning to go downstairs, seeking further details of the night's events. The man I had shot at the beach was alive, under guard in the State House, to be interrogated as soon as he regained consciousness. Both the Colonel and I had been very fortunate to receive only minor wounds causing plenty of blood but little real damage.

It had been lucky that the pistol, shot at such close range had missed, due to the boat rocking violently in the surf. The other attacker I had shot on the veranda, was dead. Investigation later that morning, showed the attacking party to be French. A frigate had anchored outside the reef. A longboat, manned by fifteen sailors, had come ashore just below the Colonel's house. Five had remained with the boat while the others carried on, with the intention of spiking the guns on Gates Fort. If they had succeeded, the entrance to St. Georges, through the reef, would have been left undefended.

With the hasty departure of the longboat, the remaining ten men had been stranded. Eight had been captured already. A search party of local militia and Red Coats combed the surrounding area for the last two. All in all, we had survived well enough, through a potentially dangerous situation. It had, however, shown up a weak point in the town's defences. I knew that this would have to be addressed as quickly as possible.

The dog which gave such a timely warning had been stabbed to death. The poor creature served us well in raising the alarm. It was a matter of no little regret to me that it did not survive the night.

On the last day of August two events caused great excitement. One was the capture of the two missing French sailors. The other was the arrival of a battered schooner, whose crew brought tales of a catastrophic storm which had swept away many of the buildings and poor souls on Turks Island, less than one week before.

A relief armada was quickly assembled and fourteen ships, including mine, sailed with all speed across the now calm sea. The scene of utter destruction that greeted us on arrival, was shocking in the extreme. Much of the stone breakwater had been broken down, none of the buildings were habitable. The score or so of survivors greeted us as we landed, each one loud in their personal tale of the misfortune that had befallen them.

Several large waves had been swept inland by a fearsome wind. It was these that had wrought such ruin, washing many people out to sea. Some bodies had been recovered although many were still missing. We spent two days trying to salvage what we could, before returning to St. George's, with our sorry tale and even sorrier cargo.

When I reported to the Colonel that evening, he was not downhearted by the bad news. By contrast he was fairly ebullient.

"An act of the Lord, John, it must have some purpose," he said philosophically. "We shall rebuild everything next spring, better than before. You can apply your sharp mind to the problem, see what improvements you think fit to suggest."

I had plenty of ideas, though needing to plan in detail. I chose not to share them with him yet.

"We are due another shipment of convict labour from England early next year, to replace those who have died. I do believe that we should settle them on Turks Island in order to assist with the rebuilding," the Colonel said.

"Mayhap, I should spend the whole season on the island myself, to insure your investment?" I asked.

"Good John, I consider that a most useful suggestion. Maybe Thomas can accompany you, it is time the lad learned more of a business that will one day be his."

I thought this to be ideal and schemed in my heart to arrange for Arabella to join us.

The plans for rebuilding the salt works must now include a fortification. England had been at war for many years first with Spain, then France and now the American colonies were in a state of unrest. On my first visit I saw that the island was vulnerable to attack and invasion by an enemy force. The works, settlement and harbour at least must have some measure of protection.

By the time that a new year dawned, I had completed my plans for the rebuilding of Turks Island and presented them to the Colonel's shareholders. They argued somewhat over the cost, enough for me to have to revise the design of the fort. It would now be a semi-circular, stone and rubble outwork and mounting only three of the ten, twelve pounder cannon needed.

The whole was to be overlooked and defended by a stone blockhouse, two storeys in height. The tower would not mount any cannon but be provided only with musket loops. I had doubts that the whole might not prove to be adequate, in the face of a determined assault and fatefully my objections were overruled by reason of thrift.

Arabella had warmed to the suggestion of a summer together. The fact that she and Thomas as well were to accompany me made the adventure highly attractive. It was Arabella who had the task of persuading the Colonel to let us all go away together for the season. In the event it was not as difficult as we had imagined it would be. The old man in his kindness and affection understood the opportunity for Arabella and I to have time together was important. We could live on the island, almost as man and wife. The Colonel made his understanding and empathy clear the next time we met. One evening, he called me to his study, at the close of a hot and humid day.

"John, I must tell you that in my old age, I would measure it a great honour and joy, should you find your obvious regard for my daughter leads you to a permanent joining."

The statement struck me, like a bolt out of the blue, long wished for but so unexpected. Marriage to Arabella would bring all of my dreams and desires together in one joyous celebration.

"Thank you sir," I replied. "I must admit, to it having been my intention, should the opportunity arise, in asking your blessing on our union."

"You have it, my boy, gladly! Now to another matter," he said in a business like tone." We anticipate the convict transport's arrival, any day. At that time, I want you to go down to the dock and look them over for me.

See that they are healthy, ensure decent shelter and food. We need them to be fit enough to undertake the work required of them. You are charged with this task because you will have some understanding and sympathy with their situation and you will be diligent in your care of them."

CHAPTER FOURTEEN

*T*hree days later, word arrived that the convict transports had anchored off Mullet Bay, south west of the town. I set out at once to take passage to them. Six sturdy sailors, indented to the Colonel, rowed me out and along the coast. I was received with all courtesy by the ship's Captain. His reception was in direct contrast to my last time aboard an English vessel. Conditions for the men, incarcerated below decks, was very poor. They had suffered a rough crossing being delayed, in consequence of which, several men had died. The remainder were looking unwell enough to follow them shortly to the grave. On regaining the shore, I set about finding secure lodging for so large a party of men, two hundred and thirty in all.

It was a lucky chance that led me to meet the commander of Fort St. Catherine while in St. Georges. He agreed the loan of the fort casements for a few days, while I arranged a more permanent solution. The following day, accompanied by twenty-five Marines with a Sergeant, the convicts were landed and signed into my charge. I also took delivery of a packet of papers, listing their various crimes and sentences. Armed with these, we undertook the five minute march to the State House.

Many of the men were very weak yet the soldiers drove them hard keeping them moving. The business of identifying each man, reading the charges and branding them took many hours. I could not bear attending this which to me was unsavoury work with too many painful memories and I chose to walk to the Fort. It was almost night by the time we arrived there.

The escort and I lodged with the fort garrison. We did not wake the prisoners till mid-morning, my hope was that with this small indulgence, they would start the new day in good heart. Once they had been served a wholesome, rich, fish broth with plenty of fresh baked bread, I instructed the Sergeant to have them gather in the Main courtyard. Climbing the steps leading to the upper works, in order that I might be better seen and heard, I addressed them:

"Welcome to the Bermudas where you have been delivered as felons. I was once as you but now am a free and pardoned man. Whatever your crimes, they are in the past."

With that I threw the packet of papers, received the day before, on to the steps beside me. I had not looked at them, nor felt the need to.

"A new life is possible here," I continued. "You are expected to work hard and in return you will be treated with compassion and humanity. My name is John, John Rigg, representative of the military commander, Colonel Thomas Tucker, for whom you will work. Should you need or want to talk to me at any time, inform the sergeant and he will arrange a meeting. For the moment we are going to escort you down to Achilles Bay, below the walls of this fort. Once there you will be able to wash off the filth of the voyage and become human again. I beg you not to think of escape. There is nowhere to go and it will only make the situation more difficult for those who remain."

I squatted in the pale sun overlooking the beach, whilst two hundred and thirty naked men cavorted like children in the clear sea. Being fresh from an English winter, they thought the sea to be warm by comparison. However, by next year, once acclimatised I knew they would not consider it warm enough for a paddle, let alone a swim.

The discarded rags of clothing were gathered up, to be burnt on the beach. Smoke rose like that of a funeral pyre, destroying the past and bringing hope. Most importantly, the lice and fleas infesting it all, also died in the flames.

The party was marched, still naked and barefoot, back to the fort, A much less sombre mood prevailed, many of them, sang together as they went. It was a truly marvellous sight. The resilience of the human spirit is, as I myself had experienced, a great wonder.

On the following morning I rose early, refreshed in both body and spirit, cleansed and renewed. Joining the soldiers in the main courtyard, I was pleased that the sun shone to warm our prisoners, newly clothed, lining up for the first roll call. The names as they were called flowed over me, almost without notice, as my mind explored the many tasks ahead.

"Daniel Bragg!"

Startled out of my reverie, instantly transported back to the open fells above Wasdale Head.

I stood on tip toe, straining to see whoever might answer.

"Aye."

A lifetime ago I would have recognised the Daniel Bragg that I knew, but what of now..?

Daniel Bragg, my Daniel Bragg, here, how?

I searched the blur of faces below me. Yes, there, a tall man with a shaggy beard and mane of hair, somehow familiar. His eyes locked with mine across the yard and I knew, in that instant, Daniel Bragg was alive and in Bermuda! The press of bodies allowed me to do no more than to stay at a distance from the man, I thought never to see again in this world. I dared not avert my gaze in case his image would fade like writing in the sand, erased by the smallest wave. He was thinner than in my memory, eyes weary and wary. His gaze held mine in a steady grip, as though he too dared not look away.

The Sergeant came to the end of his list and was about to dismiss the gathered crowd, when I turned to him.

"Sergeant, will you be so good as to ensure the prisoner, Daniel Bragg to remain behind?" He gave me a quizzical look but posed no questions. Herding the last of the prisoners from the courtyard, we were left alone. Remaining where we stood, neither able to break the unreal scene that held us so still, like statues..

"Daniel Bragg, of Hall Farm, Wasdale Head?"

There was no reaction for a heartbeat, then…

"John, 'Moses', Rigg of Ambleside?"

The spell was broken, Daniel crossed swiftly to me, gathering me up in a great bear hug, fit to break several ribs.

"Dear God Daniel, by all that's Holy, I thought you dead, four years gone."

"John, I can't tell ye, I was as good as dead 'til I saw ye yesterday!"

I stepped back, struck by his skinny body and mop of lank, tangled hair. He looked like a derelict, cast up on the rocks of life. Taking him by the arm I led him to my quarters and pushed him through the door ahead of me, easing past him to stand in the centre of the small, simply furnished chamber.

"My dear friend, returned like Lazarus from the dead, welcome to my humble home."

To my surprise, Daniel said nothing, nor did he move, yet the tears, as though released by a magician's spell, trickled from his eyes to disappear into his straggly ill trimmed beard.

"John, John, I'm a feared for my sweet Maggie. What's to do John, what's to do?"

"Come now Daniel, sit you down, your two lads will look after her well enough. All will be well anon, I promise you."

I led him to a comfortable settle and bade him rest while I went in search of breakfast. On my return, he was laid out full length, deep asleep. Throwing a coverlet over him I sallied out to find the sergeant. Wishing to acquaint him with the news, that from this time onwards, John Rigg would be taking personal responsibility for Mr Daniel Bragg of Hall Farm,Wasdale Head.

That afternoon, after satisfying myself that Daniel was still resting, I made arrangements for his care in my absence. Riding with all haste to St. Georges in order to meet with Colonel Tucker, I arrived to be greeted by Arabella.

"John, I did not expect you back yet. I miss you greatly when you are away, even if only for one or two nights."

She put her arm through mine and chattering merrily, escorted me up to the Colonel's study. At the door, Arabella turned away to return to her own tasks, but I stopped her, saying;

"Arabella my dearest, I beg you to come in with me, that you may hear the remarkable story I will relate the Colonel". The Colonel was seated at his desk and rose to greet us as we entered.

"Ah, John, no difficulties with the transfer of the new men, I trust?"

"No, Colonel, all went well, better indeed than I had expected," I reported.

"Then what is it that brings you home in such a hurry, apart that is, from the need to be with my daughter?"

As he said this, he turned to Arabella and smiled, holding out his hand. She took it, remaining standing at the side of his chair. I marvelled at her pure beauty. Her skin glowed, in the soft light streaming through the shutters. Her eyes were bright and alive with interest and expectation. Even then, in my impatience to relate the story, I paused, struck suddenly by the vision of Arabella which made my heart ache. I could however, not prevent the image of Elicia that briefly flashed across my mind.

"Colonel, I have the most strange and extraordinary tale to tell."

So it was that I recounted to the two people most important to me in the New World, the history of my dearest friend from the old. When I came to its conclusion and having answered all their questions, I made my plea;

"Colonel, as you trusted me, took me in and raised me to be a Gentleman once more, may I entreat you to grant my earnest suit and become a patron for this, my friend, Daniel Bragg?"

"Gladly John, I give you my full support and blessing. If you wish we can ready a chamber in this my house for him."

I was delighted at his immediate and generous response.

"Dear Sir, how may I ever repay your great and continued kindness?" I asked.

Arabella came around the desk with both arms outstretched. I hugged her and taking her by both hands, squeezed them in my happiness.

"Arabella, oh Arabella!"

I was lost for further words. Nodding and smiling her thanks to her father, she led me from the study. On the landing, we stopped and she raised her lips to mine, kissing me with a passion.

"You go and fetch Daniel John. I will go prepare a chamber to receive him."

"Yes, yes my love, I shall leave directly," I assured her.

Leading a mount for Daniel, I left St. Georges, heading back to the fort.

It was dark by the time I arrived and stabled the horses. Daniel had hardly moved yet a small fire burned in the grate, the remains of a meal lay scattered on the table. I took off my riding coat and boots and pulled a chair up to the fire. With a glass of light Canary wine. I sat gazing into the flames. After some time, how long I know not, I heard movement behind me.

"That you, John?"

Daniel sat up rubbing his eyes and stretching.

"Ee, that was a grand sleep, I'm more like my old self."

"Well, I am very pleased to hear you say so," I said jovially.

"John, ah beg thee for a blade, to clip this damned hair on my chin."

"Of course, I shall arrange soap, razor and hot water, I will be but a moment."

With that, I went outside summoning a servant to bring the necessary items. Once they arrived, Daniel set to with a will. By the light of the fire and candle, he restored himself to his normal appearance. The while, he talked of all that had happened to him, since we parted on that fateful morning at Wasdale.

"I were on the fell when a bevy of Red Coats burst out of cover an set after me. No sign of the Dutchman even so!"

"Could you not outrun them, knowing the lie of the fell as you do?"

"Nay, the buggers were shooting at me, every one o' them."

"I saw that and thought you killed," I remembered with pain.

"A ball in ma left thigh, brought me down, properly. Clapped in irons and hustled to the coast, an on to a scruffy little sloop."

"Aboard a ship, where were you bound?"

"Carried round t' coast to mouth of river Lune. Then to Lancaster Castle, imprisoned, nought of a trial. Nigh on five months I was there."

"Then what?

"A whole gang of us prisoners, made to labour on Turnpikes for best of half a year."

"Hard labour? I was spared that, being transported here within days of my capture."

"After that, back to Carlisle Castle. Sent to the new road along t' old Roman Wall. It was exhausting, not without danger, breaking stones in all weathers. Shackle irons on and never off. Sleeping in the open, a fair few died. Buried there and then, none cared, ah thought to join them."

"Dear God Daniel! How did you survive?"

"Ah don't rightly know John, seems some miracle. Took me back to Carlisle, tried me, and condemned to be transported. Queer it is to have fetched up here, of all places in the world."

"What did you think when first you saw me?" I asked with curiosity.

"I don't rightly know John. Ye were unreal, here in this place and in authority."

"I have been very fortunate. I was taken up and put under the protection of a most kind and considerate patron. I rediscovered my self-respect and self-worth," I told him.

"I lay awake all night. My brain not letting me rest for thinking."

"I can imagine what a shock it must have been when you first sighted me."

"The next morn, I thought it a dream. Then saw ye again, would ye notice me?"

"When I heard your name called, I did."

"I saw ye when we went to the sea to clean ourselves. You saw me not," he said.

"No, how could I? You were but one amongst two hundred and thirty."

"Likely once, you would have seen me even in such a gaggle."

"True, yet to me you were dead, never thinking to see you again in this life," I explained.

"Aye, dead, dead, a certainty, for sure."

"Once I looked at you, saw you, I recognised you then."

"It was clear ye saw me then, aye. Dared not look away for fear of losing thee".

"And me, you also."

"Once we were alone in the yard, I was as stone, an could not move," he went on.

"Now you are with me and are safe, no more a felon in chains. I have arranged to take you to my patron tomorrow. You will be treated as the friend that you are," I told him.

Daniel turned away with a great sigh and stood to look out of the small window, lost in thought, staring out across the sea.

The next morning, three days after Daniel re-entered my life and as the first rays of the sun caressed the old stones of the fort, we rode out of the gate, across the drawbridge into the woods. Fragrant with cedar, the trees were dappled with patches of the clearest light. The sea on our left shone a rich turquoise, little waves broke languorously against the black rocks. Daniel was in a happy, yet thoughtful mood, observing much but speaking little.

Passing Gates Fort, we turned toward St. George's. It was not long before cresting the hill above the town, Daniel finally roused himself.

"Tis truly a bonnie spot, John."

"Bonnie indeed, on such a morn as this." I replied.

Young Thomas must have been watching for us, for we had hardly turned into the drive, than his distant figure dashed out of the house, running to greet us. Arabella followed, waiting on our arrival, standing at the top of the broad steps to the porch. I turned to Daniel,

"I beg you not to mention Elicia,. I have found another love here. I shall explain all soon, please honour my wish for the moment."

"Surely John, whatever you want, as all ways," he concurred.

He gave me an enquiring look, I knew that an explanation would be needed, ere the day was out. As we dismounted, I introduced Daniel to young Thomas. They shook hands most formally; his slight hand was lost in the broad grasp of Daniel's. The boy smiled, looking up at Daniel with obvious admiration in his eyes. Even poorly dressed and in a weakened state Daniel cut an impressive figure.

"Well now lad, are thee in good heart?"

Thomas, still smiling, nodded his head.

"Lost thy tongue no doubt?"

"The boy is mute, Daniel," I explained.

"Ah, there's tragedy indeed for such a brave lad."

He released his hand and patted Thomas's curly head.

"Never you mind yourself laddie, it will all come right in the end."

I led the way up the steps to Arabella, who had been joined by her father. Introducing them, Daniel solemnly shook hands with the Colonel, bowing to Arabella, "Mam," he said.

Stepping into the house behind Daniel and Arabella, the Colonel clapped me on the back.

"A fine fellow John, I am pleased in my heart for you both."

CHAPTER FIFTEEN

*D*uring the next month, Daniel regained strength and health. I related to him everything regarding my new life here and of my love for Arabella. He didn't judge me, yet I felt that he considered it a betrayal of Elicia. He never put it into words, but my own feelings of guilt influenced my perceptions. Guilt is a powerful word and an even more powerful emotion. I examined my heart time and again seeking to simplify my feelings.

I did most truly love both Arabella and Elicia equally, but it was Arabella who was in my new life now, satisfying the need for the love and companionship that we both craved. I also wanted to be able to value myself as a man. The relationship with Arabella, gave me that. Had Elicia been here who knows how I would feel. Elicia might even have married and forgotten me by now three years is a long time. I mentioned this to Daniel in the first week as we stood in the garden. He was surprised.

"Don't thee know John?"

"Know what?"

"Ma Maggie, visited Lancaster goal, many months gone, past my capture, she told me the news."

"News Daniel, what news?"

"I can't honestly think ah could tell thee now, the way things stand."

"For God's sake man, you cannot leave this unsaid," I begged him.

"All right John. Elicia has had a baby, your baby, a lassie, your daughter. Christened Ruenna."

I heard a gasp behind me, turning just in time to glimpse Arabella, disappearing around the corner of the house. I turned to Daniel;

"My child?"

"Aye John, yours for certain."

"Dear God, did Arabella hear you?"

"I can't really say."

I left Daniel in the garden and went in search of Arabella. I found her sitting on a stone bench, under the coconut palms, overlooking the bay. I settled beside her, neither of us spoke.

Reaching for her hand lying on the bench, she moved it away at my touch. I placed my arm around her shoulders, at this she was shaken by suppressed sobs.

"My love, why this? Yes, it seems I am the father of a child. It makes no difference to our love but is does mean that I have a responsibility to ensure the welfare of my child and her mother."

Between sobs, catching her breath, she said;

"No, maybe not. You will want to go back to England, as a free and pardoned man. There is nothing to prevent it."

"How can you possibly think that? I love and adore you to spend the rest of my life in your arms is all I ever want."

"Do you John, do you truly? Promise me this is the true meaning in your heart."

I fell to my knees, "I declare, upon my life, that you are all I could ever desire. I ask you now, in all humility, Arabella Tucker, my love, my life. Please will you do me the honour of becoming my wife?"

Arabella looked long at me, searching my eyes for the meaning hidden there. Tenderly, reaching out, she held my face in her cool, slender hands.

"Yes, John Rigg, I will gladly be your wife. Until death parts us in this world!"

We embraced then. Hand in hand we returned to the house, to find the Colonel and appraise him of our compact. He was quite delighted, as was Thomas. Daniel shook my hand and gripping my shoulders said:

"I am happy for you John."

There was still an unspoken question in his eyes and I knew that his thoughts were of Elicia..

We celebrated that evening, with a bottle of the Colonels best Amontillado.

The return of Daniel, news of Elicia and a child, the promise of marriage to Arabella threw my thoughts into confusion. I dwelt on the things that had led to Elicia becoming pregnant with child in the first place. I cast my mind back, trying to remember every painful detail. How had it happened that day in Ambleside? I knew that if I could face up to and admit my fault, the dark shadow that hung over my relationship with Arabella, could be dispersed but only if I honoured my obligation to Elicia and Ruenna.

The day before the attack on the wad mine, we had argued, Elicia and I. Her anxiety that I held something secret had filled her with anger. In the parlour of the old farmhouse she had confronted me:

"John, John, you promised me that your smuggling days were over," so softly it was almost a whisper. She turned to leave. I moved forward, desperate and indignant. *She did not understand!* I loved her, yet must leave, my companions depended upon me. Gripping her shoulder I spun her around to face me. She was angrier now, eyes wild.

"How can you say we are betrothed? You are keeping secrets from me. How can I trust you, are you still smuggling?"

I stepped towards her.

"Don't!"

She pushed me back, I stumbled over a small stool. Finding my feet and my balance I made to grip her wrist. She twisted away and lashing out, skinned the side of my nose with her fingernails.

"Get out John, go, go to hell if you must!"

I felt confused and hurt, I could feel the anger rising in me. How did we get to this pass in so short a time?

"Go to your precious secret, whatever that is."

I struggled to control my shaking voice, it was an effort to breathe. My heart was pounding as I tried to turn our aggressive exchange into a reasoned discussion.

"Elicia, I love you, I have always loved you."

"Really *Moses*?" was her mocking response.

At that moment, something erupted inside me, lust, frustration and rage. I wanted her but her obstinacy was a challenge. Elicia's panting breast and wild expression awoke an irrational desire in me. I tried to kiss her, to force my lips on hers, to dominate her; to make everything better between us.

She screamed and fought me with animal intensity. A table fell, taking with it the stoneware jug and fresh bouquet, newly gathered, whose scent lingered between us. I pushed her back in an attempt to avoid the flailing arms. A well-aimed kick bruised my shin urging me to a greater effort. Wrestling her I bound her arms to her side in a tight embrace. Tripping, we fell together onto the flagstone floor.

All of her attempts to throw me off were to no avail, the weight of my body and single minded purpose drove me on. Lying astride her, my upper body across her breast, I fumbled behind me with one hand, pulling her skirts up. The heat of a selfish, uncaring lust carried me away. Using my knees to force her legs apart, my probing fingers found her sex.

Suddenly, Elicia was still, eyes wide open, daring me to go on. If this was an attempt to bring me to my senses it was unsuccessful. My arousal would brook no delay. When I entered her body, Elicia neither moved nor made a sound, she just stared up at me, her eyes full of contempt and hatred. Losing what little self-control that remained, in an orgy of abandon, I drove into her body again and again.

Calm and common sense returned with the fading erection and spent seed. The openly bitter judgement in her eyes contained a curse. I rolled off of her but she remained still and unspeaking where she lay.

"Ellicia?"

Even now she did not move nor utter a sound.

"Elicia? Oh my God, I do not know what induced me to behave so!"

With no response other than her unforgiving stare, shame and revulsion overcame me.

"Did I hurt you? Please…I don't…?"

The words evaporated, drifting away in the gulf between us.

Adjusting my breeches in the silence hanging heavy over us I rose awkwardly to my feet and made towards the door. Elicia's eyes did not leave my face. I tried to speak, dry mouthed, nothing! Gulping, shamefaced, I backed out of the room, unable to meet her gaze.

Running now, out into the yard, into the evening sun. Falling to my knees beside my horse, I loudly cursed myself, life and God himself for the horror of what had just happened. My brutality had been that of a stranger. How could this have been I, John Rigg?

A choked sob roused me, I looked up to see Elicia in the doorway, leaning limply on the jamb, her hair and clothing in disarray. A trickle of bright blood from thigh to ankle showed through the torn skirts. I stood up, intending to go to her but her palm was held full out towards me, fingers extended, presenting an insurmountable barrier. Tuning away, I beat my head, like one possessed, against the saddle of my horse.

Full of pathetic self-pity, on mounting my horse I urged it into a canter, wishing to depart as quickly as possible from so distressing a scene.

The image of her in the last soft rays of the sun and the lime washed house, set back into the bulk of the fell, proved to be impossible to erase.

When I reined in my mount above Ambleside in the fading light, watching the dark blue of the mountains deepen against a flaming sky, I could not resist one last look behind to where the small figure of Elicia still leaned forlornly against the porch. In the valley below, Lake Windermere glimmered with the last rays of sunlight, before they too were gone.

Chris Lane

CHAPTER SIXTEEN

*S*eeking to place the recall of the last time I was with Elicia in some sort of order, had eased my shame. I felt quieter, settled even. Admitting to myself the full horror of what I had done didn't justify it, but did make for a better understanding of how I had behaved. It was in this state of mind that I felt more able to complete the union with Arabella. Peace had returned to my tortured soul although regret was harder to overcome, as I sought to exonerate myself of guilt.

Three weeks later, surrounded by our friends, Daniel as Best Man, we married. The church of St.Georges had been built by the first settlers. Its simple and stately interior proved a worthy witness of our love. The brilliance of the sun paled next to the stunning beauty of my bride. Even Daniel was unable to stop himself saying so.

"By all that's holy John, Arabella is a glorious woman. Methinks she's stolen ma poor heart as well as yours. I cannot blame thee ma friend, what man could indeed? God give thee both a long and happy life together."

Chris Lane

The many oleander and hibiscus splashed colour brightly in the roadside's edges as we drove home from the church. Dancing and feasting lasted long past the darkening of the day.

Lifting Arabella into my arms, I carried her to our bed chamber. We were both exhausted and ecstatically happy. After a gentle lovemaking we fell asleep, entwined in each other's arms.

CHAPTER SEVENTEEN

*T*he spring came and blessed us with its promise. Thomas and Daniel became great friends. All the while the time for departure to Turks Island drew nearer.

I was becoming worried by a deterioration in the Colonel's health. He appeared to grow older with every month that passed, leaving more and more of the business to be run by both Daniel and I Colonel Thomas Tucker, was more relaxed and content than ever before, as Arabella, Thomas, Daniel and I had served to bring peace to his troubled soul. In the evening of his years, the circle of his life was nearing completion, slowing down, like an unwound clock. Many years of emotional stress had taken its toll. I felt a deep sadness for this most honourable man, resolving in my heart to do all in my power to fill his final years with love and happiness.

Needing to turn my attention to the demanding matter of the approaching sojourn on Turks Island, I was most keen that Daniel accompany Arabella and me for the whole of the season. He was an excellent overseer, well respected by both freemen and convicts. Thomas was to remain with his grandfather, despite his protestations. We wished his schooling to continue uninterrupted. His presence would also alleviate any feelings of loss that the Colonel might have, occasioned by our departure.

On the third day of July in the year of our Lord 1766 with a fair wind, we set sail in a fast sloop. The rest of the fleet carried stonemasons, carpenters, soldiers and convicts, all heading for Turks Island. As we passed Gates Fort to clear the reef, the cannon fired a parting salute. The uneventful journey lasted just four days, we all arrived safely. A lot of work had already been done to repair the previous year's storm damage. The harbour breakwater was almost complete, several buildings were fully habitable once again. The production process was underway, piles of salt lying, ready to be packed and shipped. Daniel was intrigued and impressed by all that he saw and fell to the task of housing the convict labourers with enthusiastic energy.

Arabella and I took possession of a small, stone-built cabin as our home. It was next to the site chosen for the new fort. I made a note in my mind to ensure its demolition, prior to our return to Bermuda. The new fort would require an open field of fire in every direction.

During the afternoon, we toured the salt works and visited acquaintances. Arabella had never been here before and was excited by the air of activity and bustle. I left her with a group of other wives who were eager to assist her with moving in.

The days flew by, good weather persisted and we all settled in to the new routine. Daniel made it his habit to join us in our cabin for breakfast, occasionally for supper, when time allowed. Arabella and I spent our evenings in a quiet enjoyment of our own company. We did not always need to speak, although when we did, it was to talk about something from our pasts, not mentioned before. I even found it possible to talk of Elicia, but not of the events leading up to our separation.

It was in this way that we came to know each other so very well. These evenings served to bring us closer together. Often, they would end in a slow lovemaking. Intimately exploring, each the other's body, with delighted wonder.

I worked hard on the construction of the fort. Willing to dirty my hands, I thought nothing of labouring alongside the builders and convicts in a common purpose. The construction went well, by the end of the first month the outer walls had been completed. The ordnance and powder were unloaded, the cannon mounted in the embrasures built to receive them. With that finished, to the general satisfaction of all, the workers concentrated on the blockhouse tower. It was raised quickly but we did have to send to Bermuda for joists and rafters, as Turks Island was completely bare of suitable timber. During the week lost, waiting for the delivery of the wood, I gave the convicts' time to rest, while the skilled tradesmen fitted out the additional cabins, built further away from the fort.

Arabella had made our cabin into such a cosy little home; I was loath to demolish it yet. This, as it turned out, proved to be a major mistake.

Two months into our stay on the island, with the fort tower almost complete to its full height, a strange sail was sighted to the east. The lookout on the tower saw it first and raised the alarm. Daniel joined with me and the soldiers on the roof as everyone strained to make out the vessel and the colours it was showing. The ship closed quite fast with a westerly wind behind and was soon identified as a French man-o-war. Coming nearer, we could see it was a hundred-gun, first rate ship of the line. A disorderly panic ensued, as every soul was rounded up to take shelter in the fort. We had not rehearsed this scenario, to our cost. We were not in a state of readiness and most certainly would be unable to repel a large, well-armed warship.

Further bad news was brought to me by a breathless soldier, who had run, hot foot from the magazine. The powder was damp, most likely from the voyage, none among us had thought to check its condition earlier. With no cannon we were completely at the mercy of the approaching enemy. The few muskets and pistols available would be useful at close quarters but no good if the enemy remained at a distance. Swords and small arms, we had in plenty.

The ship hove too, about half a mile offshore and anchored beyond the reef. It was obvious that they intended to stay.

That night we slept, convict, soldier, men and women, huddled together, inside the walls of the fort. Taking it in turns to watch through the hours of darkness, the day dawned without incident. We were roused by the distant discharge of a cannon, the ball hit the beach, bouncing along, coming to rest among the rocks. Another discharge, this time more than one gun, the balls came no closer. The ship was just out of effective range, armed only with six pounder guns, the maximum distance was one mile. Fired at that distance, a long shot could not be aimed and would do little damage once the velocity was spent. However, the sheer weight of a solid iron cannon ball can behead a man or cut his legs from under him.

With great care, we gathered food and supplies from the craft assembled behind the breakwater or drawn up on the beach. The residential cabins were cleared of anything that might be of use in a siege. All the while, occasional cannon fire caused us to seek cover wherever possible. Within an hour we had all returned, unscathed, to the shelter of the fort. Daniel, aided by the women, had laid out blankets on the roof of the tower and spread the damp powder on them in the hope the heat of the sun would render it useable. I realised that my choice of cannon to defend the fort had been far from ideal.

We would need twenty-five pounders, in order to be able to return fire on a ship moored beyond the reef.

The sun was high in the sky, approaching noon, when movement was noted on the warship. Two longboats full of men were launched and each was towing another, empty, behind it.

We feared that they would attempt to carry many off as prisoners, as they had in 1764.

Instead of heading directly towards our position, they veered off to land by the salt works, intending to steal the results of our recent labours. Being out of musket shot we watched, helplessly, as the packs of salt were loaded into the empty longboats. That done, a large party of heavily armed men turned their attention to us. By skirting around the rocks, they were able to take advantage of the dead ground, behind the cabin that Arabella and I had occupied.

In the general hubbub, I could hear Daniel giving instructions in a strong, calm voice. I looked for Arabella and found her inside the tower, helping clear a space for the women behind a wall of salt sacks, barrels and furniture, acting as a barricade if the outer wall was breached.

"John, are we going to be alright?"

"I'm not sure but we will do all we can to keep the enemy from reaching the fort," I replied.

A group of women joined our conversation, all wanting reassurance and determining not to give in without a fight. I was encouraged by their obvious courage and will to resist.

"Arabella, promise me that if the fort is taken, you will try to escape into the rocky hills to the north," I implored her.

"I will never leave you. I cannot live without you," she insisted.

"If I am taken or killed, you must, who knows what your fate may be if captured," I answered.

I kissed her then, with all the love and passion in my heart. Our hands slipped apart as I hurried to my post on the casements.

As the attacking party gained ground, ragged, ill aimed shots were exchanged by both sides.

Balls rattled against the stonework or whistled harmlessly over our heads. One of the convicts, a man I knew by sight but not by name, crawled to sit beside me in the shelter of the parapet.

"Mr John, I served as a Captain in the English army during the Scottish rising. I have a suggestion if you will hear me out."

"Go ahead, man. Speak freely."

"The French will over run us if they reach the walls, they have more experienced, better armed men. We will not be able to hold them if it comes to fighting, hand to hand," he warned me.

"What do you suggest?" I replied.

"A group of us who are able and know how to fight, must meet them, out there, before they reach us. I am willing to lead the attack. I have no desire to end my days in a French prison."

"That is most brave of you, tell me, what was your crime?" I inquired.

"Stealing a loaf of bread to feed my starving family."

"Your name?"

"Redmond Davey, the other convicts call me 'Red'"

"Well 'Red', you are right welcome, gather a group of good men together and I will accompany you on your adventure."

He left to do my bidding, with the promise of a speedy return. I concentrated on the approaching enemy, becoming bolder by the minute. It was going to be a desperate action, sallying out in such a manner. There really was no other option, except perhaps, surrender.

Red shouted, waving to me to join him in the tower basement.

A band of around twenty, soldiers, convicts and civilians, armed with swords, muskets and pistols stood ready at the door. The noise from the muskets shooting from the roof was tremendous, it was difficult to speak or hear. Several of the defenders had been wounded, none mortally; however, they had managed to injure at least four of the French, now working towards us, dodging from rock to rock.

Our group moved around the foot of the tower on all fours, until we reached the rear, out of sight of the enemy. Climbing from a cannon embrasure, we dropped ten feet onto the sand below. Once assembled, creeping steadily forward, using the jumbled rocks as cover fired into the flank of the French assault party. Their initial surprise did not last long, they turned about to advance head on, towards us. Shooting and reloading a fast as we could yet the French did not waver, coming on at great speed.

We were clearly outnumbered; far more men were moving among the rocks than we had anticipated. I shouted to Red and the others that it might be wise to withdraw. The man next to me took a ball square in the face, falling back, dead. I felt the panic around me, as my companions realised that our position was fast becoming untenable. In trying to retreat we found ourselves trapped.

Red, with a roar of fury, rushed headlong into the attack. With the inevitability of these things, the rest of us began to follow. At that point, when all seemed lost, a loud bang came from the fort, it was followed by a hail of shot striking the enemy in front of us. They faltered in the advance, a second shot landed in the middle of them, forcing a full retreat. Running now, we chased after them, shooting wildly and shouting loud hurrahs!

Once the French reached the longboats they halted, turning to face us. Our wild rush slowed in the face of heavy fire. We returned to the fort; losing three men fatally shot during our retreat. The occupants of the fort were on the tower, walls and casements, cheering lustily. Arabella screamed when she saw me rushing forward and flinging her arms about my neck, she asked anxiously:

"You are wounded, how badly? Where does it hurt?"

As far as I was aware, I had escaped injury and was surprised by her question. Using her kerchief, she wiped my face and it came away, bloody. I quickly realised I was covered in the blood of my unfortunate companion, shot at my side, moments before.

Daniel appeared, mightily pleased with himself.

"Did ye see them Frenchies run?"

"How did you find enough powder to fire a cannon?"

"The powder had dried. We packed a charge of nails, splinters and pebbles, it was worth a try. It worked so well we fired another!"

"As good as grape shot," Red added, joining in the general celebration.

Rising at dawn, we saw that the French warship had hoisted sail and made to the open sea.

Two weeks following the attack and departure of the French warship, Daniel and I were sitting at the end of the breakwater dangling our un-shod feet in the warm sea. The sun was setting to our right and the sky was alive with vibrant colours. A few clouds were picked out, outlined in a myriad shades of pink and gold. The air was balmy after another extremely hot day. Work had been suspended at mid-day, our fresh water was running low, and many labourers were suffering with dehydration. After clearing and repairing the damage caused during the raid, the production of salt was now in full swing. That which had been stolen was more or less replaced, ready to be shipped back to Bermuda.

The white coral sand, coloured by the sunset, glowed as though lit from within. Sitting in comfortable silence, each of us deep in his own thoughts, it was Daniel who was the first to break the spell. His thoughts were still dwelling on the past, to the fateful day we raided the mine for wad, back among the Cumberland fells:

"Ah don't rightly know John, how it was the soldiers, had knowledge of us," he puzzled aloud.

"What do you mean?" I asked, switching my mind back to the events so many thousands of miles away.

"Mean? Sold out, we were sold out man."

"How, by who?"

"I've had time a plenty, to think on it. Davey and Tickle I've known these twenty years gone, but Rob Benson?"

"I had thought him an old acquaintance of yours," I recalled.

"Nay, not been seen before four-month past. It was Tickle brought him in."

"Really, you think he 'gabbed'?"

"Worse than that, he was a spy!"

"How do you come to that conclusion?"

"Ah've seen him, seen him in Carlisle, at the jail, not locked up. Strutting around like he owned the place."

My anger rose: "My God! That does explain a lot. If I ever get back, I'll see he regrets what he has done."

"I'll run the bastard through, for sure!" said Daniel, spitting into the sea in his anger.

We separated to go to our beds, I related to Arabella what Daniel had said, not mentioning anything of returning to England or taking revenge. During the night, I lay awake going over all that had been said, seeking answers and finding none.

As the time of our departure from Turks Island approached, Arabella became restless, wanting to be more than a housewife. Limited social life combined with our relative isolation, caused acute boredom among those not directly involved in the salt production.

The weather was beginning to break, with regular spells of high wind and occasional rain. Most of all, we feared a hurricane, particularly for the return voyage. It was in order to create some diversion for Arabella, I suggested that we host a dinner party. My wish, for some time, had been to show thanks and appreciation to those who had sallied out to repulse the French.

In particular, 'Red' who, inspiring our response, deserved recognition for his bravery.

So it was, in the last week, a party consisting of the six women and their partners, Daniel, Red and two army officers, squeezed into our cabin. A tuna fish caught the day before provided a suitable feast. As we could not eat it all, the remainder was distributed amongst the soldiers and convicts. A merry evening it was indeed, aided by a small keg of rum, delivered by sloop the previous week.

Conversation around the table covered many topics but kept returning to the French attack.

Each person had their own tale, with its own particular point of view.

Daniel asked Red about his family, once he finished an account of his part in the affray.

"Red man, will ye not tell us about yourself?"

"What's to tell, other than I've come down a long way in the world?"

"That cannot be all, too little, tell us more."

"It is like this, I served my country against the Scots, was wounded for my trouble. Took a ball in my leg, the wound set bad, like to go rotten. Could have lost it, been a cripple but, Lord be Praised, recovered. The army didn't want me, no-one wanted me, too many old soldiers looking for work. My wife and three children, two girls, five and seven in years, a son, my pride and joy, at nine years of age, lived in squalor. The children begged at the roadside, my wife and I managed to find odd jobs, never enough to feed the children. None of us had eaten for several days, I went to a baker to beg crumbs from floor sweepings. He beat me, had me whipped from the village. Returning in the evening, I took a fresh loaf from the open stall. I was chased by wolf hounds, caught before I was able to reach the family, locked up, tried and transported, all in less than a month."

Shocked but not surprised, one officer guest asked;

"Your family, what of your family?"

"Don't know, likely all dead, all dead." Red, slumped in his chair, chin on chest, looking fit to cry.

The two officers, exchanged embarrassed looks, clearly ashamed;

"This is all too common a tale," said one.

"Honourable, brave men are left to rot once they are no longer needed." said the other. Arabella got up from her seat and went around the table to rest her hands on Red's shoulders,

"The world can be hard, evil and unforgiving. I will ask my father to enquire after your family."

Red sobbed, "I want to know, good or bad, want to know, need to know. God Bless You"

General words of comfort and expressions of concern were uttered by all, leaving a more sombre atmosphere than before. The gathering broke up, our guests departed with grateful thanks to Arabella. As Red made to go, Daniel placed an arm around his shoulders, pulling him close.

"Never you fret my friend, Daniel Bragg will look out for thee."

Thereafter, we packed up, setting sail for Bermuda after three more days.

CHAPTER EIGHTEEN

"John, I love you."

Waking slowly from a deep sleep, filled with dreams that were already fading from memory, I turned to Arabella.

"John?"

Arabella's face was touching mine, her nose rubbing softly around my own. The caress, nose to nose, intimate, loving, beautiful; gloriously sensual.

"John, I have something to tell you."

Stretching with a wide yawn, turning to kiss the lips so close, I said:

"Something to tell me my love, is it good or is it bad?"

"Good, always good. How could our life together be anything other than good?"

Wide awake now, I was keen to hear what Arabella wished to say.

"Tell me then, let me share your secret."

Kissing her, running the tip of my tongue, lightly along the line of her parted lips, I begged her:

"Tell me, tell all."

"I am with child."

"What? Oh Arabella, you are pregnant! How wonderful, since when?"

"Seven weeks, I thought so when we were on Turks Island, only I wanted to be certain before telling you."

I fell on her, hugging, kissing, and snuffling in her hair. Hair that smelled richly with the scent of musky cedar. Lying on our backs, side by side, holding hands, both silently engrossed in our own thoughts. A father, I properly in love, begetting children together. Arabella and John Rigg. Images of my parents in their old age drifted through my mind, had they been able to sit out the evening of their lives together. We had that to look forward to.

"You seem pleased?"

"Pleased? I am delighted. Nothing you could have told me would have been such a surprise, nor brought me such joy."

I thought for a moment.

"We can call him Isaac!"

Arabella laughed gleefully.

"Him? It might be a her!"

"That is true, a girl? What name will we give *her* then?"

"Elizabeth, my mother's name was Elizabeth, it will be good to keep her memory alive."

"Then Elizabeth it is!"

I kissed Arabella once more, rolled out of bed and paused to blow a kiss from the doorway. I realised that I was humming tunelessly as I dressed in the next room. Arabella was singing, brushing her hair in front of the large pier glass on the wall next to our bed.

Chris Lane

CHAPTER NINETEEN

The relationship between Daniel and Red developed in subtle ways. First to notice was Thomas, who told his mother in his written notes to her that Daniel had another friend. He was a little disappointed to no longer be the centre of attention himself. Arabella explained to Thomas, that expanding friendships was normal among adults. He would become a member of a wide circle of friends and acquaintances as he grew up, it was an exciting prospect. I told him that there was nothing to fear, indeed, his life would be all the more rich, because of it. Thomas accepted our advice, his face a study in serious concentration. Later that day when I had a chance to speak to Arabella alone, I commented:

"Thomas is growing up, I thought him very mature in the way that he dealt with our words."

"Yes, I am very proud of him. He has become quite the young gentleman lately. While we are talking about this, I need to say that I do not much care for the name that Captain Davey is known by," Arabella replied.

"His name is Redmond, Redmond Davey, what else would you have him called?"

"I do not know. Do you think that I could ask him?"

"Ask him by all means. However, do not be disappointed if he does not have an alternative."

"I shall call him Captain Davey, rather than 'Red' in future if that is the case," she retorted.

True to her word, the next evening, when both Daniel and Red sat down with us for supper, Arabella broached the subject.

"Captain Redmond Davey, I am aware that everyone knows you as 'Red'. May I ask, do you approve of this?"

"Madame, an interesting question. I have only been called Red since becoming a convicted felon. I do not care for the name Redmond. Red is somewhat more acceptable in a group of male peers, than Redmond. So, I went along with it," he explained.

Daniel had been following the conversation with great interest. Leaning forward, with a piece of pork on the point of his knife, he waved it in Red's direction, demanding:

"Well man, thee's intrigued me now, out with it. How do ye want to be called?".

"Well, my middle name, the one my parents always used, as did my dear wife, God Bless her, is Gideon."

Arabella, leaned back in her chair and studied him in silence for a moment,

"Gideon, a fine Biblical name to be sure. One that truly suits you. If you will be so kind as to permit me, I would like to call you Gideon, from now onwards."

"My dear Madam, nothing would give me greater pleasure. In fact, it will be a great honour to hear you use a name, I had thought, long lost."

Thus, it was that 'Red' became Gideon. It took a while, until eventually everyone knew him as such, even Thomas. Although, he was resistant at first, until that is, I told him Gideon was a famous ancient warrior.

Colonel Tucker grew weaker in body, but not in spirit as winter approached. Gideon and Daniel worked together with me on the Colonel's business; taking much of the strain and daily worry from his shoulders. During an early morning meeting with the Colonel, he surprised me with an unusual suggestion.

"John, I have a mind to enjoy Christmas in style, once more, while I am still able. This house has not hosted a Ball or party for many years and I want to celebrate, with all my family and friends, the joy *you* have brought into my life and all those I love, my daughter and grandson, Daniel Bragg and *you*, who has brought us all together, to whom I am forever grateful. The Good Lord saw my pain, sending you to heal it, to cure it, giving me a reason to live. John, you will gather a small group to assist you, money no object, to see it done."

"Of course, Sir," I replied. "I will need your guidance as to what exactly is it that you want. More detail will help in securing the celebration that you envisage."

"Leave me for now," he answered. "I will think more on it, write it out for you to discuss further."

I left him in his study, bright and happy in the expectation of what was to come.

Thomas was developing friendships with several of the local boys of his own age. Their families were seafarers of one sort or another, every boy could swim, fish or sail a boat with a skill beyond their years. Thomas had retained his early interest in boats, he continually badgered Arabella to allow him a boat of his own. Having discussed the idea at great length with me, the Colonel, Daniel and anyone else who was prepared to listen, Arabella suggested one day:

"I think that when Thomas is twelve, in December, a small sailing dinghy will be a good birthday present. I may then get some peace from his constant begging. Notes left everywhere for me to find."

She handed me a piece of paper on which Thomas had written, 'Please! Please, please, please, please. Can I have a boat of my own?' A sailboat was drawn in the corner.

"See what I have to put up with, this is the second one today!"

"Really Arabella, you must applaud the lad's persistence, surely something suitable could be found."

164

"No, I will have one built especially for him which will ensure his safety, lacking as he does the power of speech."

"Why?"

She explained that his absence of speech is a barrier to communication at sea. Also, the craft must be unsinkable.

"He is a strong swimmer, but unable to call for help should something go wrong."

I had to concede to her common sense, Arabella had considered all the possible difficulties Thomas might encounter. She went on:

"I will arrange to talk with the shipwrights at Penno's Wharf, on the south side of the town. They have built three sloops for my father and will be able to make the boat that is needed."

I accompanied Arabella that afternoon, on her visit to Penno's but left it to her to negotiate with them, regarding the necessary design.

CHAPTER
TWENTY

*D*aniel and Gideon were our constant companions, so much so, that the Colonel treated them much like favourite relations. The autumn passed into winter. We suffered the tail end of a hurricane that had swept inland, over one thousand miles to the south. High seas and strong winds restricted movement for almost one week.

A whale was blown ashore and beached on the appropriately named, 'Whalebone Bay,' attracting a great many spectators, who came to view this giant of the oceans. Whales visited the Bermudas every spring, some were caught for their oil or ambergris but the flesh was eaten also. It was unusual for them to be so readily observed on land. Thomas rode over with me to join the throng his interest and delight expressed with loud noises. On our return home, he sat down to draw a very credible representation of what we had seen.

The arrangements for the Christmas Ball began to come together. I reported to the Colonel each week the latest progress. Arabella was busy visiting ladies, discussing food, clothes and entertainment. She was five months pregnant, past the first weeks of sickness and beginning to bloom. I loved the swell of her expanding belly, in awe and wonder at nature's amazing ways. Around the last week of November two Royal Navy frigates arrived in Castle Harbour, en-route from England to the Bahamas. Severe storms to the south had forced them to take shelter here.

While on a visit to the fort being rebuilt on Castle Island, I arranged to be rowed out in order to introduce myself to the ships 'captains. The sea inside the protecting reefs and land, encircling the anchorage was calm. Both ships were moored in deeper water, south of St David's Island. I was welcomed on board the nearest vessel and taken to the Captain's cabin. The Captain was a young man of no more than thirty years, tall and well spoken. He introduced himself as Captain Robert Harper.

Over a glass of Port, he spoke of his intention to ride out the worst weather until Christmas. I told him of the forthcoming Ball, suggesting that he and his officers might care to join us. After sending a message across to the other ship, we were shortly joined by the other Captain. He was a little older, more roughly spoken, with a clear air of authority about him. Introduced by Captain Harper as Captain Eli Farrington, it quickly became apparent he was the senior officer. Our convivial meeting lasted for over two hours. On making moves to return home, Captain Harper suddenly said:

"Just one moment, Sir. I have papers here to be delivered ashore. Perhaps you will be good enough to ensure that they reach the intended destinations."

He handed me a large, heavy, tightly sealed canvas bag. I swung it over one shoulder, taking my leave with the promise to see everything distributed correctly. On returning home I delivered the bag to the Colonel, certain that he was the right person to see to the proper delivery of its contents.

Dinner had just been placed on the table, when a servant brought me a small paper package, with my name written on it. Intrigued, using a table knife to break the seal, I opened it with care. It was a letter from Elicia!

Ambleside. July 1766

My Dearest John,
If this should reach you, please reply to me my love.

I looked up to see Arabella's questioning eyes on me.

"From England," I said. She lifted her chin, as if expectant that I should say more.

I have given very much thought to you and to us. Your letter was a relief to receive, as I had expected you dead! You have a child, a daughter, she is yours. I have lain with no man since you used me so. She is named Ruenna, after my grandmother. She is beautiful and looks to have your features..

We parted in anger and shame but that is in the past, I have known and loved you since I was a child of four years. Your reaction to my questions was extreme and unwarranted. What happened between us, I have decided to forget. The love we had is too strong to resist. I want you here with me, a family, to live together as we always dreamed.

Because of what happened between us I have been cast out of polite society and it is hard to provide for myself and Ruenna. I thank God that the farm is mine and gives us enough to live on day by day but the winters are more difficult.

I will survive and have vowed to take no other lover. Despite everything you and you alone are all my heart will ever desire.

Sealed and sent in hope and love
For ever yours

Elicia xx

I looked up, everyone around the table was watching me, conversation and eating had paused. I felt a tear slowly escape to run down my cheek but could not speak. Arabella stood up, pushing the chair violently back. I held out my hand and said:

"Arabella?"

She rushed from the room, clasping her belly and sobbing. *She knew! How did she know?*

Daniel was the first to break the spell, "Elicia?" he asked.

"I never thought…" Of course, Daniel would have told Arabella about Elicia. How could I not have suspected that he might?

"What does she say?"

"She says she still loves me," I said. She wants me to go home. More importantly of all, she has found it in her heart to forgive me. I thought that she never could or would."

"What are ye to do John? Get yourself to Arabella, reassure her, *Now!*"

Taking the letter with me, I found Arabella in our bed chamber, lying face down on the bed.

"It is from Elicia, written as a reply to the letter that I sent some long time ago, before you and I knew each other."

Between sobs, Arabella asked;

"Will you leave me, go back to England. Do you love her?"

"I still have feelings for her it is true," I answered with honesty. "Yet my life is here with you, for ever. There will be no going back to England for me. I love you more than anything in the world. I will never leave you!"

Arabella sat up, wiping her eyes with the sleeves of her jacket.

"Do you really mean that? Promise me, you mean that."

"I promise, I promise. How can you think that I do not mean it?"

"You will never leave me?"

"Never!"

I lay down beside her, my arms thrown over her, my lips kissing away her tears. We fell asleep wrapped around each other, drawing comfort in the sense of oneness. Thoughts of dinner were left forgotten and of the group around the table wondering how such a thing had happened.

Their muted conversation continued for a while, until one by one they drifted off, each to their own bedchamber.

The addition of a group of naval officers to the social life of St. George's was most welcome. The excitement caused among Bermudian society was extraordinary. From mature matrons to hopeful young maids, the talk over the tea tables was of little else. Even Arabella expressed her pleasure when receiving the two Captains, accompanied by several officers. She sparkled in their company, considerably expanding her group of admirers.

The tiers of Bermudian society was complex, the native families descended from the first settlers comprised the top rank. Next it was those who arrived later from Portugal, England and other parts of Europe including those of mixed race like Arabella. Incomers from the Americas' also mixed in this circle. The labourers were predominately Negro but many of them had improved themselves by becoming sailors, craftsmen and even pirates.

The slaves and convicts occupied the lowest level of society being neither free nor valued except as beasts of burden, to be worked to death.

The contribution of the Navy to my task of fortifying the main harbours, was very much appreciated. My experience as part of an English army turned smuggler was useful but far from that required by a designer of forts. Captain Farrington, in particular, showed a great deal of interest in the designs so far completed.

Several days spent in his company brought me to admire and respect him. In his career he had experienced the cold far north, as well as the heat of the tropics. He understood both the demands of the Navy, also the art of coastal defence. We quickly became great friends, I always looked forward to his visits with pleasure.

It was during one of our meetings that he talked about the coming rebellion of the American Colonies. I had never considered this a possibility but he convinced me that a military confrontation was inevitable. I pondered his words for a week before sharing my thoughts with the Colonel.

"Colonel, I wonder, have you heard anything regarding the American Colonies that would cause you alarm?"

He was silent, looking down at some papers in his hand. When he raised his head, I could see some concern in his eyes.

"There is, I know, great resentment towards the demands of the mother country. Taxation is becoming unreasonably high. The difficulty is in forcing the government in England to understand a situation as exists three thousand miles away."

"I admit to having overheard conversations in the coffee houses and thought it purely bluster," I said.

"No, quite definitely not bluster. There is an element here on this island which would like to see our ties to London severed. We are closer to the America's than to England, it might seem to some that we should look to the new west, rather than backwards."

"What is your position in this then sir?"

"I John am a loyalist, my ancestors supported the King, fighting Cromwell's Commonwealth. They rejoiced when Charles the Second became king. We are a Crown Colony, long may we continue to be so. However, our main markets for export are the American Colonies. War would mean loss of our main food supply, which comes from America. There are many here who do not wish to see trade ruined, who also sympathise with the colonists."

"It is obvious then, that I should pay more attention and be guided by your wisdom, sir," I ventured.

"If you wish to worry about something, may I advise you to advance the fort construction work because pirates are the immediate threat," replied the Colonel gravely.

I left him writing letters in support of his business interests. He was a wise man whose experience, skill and foresight, guided all my actions.

Gideon and Daniel took on responsibility for the fort improvements at the western end of the island. Particular attention was to be paid to the coast around The Great Sound. The island of Somerset Parish was vulnerable to attack, as was Ireland Island further north. Consequently, they were away for days at a time supervising the defence works. It was with some surprise therefore, that Daniel's voice carried up to the study where I was working. I had not expected him for several days and wondered what had caused his early return. He clattered up the stairs, bursting through the door, from his attire and demeanour he had travelled in haste. Dreadful possibilities rushed into my mind before he had spoken a word.

"John, John, ah must tell thee, a report, pirates, pirates in the islands," he said urgently.

"Islands, what islands?"

"On the other side of the Great Sound!"

Gasping for breath he was unable to continue for a moment.

"Sit down Daniel, calm yourself, take a breath and tell me all."

Daniel scrabbled in his pockets until he found the sheet of paper he had been searching for. Passing it to me, he sat back waiting on my response. Unfolding the paper revealed it to be a rough chart of the Great Sound. A string of twenty or so islands running out from the shore reached into the centre of the great bay. Those further out gradually reduced in size, until the last, Pearl Island, no more than a few hundred paces wide, marked the point.

"Fisherman brought it this morning, an I thought best to get it to ye."

The reverse of the chart was a larger sketch of Pearl Island, drawn as viewed from a boat. It was heavily wooded with mangroves on the margin, smoke billowed above the trees and several longboats were drawn up on the small beach. The pirates, if that is what they were, did not expect to be observed, it was a matter of good fortune they had been spotted.

Daniel and I went, immediately, in search of the Colonel, only to discover that he had left to visit Gates Fort half an hour earlier. Horses were quickly saddled; we made all speed following the Colonel's route.

Arriving but ten minutes behind him, I was pleased to see that Captain Farrington was in attendance also. Daniel repeated his tale, producing the rough chart for examination. A long discussion ensued, finally it was agreed to do nothing other than mount a constant watch from Spanish Point, a mile or so distant, across the bay. Captain Farrington offered to provide a small detachment of Marines for that purpose. His offer was gladly accepted, the meeting dispersed. Daniel returned to Somerset Island, I to my office and Captain Farrington to his ship. It was some time later before I had cause to reflect on our failure to deal with the pirates immediately and wonder what the outcome of our omission might be.

CHAPTER TWENTY ONE

*M*y talk with the Colonel had interested me greatly. It was not the first time that I had heard mention of the island's dependence on the American Colonies for food. During my weekly travels round the islands, the investigation of this trade became the main question in any conversation. Salt, as I already knew, was the staple export to the Colonies. In exchange they sent corn, bread, flour, pork and lumber.

Bermudian farmers grew cabbages and onions which were shipped to the West Indies, returning with rum, molasses and cotton. This trade did explain the close ties with America, also the Bermudian empathy with their expressed grievances of English taxation. The Colonel was always loud in his condemnation of slavery as it existed in the Colonies. In his beliefs as a Quaker, all men were equal, whatever colour or creed.

Preparations for the Christmas ball were overtaken by the arrangements for Thomas's birthday celebration and his present. Arabella went to approve the boat builders' progress, returning excited and pleased with what she had seen. We asked that the dinghy be delivered the evening prior to December fifteenth, leaving it in the middle of the carriage drive.

Thomas rose early that morning. He squealed with delight when he saw the little craft in the garden, waking the household in his enthusiasm.

He persuaded Arabella that it should be launched right away, sailing with his friends in the harbour for the remainder of the day. Whenever the weather permitted, the boys spent all day exploring the ring of islands between St George's and St David's. Arabella's initial fears over Thomas's communication skills proved unfounded and she gained satisfaction and joy from the obvious happiness that these expeditions gave to Thomas.

Christmas day dawned bright and clear; the sea lay calm with hardly a wave to break against the shore. I left the bustle of the house to walk down to the beach. Sitting on a rock ledge, my thoughts turned to the events of the past. It was in this state that Daniel found me. Sitting side by side, no words were exchanged in silent understanding that both of us had loved ones left in England to occupy our minds. Sighing, I turned to Daniel, whose gaze was focussed far away.

"This is a very beautiful place," I said. No answer! "I could live here for the rest of my days."

He stirred. Looking at me absently he murmured, "Your pardon, John?"

"I said I could live here forever."

"Live here forever? Mayhap ye may?"

"It is beautiful, is it not?"

"Ay 'tis so."

"Would you stay if you had a choice?"

"Nay, Maggie, ma dear lass, breaks ma heart to think on it!" he replied.

"Well, whatever, we are here now and will have to make the best of it."

"Best of it, ay, Best…" His voice trailed away, the remainder unsaid.

Placing my arm over his shoulder I said, "Come Daniel, we are here for now and it is Christmas. Let us join them up at the house."

He rose slowly and stiffly, taking one long last look at the horizon then we strolled, arm in arm back to the house.

Guests were arriving, dogs barking and the general hubbub that rises up from a happy gathering. Christmas 1766, four years since my last in Ambleside, an age past and I, no longer the man I was then.

Changing quickly, we joined the Colonel's household walking to St Peter's Church, meeting with friends and neighbours along the way, all heading to Christmas service.

Returning to the house afterwards was an animated crowd of party guests, Bermudian traders, local fishermen and ship owners all with their families. Officers of both the

Navy and the military accompanied us, it was a jolly, festive scene.

The Colonel's house had been decorated that morning, with swags of flowers entwined in cedar boughs. Candles lit every corner and aromatic fires burnt in each fireplace. Platters of food were laid out in beautiful array, on tables constructed by the carpenter the day before. So merry, so bright-the atmosphere filled me with the spirit of Christmas, joining in the dancing with enthusiasm.

Arabella looked so fine dressed in robes of scarlet. Thomas wore his best waistcoat and breeches in dark blue and canary yellow. Daniel and I chose to be dressed in more sober colours but had not been able to resist silver threaded waistcoats with red cravats all purchased from the skilled seamstresses of St. George's. The laughter, dancing, music and wine whirled us on through the day from noon to night. I had not had so much fun for many a year. Midnight came too soon, guests began to take their leave singly and in couples.

With little remaining energy and a heavy head, I sank into the nearest chair, dozing lightly. Arabella woke me, shaking my shoulder so fiercely, I thought my head would come adrift.

"John, John, have you seen Thomas?"

Fighting to clear my head and to focus my eyes on Arabella, I sensed her panic.

"What, is something wrong?"

"When did you last see Thomas?"

"I don't know, I cannot remember. Have you looked in his chamber? No doubt he has tired of the party and taken to his bed," I said calmly.

"Not so John, I have looked everywhere, there is no sign of him, he will not answer, although the servants have been calling all around the house and gardens."

My befuddled brain cleared in an instant.

"Not in his room?"

I leapt to my feet, suddenly very concerned.

"Perhaps he has gone with a friend, staying in their house for the night?"

Attempting to sound convincing I suggested we dispatch servants to discover if he was in another's house. Daniel arrived, he had been appraised of the news that Thomas was missing. Having overheard my last remark he offered to go directly to seek out the friends that Thomas might be with.

Arabella had calmed herself, comforted by the possibility that her son was safely ensconced with another family.

"Daniel, please go with all speed, bring him back home that I may rest easily in my bed tonight," she implored him.

She sat down, wiping her eyes with a lace trimmed handkerchief and then turned to me.

"I am so sorry my love, I had thought the worst and panicked as any mother would."

I sat beside her, taking her hand.

"Don't apologise, I understand. He will be found soon, let us prepare to retire while we wait on his return."

"No! I cannot until he is safe, please! Sit with me 'til that is so."

"Of course, my dearest, whatever you wish. Come to the fire, we can sit here awhile."

Moving into the parlour, where a dying fire glowed weakly in the hearth, we sat together on the settle, holding hands. A short time had elapsed before we were roused by a commotion in the passage outside. Daniel entered, his face anxious. Arabella saw it too and started sobbing, even before Daniel reported that there was nought found and that three of the other lads were also missing.

People began to crowd into the room, our remaining guests, including the two naval Captains and some Red Coat Officers. The sound of the worried babble was pierced by a long scream, a primeval cry of pain straight from Arabella's heart. Every other conversation stopped for a second, she collapsed in a faint, falling almost into the fire. I barely managed to catch her. The effect of a joyous evening spoiled, the protective love for her mute child and for the baby she carried, as yet unborn all conspired in weakening her spirit. Captain Farrington took command:

"Quiet for God's sake! This must be discussed properly, but not here."

Whilst the ladies present looked to Arabella's comfort, the men removed to the dining room; where more detailed information was demanded of Daniel. Those who could, found space to be seated around the table, still laden with leftovers of the party feast. The remainder stood, as many as were able to squeeze into the limited space against the walls. Daniel recounted his visits to the homes of Thomas's friends. Three of them were also missing. It was assumed the boys had all gone out for a sail in the dinghy during the afternoon. "At least we may be assured the boat is unsinkable," I said. "More than likely they will have moored up somewhere, once darkness overtook them. They are experienced sailors, sensible lads. No doubt we will find them safe and well come tomorrow."

Captain Farrington offered to despatch armed cutters, to search as far as Castle Harbour once it was light. The general mood was one of relief, all felt confident in the boys' discovery, unharmed, next morning. That was until the missing boys' parents joined the gathering their worried exclamations and demand for information added to the general hubbub, it was they who suggested that pirates might be involved in such a disappearance.

Arabella would not be comforted. Once recovered from her collapse, anger overcame her, demanding a search be commenced at once. It proved impossible to deny her in the face of such determination. Several groups set out in different directions. The Colonel, finally aroused by the rumpus downstairs, descended to ascertain the cause. He shared my opinion, that the boys were holed up nearby, waiting for daylight.

A long night spent without rest passed, before dawn brought light and renewed vigour to the rescuers. The search ranged as far to the south as Hamilton Sound. Every bay, inlet and beach was explored, along the whole coastline. By noon, without anything further to report, I started to think that the unthinkable had happened to the little craft and crew. I chose not to share my thoughts with Arabella, who was becoming more distressed with every hour that passed.

The Colonel took me aside to say that he was concerned for the child Arabella carried.

Mid-afternoon, a messenger arrived from the commander of the Marines camped on Spanish Point. The note he delivered brought news that two longboats had departed from Pearl Island at noon yesterday. The same had returned at dusk, towing a small sailing dinghy. At last, there was something positive to consider. Captain Farrington and the Colonel summoned everyone to a counsel of war in the dining room. The suggestion was that the longboats might have some connection with the pirate's camped on Pear Island.

"My Grandson is more important to me than almost anything," he said in anguish. "I want to make it clear that every possible avenue must be considered in any attempt to have him and his companions returned to us unharmed."

Captain Farrington interjected;

"Without doubt, we need to act quickly otherwise the boys will be spirited away from these islands, to God knows where."

"What is the possible purpose in their abduction?" I asked.

"Slavery and who knows what else besides," answered the Colonel. "Young lads are worth gold coin in some places, they are a valuable prize. It is possible that a ransom demand will be made."

The comments and conversation rose in volume while the possibilities were debated and discussed by everyone in the room.

Captain Farrington called for quiet:

"I have Marines and Sailors at my command and am willing to set out at once on a rescue mission. Who here will join me?"

"Wait, wait!" cried the Colonel. "I am sure that a large assault will end badly for the boys.

Their throats will be cut, and the pirates if that is what they are, escaped before we get close. I will lead a small raiding party myself. A body of hand-picked men will have a far greater chance of success in this enterprise."

"I will come with you." I said.

"And I," said Daniel.

Captain Farrington acquiesced, offering every help and support.

"I will join you with however many of my men you think fit. My dear Colonel, I understand your wish to take part in the expedition but would urge you to allow younger fitter men to undertake it."

"No!" Was the Colonels reply, "I will see Thomas safe, or die in the attempt. That is the top and bottom of it. No more discussion, let us prepare with all haste."

The meeting broke up, the messenger returned to the lookouts camped on Spanish Point, with instructions to keep the raiding party informed of any movement from the pirates. The group of twenty marines, sailors and others chosen to attack the pirate camp hurried away to arm themselves and reassemble three hours before dawn. Daniel and I collected pistols, daggers and a sword each from the armoury at Gates Fort.

We both looked like a couple of desperado cut-throats once we had darkened our faces with charcoal. When Arabella found us, waiting in the hall, had the mission been any other, she would have laughed, to see us.

"Bring him back, John. Take care of yourselves and my father, look after him, his heart is strong, but he is an old man. I fear for you all, may God be with you, I shall pray until you return safely to me."

She hugged Daniel, then turning to me she held me in a tight embrace, as tight as the child in her belly would allow. Lifting her face to mine we kissed and for some moments we stood looking into each other's eyes. Without another word, our hands touched briefly before I joined Daniel and the rest of the party waiting outside.

Men were whispering quietly, others stood apart lost in their own thoughts. Each man was heavily armed, dressed in dark clothing. The Colonel spoke to us, laying out the planned route to Pearl Island.

Four fast cutters had been brought around to the north of St. George's Island where we would embark to sail around the coast to Spanish Point. From there a short overland march, leaving the boats to be rowed around the point to pick us up again. Captain Farrington had considered it prudent not to undertake to sail all of the way to Pearl Island. If we rowed from Spanish Point to Omega Rocks and from there waded through the shallow sea to Pearl Island, there was less chance of our being discovered.

The armed cutters were to patrol to the north in order to prevent the pirates escaping by boat should our approach be observed. It was a good plan, well thought out and very likely we would be in position before first light. We set out with all speed and once aboard the cutters, a following wind whisked our little flotilla along at a spanking pace. We made good time to Spanish Point, trekking to the Marines camp within ten minutes. Once joined by the cutters and rowed out to the rocks it had been a mere two and a half hours that had elapsed since departing from St. George's.

We still had an hour of darkness before the dawn. The sea glowed enough to show us Pearl Island as a silhouette on the horizon. Slipping into the sea from the rocks was hazardous. They were rough and sharp, enough to snag a man's clothing or slice flesh.

The sea was cool and the rocks uneven underfoot. With water only three to four feet deep, it was possible to keep the powder dry, providing that an unwary step into a deeper pothole did not soak you. It was more difficult going than anticipated. Captain Farriington led the way, a rope about his waist and carrying a long wooden pole to test the way before each step. The rope was uncoiled, the other end tied to the last man. The rest of us used it to guide and steady our progress. It was slow and difficult work, stumbling amongst the blocks of coral. Muttered curses could be heard as men struggled with the uneven footing. An eerie luminescence flickered in the water disturbed by our passing.

The Colonel required the strong arms of those on either side to prevent him falling at every step. It was obvious he was fading fast and required assistance for the last few yards onto the beach. He sat down heavily, struggling for breath. We were pleased to see the pirates' long boats still drawn up out of the water, with Thomas's sailing dinghy alongside. No sentry had been set, the pirates thought themselves unassailable.

Once the last man had waded ashore, we checked our weapons and split into two groups. Captain Farrington with his Marines and crewmen, ten in all set off to work their way around the rear of the small island. The Colonel, with me, Daniel and seven others were to go to in the opposite direction. It was agreed by all that pistols must be a last resort, to avoid shooting each other in the melee.

The smell of wood smoke warned us that we were close to the campsite. Apart from the waves breaking softly behind us there was no other sound. Once in a position from where we could see the clearing, we waited for the agreed signal from the Captain's party. It was to be a whistle. While we waited, I became aware of the increasing glow on the eastern horizon, it would soon be light.

Scanning the clearing as every detail became clearer, Daniel noticed a crude cage off to the left-hand side. There were dark figures lying in it but too dark to identify at present.

"There are the lads for certain." he whispered. "In the cage, must be!"

I tapped the Colonel on the shoulder, pointing to the cage and whispering,

"The boys are in there we think, Daniel and I will work around to it. If we can release them before the shooting starts, so much the better."

I signalled to Daniel, setting off in a crawl towards the cage with him close behind me. Keeping to the undergrowth as much as possible, even so, the occasional open ground had to be crossed, very carefully. It was on the last of these that the captain blew his whistle and all hell broke loose.

A large dog lying between Daniel and me jumped up at the sound, barking furiously. Although chained to the cage it strained towards us, teeth bared, jowls flecked with foam. Shouts of roused occupants were followed by wild shots into the bushes around us. The pirates burst into the clearing firing wildly in all directions.

The dog's attempt to get to us was breaking the wooden bars to which it was chained and the whole cage was shaking and creaking. Daniel stood up and leapt over me where I lay. He landed on top of the dog, crushing it with his weight, stabbing in the same movement. Leaving the dog, he crawled to the cage, tearing at it with his bare hands, I scrambled to join him. With both our efforts the cage soon disintegrated on one side, enough to pull the terrified boys through the gap created. They had been woken by the sudden eruption of barking and shooting. Confused and frightened they had huddled together in the corner of the cage, opposite from the dog. It was a miracle that none of us were, so far, injured.

"Juh, Juh, Jon?" muttered Thomas haltingly, throwing his arms around my neck.

Daniel gathered the other boys in his arms, setting off in a run towards the beached boats. I followed, Thomas on my back, another running beside me. The shouting and shooting intensified, forcing us to run faster. On gaining the comparative safety of the beach I put Thomas down, asking Daniel to remain there to look after the four boys and returned to the scene of battle.

Bodies of eight pirates lay unmoving in the clearing, while the two who still lived, were being held roughly against the trunk of a tree by the Marines. Captain Farrington was beating the undergrowth for anyone hiding there. He was bloodied about the face and hands. Two of our men were injured and being cared for by another with bandages improvised from strips of linen..

We had won the day, without too much loss to ourselves and the boys were safe. With daylight now fully upon us it was possible to appreciate the defensive situation of the island in the Great Sound. Visibility all around was excellent and by a lucky deduction, we had chosen to approach from the least expected direction. The sea was too shallow for any sort of craft and none would have thought us foolhardy enough to wade across under cover of darkness.

I became aware that the Colonel was not with us and asked if anyone knew where he was but to no avail. Resolving to find him, I charged two fellows to assist me in searching the area where he was last seen. It did not take long. We found him where he had fallen, almost hidden by dense undergrowth in a shallow hollow, enough to disguise him from chance discovery. The Colonel had been mortally shot in the chest although he still clung to life. I knelt beside him, cradling his head on my knees. A pool of blood spread under him, his breathing shallow and laboured.

I sent one of my companions to find Captain Farrington and bring him to me. Colonel Tucker opened his eyes, already clouded by imminent death. He tried to speak but the words were lost in bubbles of blood and froth. My heart was heavy to see him thus. A man beyond any other I had ever known, he was honourable, honest, generous and loving and I knew then, that I would miss him more than I can ever say.

Captain Farrington arrived and falling to his knees, he took the Colonel's hand in his, questioning me with a look. When I shook my head, he bowed his own head in sorrow, quietly praying. The Colonel drifted peacefully from this life, comforted by two people who respected and loved him.

There was no time for further reflection as shouting and the discharge of firearms reached us from the beach. Captain Farrington and I accompanied by others ran toward the noise. Bursting out onto the beach, a shocking sight greeted us. Daniel was prone on the sand, covered in blood. Out at sea, Thomas's dinghy was under sail and moving fast. Lined up on shore some of our men were shooting ineffectually after it, while others struggled to launch the beached longboats; unsuccessfully, as the bottom of each one had been stove in. We watched helplessly as the pirates escaped with the boys, despite the losses we had suffered to rescue them. Returning to where Daniel was lying, I was relieved to see he still breathed. Cheering from those behind, prompted me to look out to sea where the cutters were speeding to intercept the dinghy as the sound of shots reached us across the water.

A round- about chase ensued. As wading ashore had shown us, the Sound was very shallow in places. The dinghy came to a sudden, jerking halt as it ran aground. More cheering from those on the beach as the cutters surrounded and took the dinghy, pirates and boys safe into their custody.

Satisfied that the boys were now back in our hands, my attention returned to Daniel. Two sailors were attending him and as I asked them the extent of his wounds, they told me he had been stabbed twice in the arm and side. His hands were bloody and lacerated. It was obvious, Daniel had put up a determined fight trying to protect his charges, even grabbing the pirate's knife blade in their defence. His breathing was irregular, the skin of his face had taken on a greyish hue, I was very concerned for his survival. Those who had been watching the drama play out in the bay now gathered around Daniel. The clamour was silenced by Captain Farrington, who, taking charge, ordered Daniel be bandaged and made as comfortable as possible while we awaited the arrival of the cutters.

Even now the cutters were working their way between the shallows to reach us, with the dinghy in tow. During a quiet moment the Captain appraised the assembled group of the death of the Colonel. The news was received in shocked silence, a feeling of gloom settled over us all. After ensuring that Daniel was well cared for, I guided a party back to where the Colonel lay. Forming a cradle with our arms we hoisted the body back to the beach, laying it next to Daniel. It was then that the full horror of his plight hit me. It seemed that I was about to lose Daniel again, as well as the Colonel.

What to tell Arabella? How to comfort her, even though Thomas was safe, such a great loss.

The cutters anchored in the shallow sea, just off shore and the boys were carried, shoulder high to the beach. Thomas ran to me, arms outstretched, gripping me so tightly, I could not move.

It was decided to send the boys and Daniel back to St. George's directly by fast Cutter. The Colonel's body was to be escorted overland. I wanted to stay with the Colonel for this last journey. Leaving the island to cross to Spanish Point, I looked back at the rising smoke where the pirate camp was burning, my heart filled with the most profound sorrow. Once on shore, we set about making a litter to carry the Colonel's body, it was to be draped with a Union flag. Sailors and Marines formed the escort and bearers. According to the Colonel's timepiece which I carried we started out on the ten-mile march at half an hour past eleven-o-clock.

There was a brisk wind blowing, enough to cool us in the weak sun. Word had spread quickly and very soon our sad cortege attracted spectators. Some lined the road as we passed, others joined with us to follow on behind. Hardly a sound was uttered, just the steady tramp of feet and quietly whispered words when bearers were changed. It was near four-o-the clock when St. Georges came into view. Our party now numbered many hundreds, as at every building and hamlet, more joined us.

The whole population of St George's lined the streets with bowed heads. Somewhere a child bawled or a dog barked, otherwise all was silence. Approaching the Colonel's house, the servants had crowded out into the street, Arabella and Thomas stood among them. Rushing forward as soon as they saw me, we linked arms, following the litter in through the gates to the house. Once the Colonel's body had been placed on the dining table and left to the ministrations of the women, the escort party was refreshed by the beer and food brought out for them. Muted conversations trailed away as the gathering broke up, leaving the house to an unusual, expectant quiet. Arabella, Thomas and I had retired to the Colonel's study as soon as we could. Sitting together on the sofa, we held each other close. Our tears flowed, unstoppable, we were wrapped in our own storm of emotion. Finally, I recovered enough to ask:

"What of Daniel?"

"He will live but may be confined to his bed for some weeks yet."

"And Thomas, how are you, recovered from your ordeal?"

The boy nodded, eyes red with crying, he looked up, leaning forward pressing his cheek against mine. His last tight embrace of me as he was rescued suddenly flashed in my memory. *On the island he spoke, attempted to say my name!*

Had I dreamt it? No, I was certain not! Holding him away from me I looked into his eyes.

"Thomas, do you remember, on the island, you said my name?"

He shook his head.

"Thomas think! You *did* speak, I know it."

Arabella stared at me incredulously but said nothing. Her gaze turned to Thomas, regarding him intensely. Thomas continued to study my face, a frown of concentration furrowing his brow. His lips moved, forming a sound,

"Juh, Juh…"

Arabella leaned closer to him, her hands either side of his cheeks.

"Thomas, are you trying to say John?"

His lips shaped the first part of my name again, all the while holding his mother's gaze. Tears started from his eyes, I hardly dared breathe. Arabella said;

"Oh my darling, don't fret."

She pulled him to her breast, stroking his hair,

"You are home safe that is all that matters. My two men are safe, her voice trailed away in a wracking sob…my dear father…I would I had the three of you here with me now."

All I could do was to sit with them, holding them in our shared grief. Never again would I spend a convivial evening in this room with the Colonel. Although evidence of his presence was in every corner, the vital spark of his spirit had gone.

CHAPTER
TWENTY TWO

$\mathcal{J}$t was on the day of the Funeral and burial of Colonel Tucker that Daniel regained consciousness. Gideon had been left in charge while the household, joined by most of the Island's inhabitants, attended the service. He met us on the way back from St. Peter's Church, beaming broadly and much excited.

"He is awake and asking for food, though still too weak to sit up unaided."

I could not restrain myself, grabbing his hand and thumping his back.

"Really, Daniel is awake? If he is wanting to eat, he must be on the mend."

I looked back at Arabella, who sensing my impatience, smiled lightly and waved me to go on ahead. Taking hold of Gideon's arm, we ran all the way back to the house.

Rushing upstairs to the invalid's room, I hurried in without a pause. Daniel lay on the bed, head slightly raised, resting on a bolster. He opened his eyes as the door burst open with the force of my entry. His arms lay at his side on top of the bedcover. He looked very thin and pale but raised a bandaged index finger in greeting, nevertheless.

"Daniel, my dear friend, me thought I had lost you for good, this time."

Gideon had followed me into the room,

"Come John, now you have seen him for yourself, he must be left to sleep."

I allowed myself to be led out, pausing to take one last look back as the door closed.

"Don't worry John, I will care for him and see that he wants for nothing. He is my friend also, I owe him much."

Gideon caught at my sleeve, holding me back in the corridor, I stopped and turned towards him.

"John, I have been meaning to tell you, these two days gone," he paused. "Did the Colonel inform you?"

"Inform me of what?" I asked. "It has been a difficult few days, I have hardly had time to converse intimately with him."

"Inform you of the letters he has had back from England."

"Letters?"

"Yes, the request he sent about my family."

I waited for Gideon to continue.

"My family have gone, dead, every one"

"Oh Gideon, I am so very sorry to hear it," I commiserated.. "They did not deserve the fate they were dealt, nor you, even."

"It is well that I know the truth. One day I will return to England to find their graves. I will gather flowers to place there and water them with my tears," he replied.

I did not know what else to say, words were not enough. Instead I embraced him for a while, then we parted to go our separate ways, he to his patient and I to join the gathering below, celebrating the life of Colonel Thomas Tucker, Quaker, Military Commander of the English Crown Colony, of Bermuda.

CHAPTER TWENTY THREE

*T*he New Year came, 1767 but it did not bring much joy. Everyone was raw with the pain of the Colonel's passing, the whole household in deep mourning. Arabella went each day to visit the Tucker family vault in St. Peter's graveyard. Occasionally I was able to accompany her, sitting quietly as she prayed.

The pregnancy was increasing the size of her belly, making walking laborious. As January passed into February the visits became fewer, until they were no longer practicable. Daniel slowly recovered from his wounds, although his hands would never again enable him to hold a tool or weapon effectively. Gideon took on the task of completing the improved fortifications and Thomas spent many hours alone, by the sea or in the garden when the weather permitted. He did not express a wish to sail out in his dinghy, which had been repaired and was moored in the harbour.

My time was taken up in the Colonel's study, working through the thousands of documents stored there. The wide-ranging business interests and numerous financial affairs had to be itemised and dealt with in order. Arabella often joined me, lying on the sofa, while I worked. She complained of back ache more often now, sleep was difficult, she could not find any position comfortable. It happened in late February that she lay on the sofa as usual, dozing, shifting her body every few minutes. A sharp cry escaped her lips, I looked up from the paper I was reading, to see her sat up eyes wide, gripping her belly.

"John! Oh John, the baby is coming, my waters have broken!"

Leaping to my feet, I rushed around the desk to kneel beside her.

"What shall I do?"

Another sharp cry of pain, more urgent this time.

"Go! *Quickly!* Send for the midwife. Help me to my bed, now, *now!*"

It was plain that I needed to act but panic and concern froze my mind, making me dither.

"*John NOW!*"

Helping Arabella to her bedchamber took several minutes, stopping every few yards when the contractions came. I called for help while trying to support her, my shouts becoming louder and more insistent when unanswered. It seemed an age before the servants answered my call. I dispatched one to fetch the midwife, handing Arabella over to the women who were milling about, taking charge, and pushing me from the room.

Daniel led me into the downstairs parlour, pouring a good measure of Canary wine as we sat in front of the fire, to await events.

"Don't ye fret John, the women will set all well. I've seen it with ma Maggie. We have nought to do, bar wait."

I did not feel encouraged, if anything felt even more nervous.

"God in heaven Daniel, why are we left thus, I feel so helpless and useless," I complained.

Loud noises from the front door and hall, announced the arrival of the midwife who immediately clattered up the stairs. Apart from the creak of floorboards and murmured voices from the room above, everything appeared normal. Daniel poured us another drink, I swallowed it at once, without thinking.

"John, John, slowly man, you'll get yourself as drunk as a bishop, if ye don't take care."

He filled my glass again, leaving it to stand on the table I began to pace about the room.

"Sit down man, for heaven's sake. You're making me right giddy."

I collapsed into a large leather chair, taking my wineglass with me, settling to stare into the fire. Daniel tossed more logs on, sending bright sparks up the chimney, such as a blacksmith strikes from hot iron.

The candles had been lit, the fire stoked, the shutters closed. Dusk was washing the colour from the sky before we were roused by the cry of a new-born child. By then we had drunk two bottles of wine and had started on a third. The warm glow of the fire aided by the wine dulled our brains, causing us to rouse ourselves with less speed than we might.

Footsteps on the stairs, followed by movement in the hall heralded the approach of a messenger. The door was opened by one of our female servants, she smiled broadly as she announced the completion of a safe delivery.

"Is Arabella alright, can I go up to her?"

"Not quite yet Master John, we women have things to do, you will be called soon."

"What is the child, boy or girl?"

The messenger giggled, raising her hand to her mouth.

"You will find out soon enough."

With that she bobbed a quick curtsey and turned from the room, leaving us to our thoughts.

"Daniel, what can that mean? I am confused."

"I don't feel able to say John, it is a mystery indeed."

Above half of an hour had elapsed when our messenger returned.

"You may go up now sir."

She giggled again, continuing to do so as she hurried off down the corridor. Leaving Daniel, I ran up the stairs, taking them two at a time. Pausing on the landing to catch my breath, I made a more dignified entrance, which belied the state of my thoughts.

The room was quiet and calm, Arabella lay on the bed, tired and drawn and she smiled weakly, turning her head to the left. A servant woman bending over the wooden cradle by the side of the bed stepped back when she saw me. Approaching the cradle with trepidation and peering in, I gasped, for there, toe to toe, tightly swaddled were *two* babies!

"You are the father of twin girls, John Rigg!" Arabella announced.

"Oh my dearest Arabella, how can this be, what are we to call them? We only have one name."

I sat down on the bed next to the cradle, reaching behind me to hold Arabella's hand. Their skin was coppery gold, with copious heads of dark coloured hair.

"They are beautiful, we have been blessed, my love, it is just that I had not expected two daughters or even *two* sons."

"I know John, it does explain how large my belly became, me-thought it was one big child inside of me!"

"We must think on the other name I mused, Elizabeth was your choice yet perhaps Thomas needs to be consulted. He is desperate to see you; shall I call him up?"

"Please, do not to stay long as I am very weary."

When Thomas came in, full of excitement and curiosity, he had to be restrained from leaping onto the bed with his mother.

"You have two sisters Thomas, go and greet them."

He went to the cradle, peering in, inspecting the new arrivals, looking very serious. Touching the babies faces gently, he leaned down to kiss them, each on the forehead. Looking up at his mother, eyes bright, he smiled and clapped his hands with delight.

"Come Thomas, we must leave your mother to rest."

Thomas hugged Arabella while I kissed her long and full on the lips, my heart bursting with gratitude and love.

"Sleep well my sweet, we will return later, after Thomas has had time to think of names." Going downstairs, Daniel greeted us, glasses filled with rich ruby wine.

"Here ye are, a toast: To Arabella, and the newest additions to the Rigg family"

Clinking glasses, echoing the toast, the full realisation of my new life left me with a foolish smile on my face for the remainder of the day. Now, I was the father of *three daughters*! The effects of two and a half bottles of wine helped the day pass in a blur.

After explaining to Thomas the need to find another girl's name, he took pen and paper,

retiring to his room to write down those he fancied. The evening was well advanced when he finally came to the bed chamber where Arabella was feeding the babies. I lay across the foot of the bed, taking great pleasure in watching the display of motherhood. As they looked identical, how were we to recognise one from the other? I put the question to Arabella.

"Have no fear, I shall know them apart, even now their characters are not identical."

"I am glad to hear you say it, for I know not if I can say for sure, which is which."

"So, tell me which Elizabeth is?"

"This is Elizabeth." She said, raising the child attached to her right breast. "She is more spirited than her sister, also the noisier."

Thomas was keen to show his list and taking it from him, I was surprised by the number of names he had written there. Holding it up for Arabella to read, catching her eye, we both laughed. Thomas looked hurt; Arabella reassured him.

"Don't be upset Thomas, we laugh with surprise to see such a long list, we are not laughing *at you!*"

Eighteen names in all were listed in alphabetical order.

"Which do you favour?" I asked him.

Taking the list from me he regarded it seriously for a minute, finally pointing to AURELLIA. Changing his mind, a moment later, he pointed to EULINA, then his finger hesitated moving to ARETHUSA.

"Thomas would like his sister to be called either Aurellia, Elunia or Arethusa," I said.

"What do you think, my love?"

"I am not sure John, give me the list, once Elizabeth and her sister are back in the cradle." Arabella tucked the babies in, watching them for a moment before taking Thomas's list from me, speaking the names out loud as she read them.

"John, look, tell me your preferred name?"

Moving to sit beside her, we scanned the names together. Arabella ran her finger down the list, pausing at ELOISE. Jabbing it twice she turned to me with a questioning look. I shrugged, indicating my agreement.

"Thomas, would you be happy if we called your sister Eloise?"

He nodded, clearly relieved that the decision had been made for him.

"Eloise it is then, we are in agreement."

Saying which, I rose, kissed Arabella and the twins goodnight and ushered Thomas out of the room.

CHAPTER
TWENTY FOUR

*A*rabella struggled to breast feed the twins. A wet nurse was found and engaged to help, taking the major responsibility from her. Thomas visited the nursery each morning to see his sisters, in whom he exhibited enormous interest. He was growing into a handsome young man, with his mother's dark fine hair, his father's deep brown eyes and a Mediterranean tone to his skin. It was of some concern to Arabella and me that Thomas spent many hours alone, He showed no desire to venture out onto the sea again. When asked what he had done during the day, his answers we vague. Arabella thought that he was hiding something from us and she urged me to talk to him. He rarely mixed with his sailing companions any more. His solitary pursuit, whatever it was, occupied every hour spare.

I resolved to enquire of the servants, also seek out both Daniel and Gideon in the hope of an answer. This took several weeks as I had no wish to raise any suspicions on the part of Thomas. Intriguingly no one was able to explain the behaviour, although it had been observed that he was reading a great deal. New books were taken from the library, read and returned almost daily. One evening the opportunity arose for me to broach the subject.

"Thomas, I am pleased to notice that your desire for knowledge has led you to the library, which subject do you favour?"

He regarded me for a moment, his eyes luminous in the candlelight. Dropping them to regard his feet, he shrugged his shoulders. Was there a hint of embarrassment? I considered what to say next.

"It is good to have an enquiring mind, to thirst for knowledge."

He looked at me again, smiled. Leaning forward to hug me, holding on for more than a minute he then resumed his seat. It was clear, I was to have no satisfactory answer! Deciding not to press him further, the conversation being mainly on my part. Thomas responded with nods, smiles or shakes of his head, which ended when we retired to bed. I reported to Arabella, who was as mystified as I was. We fell to discussing the need to christen the twins as soon as was possible.

I volunteered to go the next day in order to make arrangements with the priest. He suggested the following Wednesday, agreeing that it be a quiet family affair as we were still in mourning. Arabella wished both Daniel and Gideon to be Godparents. We could not agree a third until Arabella suggested Thomas.

"Perhaps it will give him something to look forward to, raising him from melancholy."

"An excellent idea, I totally agree, my dearest love," I replied.

I lost no time sending for Thomas, who was clearly pleased to have been asked.

The day of the Christening arrived, windy and cold. Wild scurries of ragged cloud sped across the sky, masking the sun. The small gathering, huddled together in the empty church felt a little sad, marking what should have been a joyous occasion. The Godparents had their words written out for them, each his own responses. Thomas knew to show his agreement by signs or nods and was very excitable. Before the service began, he fidgeted to such an extent that Arabella scolded him.

"Thomas, my son, what has got into you? Sit still or you will have to stand outside."

He quieted for a while, until the priest stepped out to conduct the baptism. Thomas was bursting with nervous energy, rocking back and forth, shifting from one foot to another. As the service proceeded, the moment came for the Godparents to give their assurances. Daniel and Gideon did their part, it was now the turn of Thomas. Nothing! He stood stock still and there was a long pause as all eyes fell on him. The priest coughed, indicating that the service of baptism required a response from Thomas. Thomas returned our puzzled looks, then taking a deep breath *he spoke!*

"I promise."

A stunned silence ensued, after a curious glance, the priest cleared his throat, continuing with requests of the Godparents. All eyes were on Thomas, his turn to speak came again.

"I will."

A clear, steady voice rounded and sweet. He reddened under the gaze of all present. Arabella exchanged looks with me, I with Daniel and Gideon. Daniel raised his eyebrows, shaking his head in disbelief. As the service ended, all was quiet for a heartbeat, then, the gathering erupted.

"Thomas, how comes it, how long have you been able to speak?" cried Arabella, confusion and joy fighting for possession of her face.

"I found my voice when the pirates took me, I have been practicing, on my own every day. My words needed to be perfect before sharing them with you."

Of course, now his strange behaviour over the past weeks made perfect sense. Thomas was embraced by the whole group, holding him, laughing and crying. The church filled with happiness, dispensing the previous gloom. Thomas chattered nonstop as the happy throng sang and danced all the way home, despite the worsening weather.

During that evening, we all gathered in the parlour to have Thomas recount his miracle to us. It was on being captured, when extremely distraught, his sounds became words, ill formed, coarse, but words, nevertheless. He resolved then and there that he would not share his discovery until perfected. Catching Arabella's eye, I saw that tears of grateful happiness shone there. I had never seen her look as beautiful as she did that night. Going to our bed later in the evening, we made slow, wonderful love, for the first time in several months.

CHAPTER TWENTY FIVE

*E*lizabeth and Eloise proved to be happy and contented babies. As they grew, the differences in character became more evident. Dark baby eyes changed to grey-green, much like mine. It was wonderful to be the father of such as these. Thomas began to sprout; it was likely that he was to be taller than me eventually. His voice started to break, now able to express himself through speech, we all found his constant chatter tiring. The years of mute communication had not fitted us to tolerate such a talkative young man.

The household's period of official mourning came to an end, coinciding with the return from the American Colonies of the Tuckers' lawyer, Sir Robert Sandys. At last, the Colonel's Will could be read, his Estate settled. Arabella met with him, on her own, in the Colonel's study. Thomas, Daniel, Gideon and I were invited to join them after an hour had elapsed. We were all very curious as to the way in which the Colonel had wished his Estate to be divided. There was no expectation on either mine or Daniel's part, certainly none whatsoever on Gideon's. It was a surprise for us to have been invited at all. Therefore as we sat waiting in the Colonel's study, an atmosphere of suspense filled the very air around us. Sir Robert peered over the rim of his spectacles, coughed and began.

The last Will and Testament of Colonel Thomas Henry Tucker.

In the name of God Amen. I, Thomas Henry Tucker of the Parish of St. George's, in the Crown Colony, Bermuda, gentleman and Colonel, Military Commander of the said Colony. doe this fourteenth day of June in the year of our Lord one thousand seven hundred and sixty five. Being of sensible and disposing mind and memory (thanks be to almighty God) doe make this my last will and testament in manner following (that is to say), first I give and bequeath to my dearest daughter Arabella this my house in St Georges, and all goods and chattels therein. I give and devise her the sum of five thousand pounds as a portion of proceeds of the sale from a full seasons salt to the American Colonies. I ask that my daughter Arabella is to hold the above individually and separately of her husband John Rigg Gentleman. Item my will is that I require on taking possession of the afore mentioned house.

Arabella grant full and complete freedom to those indented servants and others remaining in my household.

I give to my grandson, Thomas who has brought me great joy, all of my businesses and business interests both in Bermuda and abroad, I leave my fleet of nine trading sloops with all licenses and connections appertaining to the same. To be administered in his stead by Mr John Rigg until Thomas shall reach his age of maturity at eighteen years of age. Mr John Rigg to draw annually the sum of one thousand pounds and five percent of profit from the said businesses in remuneration for his management of the same.

I give and bequeath five hundred pounds, my two fishing vessels presently moored in Flatts Inlet and the cottage on Smiths Island to my dear son-in-law John 'Moses' Rigg in grateful thanks for his loyalty and friendship.

I give and bequeath a Royal Pardon and one hundred and fifty pounds to Mr Daniel Bragg.

I give and bequeath a Royal pardon and one hundred pounds to Redmond Gideon Davey.

I give and bequeath to each and every member of my servants and estate workers five pounds.

I give all the rest and residue of my personal estate (subject to my just debts legacies and funeral expenses) to my daughter Arabella to be distributed and disbursed as she wishes.

Signed sealed published and declared by the above named Thomas Henry Tucker to be his last will and testament in the presence of

Sir Robert Sandys
Arabella Tucker
Richard Smith

An audible sigh escaped from the assembled audience; glances were exchanged. Sir Robert looked up, no one spoke, the enormity of the Colonel's generosity stunned us all.

Colonel Tucker had been a very wealthy man and his provision for those he loved showed for the last time, how astute and caring he truly had been. Sir Robert pulled two, heavily sealed parchments from his pouch, handing one each to Daniel and Gideon. Daniel opened his to read, Gideon sat with his on his lap, in something of a daze. Arabella squeezed my hand, resting her head on my shoulder. We were going to be comfortably provided for financially, for the remainder of our lives. I resolved to inquire into sending some money to assist Elicia in looking after herself and Ruenna.

The spring came, slipping slowly into summer, while we each travelled extensively in the tasks of running the late Colonel's business interests. Elizabeth and Eloise continued to thrive, loved equally by us all, although, Gideon, in remembrance of his lost family, indulged them more than most. Thomas grew to become the typical young gentleman, more quickly than I could ever have imagined. His speech, apart from an occasional inflection, was perfect. He spent many hours with Daniel, Gideon and me, asking questions about our previous lives. Endlessly inquisitive, his bright, agile mind, drank from the pools of our knowledge, filing everything away, to be revisited later. I was constantly surprised by his sharp memory and in no time he became most dear to me, my son in all but paternity.

Arabella ran the household in her own gentle way, earning the love and respect of all whom she commanded. She was a wonderful mother to the twins, most evenings we sat together in quiet companionship, while Thomas read to us from a favourite novel. This was a level of domestic bliss to which I had never dared aspire.

The transfer of money to Elicia was easily arranged and the documents required to authorise bank payments were dispatched on the first ship bound for England.

In the months from March until October the islands were a blaze of exotic colour. The native flowers grew everywhere in profusion which I had hardly noticed before. Purple Morning Glory vines spread luxuriantly over every piece of wasteland, while a plant, unique to these islands gladdened my eye. It was but a small thing, resembling a miniature Iris, with delicate blue flowers bearing a yellow eye named 'Bermudiana;' blooming among the rocks and sand dunes. Oleander, Mimosa and Acacia grew in the cedar forests, while colourful Hibiscus shrubs filled the hedgerows with red, pink and yellow flowers. Poinsettias added their rich red in December. There was no autumn, no time of bare, grey branches, no winter as in England, Bermuda was an ever golden world. With eyes newly opened I appreciated the beauty around me as joy and contentment filled my heart and soul.

A tutor was engaged to instruct Thomas in the sciences, arts, geometry, Greek and Latin his enthusiasm to learn was undiminished.

Journeys to Turks Island became a regular part of my life, taking Thomas with me whenever possible, that he might fully understand the whole of the salt making process. In trade he accompanied me on two visits to the American Colonies to deliver salt, bringing general supplies back on our return. I came to consider that it would not be long before he would be able to undertake these voyages without me.

Daniel completed his military construction labours, the islands were now as secure as possible, well able to be defended from a seaborne attack. Indeed, the fortifications were tested twice in the year, proving the construction and design to be well done, the raiders being defeated long before any successful landing.

By Christmas 1767 our little group had managed to increase profits, developing business affairs with creativity. Both Gideon and Daniel had used some of the inheritance to invest in other operations, building a business income of their own. One hurricane reached Bermuda in late summer. Sitting out the violent storm huddled in the cellars was tedious, as was the work of repairing the damage once the storm had passed. However, none of our properties suffered seriously and we were back in operation within a few days. Arabella possessed a tidy and orderly manner of thinking which proved most beneficial when dealing with disaster of whatever nature, be it domestic or otherwise.

CHAPTER
TWENTY SIX

*D*uring the January of seventeen sixty-nine, while sitting as we were wont at the fireside after dinner, Arabella, staring into the flames for some minutes, suddenly asked:

"John, have you thoughts for the future?"

"In what way, my dearest, why do you ask?"

"I don't know. Only I often look to the future, our future, wondering what it might hold for us."

"Much the same as at present I would hope, God willing," I replied.

"Easily said, but really, where shall we be ten years hence, you, I, Thomas, the twins?"

"Here, surely here, you and I, our family and friends, together."

"John, my lover, my dearest friend, I feel a darkness in my soul, coming closer. My dreams are full of foreboding."

Arabella came over to sit close beside me, laying her head on my breast, holding my hands in hers. "John, truly, I fear for the future. Our life seems too perfect to last. I have known more happiness in the last three years than in all the years before, everything is just too good to last."

"Saying so, does not make it so. My darling Arabella, you deserve to have a good, long and happy life. I will never leave you, could never leave you. You are adored by everyone who knows you. I love you with every particle of my being, you are all that I live for.

I have no regrets, would do the same again had I my life over."

Kissing her eyelids, cheeks and nape of her neck, I hugged her tightly to me, resting together in this way, until going to our bed. There we cuddled together kissing with an urgency, almost desperation, to dispel the shadows endeavouring to come between us.

The morning dawned as always, the sun shone as ever and we rose as usual to speak no more of our fears. Yet I pondered often on the words shared with Arabella the previous evening.

In April, a packet ship arrived in St. Georges harbour, bringing tidings and letters from England. Among them were several for the Colonel, written ere the news of his death had been generally announced. I was delighted to find a letter for Daniel. Losing no time, a horse was saddled that I might ride to Fort St. Catherine and deliver it to him. He was in the Keep holding a meeting with the Governor. Obviously startled when I burst in, he leapt to his feet, knocking his chair to the floor.

"God's blood John! What's thee so lathered, what's afoot?"

"Daniel, Daniel such good news I bring," I said." At last a letter for you, from Maggie, I believe."

Taking the letter from me, without a word, turning to the window, he read it, several times.

"Is everything alright, is it from Maggie, is she well?"

"Aye John, it is good, to hear all's well on the steading. I thought never to hear aught again."

The tears in his eyes told of his pleasure and emotion and I was happy for him, clapping him on the back, shaking his hand before I set off back to St. George's.

Returning to the house, Arabella was waiting for me in the study, an unopened letter in her hand.

"John, is Daniel alright, was the letter from Maggie?"

"Yes, I am so pleased to say it was. What is that in your hand, is it for me?"

"Yes John, yes it is for you, from Elicia!"

Placing it on the desk she moved as if to leave.

"Wait, wait Arabella, read it with me. I have no desire to hide anything from you. I need you to know what she has to say."

Noting that it was dated June seventeen sixty-eight, I eased it open at the seal. Reading through once, I read it again, aloud this time while Arabella sat in the Colonel's chair, her hands clasped in her lap.

Ambleside June 14th 1768

My Dearest Love,

I received your letter and my heart is torn in two. I wish so very much to be with you, to share every possible minute with you. I love you so much I could set sail to join you in Bermuda. Please write again, tell me all that you do, that I may imagine every day your doings there.

Your daughter, Ruenna is a beautiful child, I often tell her of her father far away, in a distant land, so she will know you when you come back to me. All I have told her is that she was conceived in love. When will you come back to me? I cannot bear to be parted thus and wait patiently for your return.

Thank you for the three gold guineas' that I receive from your agent each month, it has made a deal of difference to our situation here.

Know that I am now and always will be yours, and yours alone. Come back to me my love, I implore you, come back to me.

Your ever loving

Elicia

When I finished reading, Arabella sighed, rising from the chair she came to embrace me. We held each other for a while, neither spoke. At last Arabella said:

"Poor woman, John, she loves you much as I love you. I understand her pain. What do you feel about what she has said?"

"I, as you, feel compassion and concern," I answered carefully. "She was once very dear to me, we had a happy childhood together, I cannot be totally unmoved by her situation."

"Good, right glad am I to hear it. The John Rigg I know and love is not an unfeeling man. You must write to her, tell her about me, about us. Relate to her your experiences and life here, tell her everything, it is only right. I am happy to know that you send her money to support your child."

I thought my heart would burst at such a generous reaction from Arabella. Her womanly empathy for Elicia's plight made my love for her stronger still. Elicia needed to know that I would never return to her, her suit is pointless.

I replied to Elicia,s letter but also asked that Arabella should write too, so that Elicia should be in receipt of them together.

CHAPTER
TWENTY SEVEN

*I*t was later in the week, while searching for Arabella, who had left to visit friends in Flatts, I chanced upon Daniel and Gideon in the Colonel's study. Many charts and maps were spread out on a table and they both looked embarrassed and sheepish at my arrival.

"Well now lads, what are you about?"

"Tis nought John, a little treat for ourselves."

"Aye John, we took a liking to see the old country, revisit old haunts."

My curiosity was aroused, "I'm intrigued, what is it you are looking at is?" I inquired.

"Maps of England, John, there is nothing in it, just two ex-convicts yearning for home."

"Aye John 'tis rightly so."

"Well let me share with you, come show me," I said.

The charts were mainly of England and Ireland, a large-scale map of the whole of the British Islands was prominent in view, attracting particular attention. Gideon pointed out his old home near Bristol while Daniel searched for familiar names in Cumberland and Westmorland. It was a nostalgic distraction, one that I was pleased to indulge in. Seeking the names that we knew so well brought long suppressed memories to the fore.

"Daniel, what do you wish when you look at this map?"

"Ah now John, that is the question. For myself ah wish to be on ma own steading, with ma lass on the fells. Ah never thought to see ma home again. But now with the coin that the old Colonel gifted me, well I may yet. May happen, ah may John it may happen," he mused.

"So Daniel, you would return to England, now that you can afford to, with the Pardon and your inheritance?"

"Aye John that would be mighty fine."

"I understand. Nor will try to prevent it."

I was saddened by Daniel's obvious wish to leave but understood that he needed to return to his farm and family. I had thought for some time that this would be the outcome, once he was free and able to look to his own destiny. Gideon had listened to our exchange and after a moment's pause he said:

"I, for one, have no reason to return, I will stay here, make my fortune and die a rich old man."

"What of thee John?" Daniel asked.

"I must admit that I miss the crisp cold of a morning's frost, snow on the Fells even. In my dreams I hear the sound of wind in the bracken, bells on the trod from a packhorse string as I lie just on the edge of consciousness. I have always looked to the mountains as the limit to my horizon. This place is pretty, beautiful even, but it is not magnificent. However, having said all of that, my life, my love, my family is here, so I shall never have need to leave".

I looked at them both, dear friends. We three had been each other's rock, anchor and support through such a deal of danger and sorrow. How would it be without Daniel? Much like the loss of a limb, I would guess. What would Arabella think, she was certain to have much to say, I was sure. Could she support Daniel in his wish or perhaps resent his lack of loyalty. No! Daniel was never disloyal.

We were interrupted by the arrival of Thomas. He looked from one to the other an unspoken question in his eyes. Glancing at the maps laid out on the table, he looked hard and long at me before saying;

"John, you are required below, Captain Farrington has returned from the Colonies, The Repulse is entering St George's harbour, even as we speak".

I took my leave, crossing the hall to the reception room where Captain Eli Farrington was waiting.

"Eli, it is good to see you again."

"John, the pleasure is mine, I can assure you. May I enquire after Arabella and your family?"

"They are all in good health, thank you for asking. Will you take a glass of Canary wine?"

"Yes, but might we speak in private somewhere as I have much to report."

"We will repair to the study, where there is no fear of us being disturbed."

Calling for wine to be brought up to the study, I led the way wondering what might be of such import that had brought the Captain in haste to my door. As we entered, Daniel and Gideon came out, their arms full of maps and charts.

We settled opposite each other, sipping our wine. Captain Farrington studied me over the rim of his glass.

"John, I have come directly from the Provincial Congress of Pennsylvania but felt compelled to meet with you before I set sail for London. There is a great deal of dissatisfaction with the demands that England makes of the American Colonies. I have myself, experienced, at first hand, real anger among some members of the aristocracy. Knowing to what a degree this island depends upon goods brought under sail from the Americas, I thought it best to warn you, as a friend. I believe that unless concessions are given by London, a revolt is inevitable. Maybe not this year or next, but soon enough. You and all here will suffer great hardship unless preparations are made now, to ensure your independence in food production."

I was not unaware of the situation, although a revolt had not seemed the likely outcome.

"Eli, I am not ungrateful for your concern, it is a pleasure to have your company for whatever reason yet how can there be a war between two parts of the same country, it does not appear the differences will lead to such a pass."

"You forget John, it is not so long ago that the whole of England was at war with itself, King against Parliament, neighbour against neighbour, brother against brother. America is a long way from the mother country, it is rich, successful, vibrant and becoming more independent with every year that passes."

"Well, I must take your advice in this," I replied. "You are in possession of an overview, a knowledge of both sides which I do not have. I am right grateful you chose to bring this information to me directly. I will ensure that the islands take note and endeavour to make contingency plans for the future," I promised.

"John, I know only this, that if the right leader emerges, someone to attract the rank and file to support him, God knows what will happen in such a volatile situation."

We sat in conversation for a further two hours and before the light had faded into evening, Eli took his leave, informing me of his intention to depart for England as soon as fresh rain water and victuals had been loaded aboard the Repulse.

I decided to keep this news to myself, but to set about ensuring that the island was growing enough food to sustain us, at the very least. It was not going to be easy.

Arabella quizzed me that night as we lay abed. Thomas had spoken to her regarding what he had overheard in the dining room.

"Is Daniel wishing to leave us, to return to England?" She asked.

"It is difficult to say. He has a family, a life that he would want to recover, also the riches to enable its execution."

"You will miss him?"

"Of course, much so!"

"Does he wish you to go with him?"

"No, he knows full well that I can never return to England, my everything is here. Why would I want to leave you, our children?"

She lay silent, I turned toward her, wrapping my arms about her. Rolling on top of her, supported on my arms, searching her face. She was heart achingly beautiful in the pale glow of the candle. It was impossible to resist the velvet lips, the love in her eyes, her quiet, passive femininity. Sliding into her body, we lay, closely connected enjoying the sensation of oneness.

I began to move, reluctantly responding to the thrust of her hips, relishing each moment our bodies touched and withdrew. Arabella moaned softly, rising to meet my thrusts with a violent urgency, crying out together as we both reached fulfilment simultaneously. Neither of us moved for several minutes, eventually, I pinched out the candle. Both of us sated, content, we lay, our arms and legs loosely entwined.

Quickly falling into a deep dream-filled sleep, I was on the high fells of home, vainly pursuing a distant figure. My legs moved as though in deep molasses, preventing me from running. Arabella, if it was she, left me far behind. Suddenly the open shaft of the Wad mine yawned in front of me. Stumbling headlong into it and falling into the blackness, I awoke with a jolt.

Eyes wide open, staring into the darkness of our bed chamber, my racing heart slowed. As the reality of the dream passed, I became aware of Arabella's measured breathing beside me. She turned in her sleep, throwing an arm across my chest. I lay thus for some time until sleep overcame me once again.

CHAPTER TWENTY EIGHT

*A*s the year progressed, Daniel became increasingly unsettled. His conversation turned to his farm and family very often. I knew in my heart that it was only a matter of time before he would decide to leave for England. It was no surprise therefore, when he came up to the study one morning in early September.

'John, 'Moses', ah have come to the conclusion ah cannot really stay, when all ma head is full of thoughts of Wasdale Head. Ye are ma greatest friend in all the world, and ah don't wish to desert ye. But ah must, and can no longer deny it!'

"Daniel, you are the only true friend I have ever been fortunate enough to have in my life.

I regard you as a brother. I know that you are desperate to return home, Bermuda can never be that for you, as it has become for me. Go with our blessing, go in joy, be with your family.

Never fail to remember me and all we have shared together."

Saying this I reached out, gripping his shoulders and he responded in an embrace. As we drew apart, the tears in our eyes showed the deep emotional bond that we shared.

"Ye daft bugger," said Daniel, knuckles wiping his eyes.

"No more of a 'daft bugger than you," was my retort.

We shook hands solemnly, Daniel left to watch over the twins, playing in the garden. leaving me to sit, staring out of the window at the coconut palms swaying in a stiff westerly breeze.

CHAPTER
TWENTY NINE

*D*aniel arranged a passage back to England, leaving in late October. The whole household anticipated his departure with sadness. Daniel had become highly respected and loved by servants, Bermudan merchants, the twins and Thomas. Yet Arabella became livelier as the date approached, but I knew it to be a brave face, she did not wish to let Daniel see what a gap his leaving would make in our lives. I too tried hard to be positive and supportive, with a heavy heart, nevertheless.

Having thought him lost to me once already, I had no desire to lose him again. We had been through so much together, in good times and in bad.

Coming down to breakfast on the last morning, we were greeted by a stack of trunks and boxes ready to be transported to the harbour. Daniel stood in the middle giving instructions, all the while, coping with the twins wrapped around his legs. Thomas sat on a trunk, sadly observing the servants as they carried more boxes into the hall.

"Are you taking all of Bermuda with you?" I asked, laughing at the chaos the scene presented.

Arabella came to stand beside me, arm around my waist. She could not help but laugh at Daniel dragging the twins to and fro, still clamped, limpet like, one to each leg.

The cart arrived, everything was loaded, and we all set off in a colourful parade escorting it to the harbour. The twins rode on top of the luggage, as the cart led the way into St. George's.

At the harbour many more people had gathered to say their farewells. Daniel could not have been insensitive to the warmth of feeling that he had inspired in everyone who knew him.

Once loaded the ship edged away from the quay with the sails set, it began to make way towards the islands strung across the harbour entrance. Puffs of smoke followed by a loud report, erupted from the fort on Paget Island, well known to Daniel, signalling its own message of God speed. All the while Daniel had stood at the stern, waving occasionally until at last the ship passed the outer islands, in full sail, riding onto the open ocean.

The farewell committee slowly dispersed, until Arabella, Thomas, Gideon, the twins and I were all who remained. With one last look toward the fast disappearing sail on the horizon, we made our way home in a sober mood, apart for the twins, Elizabeth and Eloise, holding hands and giggling together, trotting along beside' us.

It took more than a month to accustom myself to Daniels absence, even so, he lurked forever within my sight, just out of focus. My heart leapt whenever a figure or a face reminded me of him. Slowly however, these imagined sightings lessened as memories of Daniel became less frequent.

We, Arabella, Thomas, Gideon and I, talked of Daniel during evenings spent together after dinner. It was then, when full of food, relaxed and content that those reminiscences of him came more freely.

The last months of the year of grace 1769 passed unremarked. Everyone had settled into the new way of life. Thomas celebrated his fifteenth birthday quietly with family and friends, though, Daniel was remembered when raising our glasses in the after dinner toasts. The twins were both talking well, choosing to call me 'doodah', causing plenty of merriment, but I have to admit that I loved it. Arabella told me that this would not last, urging me to enjoy the name while I could.

Many mornings we were woken earlier than we might have wished by Elizabeth and Eloise leaping on to our bed. Occasionally, Thomas, still in his night clothes, would join us, tucking himself under the covers at the foot of the bed. It was at these times that many family decisions were made, or problems dealt with. When the wind howled about the house, whipping the palm trees into a frenzy, we were cosy indoors, with rain rattling against the casements. These made the best moments that any family could possibly treasure.

CHAPTER THIRTY

*T*he year of our Lord 1770 arrived in a series of great storms, restricting communication with the outside world. Fishing became dangerous beyond the reef, merchants had to be satisfied with counting stock or filing accounts. Grain became scarce, causing much hardship to the poorer families. Arabella went out every day, taking the twins with her, to deliver food to those neighbours in need. Thomas repaired to the library, spending the daylight hours in research. Now and again he would join me in the study, either to assist as my clerk, or to chat about something he had read.

In early March the weather improved, the sun offered enough warmth to enjoy sitting out in the garden. Ships began to arrive from the American Colonies, carrying news of unrest and disaffection.

The first Mail Packet of the year brought a letter from Daniel, informing us of his safe arrival. It was a great relief to know that his journey had been without incident. He wrote of the farm, Maggie and the boys, the magnificence of the

Lakeland scenery. He also wrote of his attempts to locate Rob Benson, so far unsuccessful. I scribbled a hasty reply, in order to catch the ship on its return to England.

My concern was that if Daniel found Rob Benson he might do him harm, only to end up in prison once more. I urged him to be careful, not to act rashly.

A visit to Turks Island needed undertaking within the month of April, therefore I broached the subject with Arabella over dinner one evening.

"It will soon be time for me to return to the salt works," I said. "After the recent storms it may be that a great deal of repair, rebuilding will have to be done. I may have to be away for more than a few weeks."

"Will you take Thomas with you?" She asked.

"Yes, I think so, he must shoulder responsibility, learn to direct and control the workers."

"Then, I will come with you also.

"My dearest wife, is that wise, what of your duties here, what of the twins?" I asked anxiously.

"Duties here can be set aside, the twins can accompany us."

I was taken aback by her reply, I did not consider it safe to take the twins nor did I feel the risk to Arabella was worth taking.

"My love, it is risky, dangerous, as you know. I am unhappy with the suggestion that you or the twins should come with Thomas and me."

"Really John, I want to be with you, share your life. The twins have not been off this island yet and this may be the ideal opportunity. We will all be together, it will be fun, a good place for the twins to learn."

"My dearest Arabella, I know full well that if this is your mind, then there is little to be done that will change it. I agree but do not approve."

Arabella reached out to hold my hand. "Don't fret my love, all will be well, I promise."

I sighed, without Daniel's stolid presence to support me, I felt exposed and vulnerable. "I will make the arrangements; Gideon will have to remain to run things here in our absence."

Three weeks later, we embarked, sailing south on the one thousand mile journey to Turks island. Our flotilla consisted of four large merchant ships, with an assortment of eight other craft. Traders, some with their families, builders, convicts and soldiers totalling two hundred and fifty souls, undertook the journey with us. On the second day, the alarm was raised by the sighting of sails far out to the east of our course. Our Bermudian built ships being fast and manoeuvrable, we left the unfamiliar sails far behind, arriving safely two days later.

The usual muddle of damaged buildings, blocked salt tanks and windblown sand were the first priorities and after two days' hard work everything was repaired and salt production recommenced the following day. Arabella, along with the other wives concentrated on cleaning the accommodation, sorting supplies and looking after the children. Thomas worked with the convicts to get the salt works up and running. Thus, by the evening of our third day on the island we were able to relax and enjoy a fine supper of fresh fish accompanied by a bottle of good wine.

Elizabeth and Eloise relished the freedom being on the island offered. They spent many hours scrambling among the rocks above the beach, not without scrapes to knees and elbows, however. They were robust, sturdy children, rarely coming to Arabella or me for comfort after a fall. Even with the chores that we all had to complete each day, there was a closer bond between us, a greater feeling of family. It was a wonderful, special time, one to be oft remembered in the years to come.

Without the normal distractions, Arabella spent the evenings, once the twins were in their bed, sitting with me before the fire. Occasionally we would read but more often sat hand in hand, lost in thought, staring into the flames.

At the end of the first month, two merchant ships, loaded with salt for Bermuda and escorted by three armed sloops left at dawn for the long journey north. The following afternoon, a cannon fired from the roof of the fort gave warning of approaching danger. All work ceased while everyone who was able, either climbed to the battlements or ran down to the harbour. A battered sloop limped into the bay, shot holes in the sails and a smashed boom were evidence of a violent fight. While the injured crew were tended to, I went aboard to obtain a report from the captain.

"By all that's holy John, I declare, we are most fortunate to have escaped," he said.

"Tell me in as much detail as you can."

"We were heading back to St Georges, a slight sea with a good following wind, when a French man-o-war drew up on the starboard beam, leaving very little sea room to manoeuvre. Had we not been escort we would have been able to evade them but attempting to shield the merchantmen while drawing off the French proved an impossible task. We took a full broadside in the rigging, forcing us to pull away."

"What was the fate of the others, did you see?" I queried.

"One sloop was gravely struck, that I do know."

"The salt, what of the salt?"

"The merchantmen were trapped by a second man-o-war coming in from the North West. They were waiting for us, it was well done."

"We must therefore assume the loss of both ships and their cargo."

Looking up, I discovered that a crowd had gathered, meanwhile around us and been party to our conversation. A general uproar broke out with cries of concern being expressed by all.

"Wait, wait!" I shouted. "We need to prepare for our defence. I cannot but consider it very likely the French will turn their attention to us here."

Confusion prevailed for some minutes. I thought how, at this time, Daniel's presence would make such a difference. Alas it was not to be, we must look to our own resources,

"Everyone, return to the fort NOW! We must call a meeting to decide what to do, how to defend, protect ourselves."

There was a general rush back to the fort and the relative security it offered. Several people scattered to rescue family or belongings from the outlying buildings. I looked for Arabella, Thomas and the twins, finding them already gathered within the tower of the fort. We embraced briefly, Arabella holding me longer than expected. She whispered in my ear;

"John, I am a feared for us all. We were lucky the last time but…?"

Her voice trailed away leaving much unsaid.

"I admit that this is an unexpected turn, I had thought us safe for a month more at least," I admitted.

Elizabeth and Eloise were frightened by the atmosphere of alarm and panic in the room. They did not understand what had brought it about nor was it possible to explain to them the danger that threatened us. Thomas set off to go up onto the roof where a better view might be had of the enemy. Five minutes later he came down to report that the ocean was clear of any sail, friendly or otherwise.

It was with trepidation that I searched the horizon the following morning. My fear was unfounded, the ocean was empty of shipping as far as I could see. Posting sharp-eyed lookouts on the roof of the tower, I asked Thomas to restart salt production, leaving myself to go in search of the senior military officer for a council of war.

Not finding him in the fort, I was directed to a small hill of sand and rock one hundred yards to the north. Major Da Silva was a tall individual of Portuguese decent, an ex-officer in the King's army who had served in the Americas for twenty years. Born and bred on Bermuda he carried an air of dependability. Obviously, a capable soldier, I respected his opinion, being eager to avail myself of it now. He stood on the crest of the hill pointing to the north, in the company of the salt works surveyor.

"Major, I am pleased to have found you here. It is important that we talk about the threat facing us."

"Yes, Master Rigg, as you say. It had been my intention to seek you out after coming up here."

"Are we able to mount an effective defence if attacked in force?"

"We are in possession of a good amount of powder and shot," he said. "There are twenty capable soldiers as well as a further thirty or so experienced men like yourself. Enough I would say, to keep a landing party at bay for several days. My main concern is bombardment from the sea, we can return fire as long as the fort walls are able to withstand it."

"The civilians, women and children will not all be able to shelter within the safety of the walls," I worried.

"Hence my investigation of this eminence. It is a good place to keep any of those safe. A redoubt here will protect our rear, also provide the overflow sanctuary required," he replied.

"Will it be out of range of a man-o-war?"

"I am certain of it. I have observed that the salt works have been re commenced, may I ask that you stop that and deploy the workers and convicts to the construction of the redoubt up here?" he suggested.

"Of course, without delay."

"I will leave the surveyor to oversee and direct the undertaking," he decided. "Come, accompany me back to the fort, where spare hands can endeavour to make it as secure as possible."

With that we walked down to the fort, I was pleased to note that the top of the tower overlooked the site of the redoubt. The occupants would be in view as well as supported by gunfire, should the need arise.

That evening, once the twins were asleep, Arabella and Thomas sat with me to talk about our roles in the event of an attack. It was decided that the twins would go to the redoubt with Thomas while Arabella remained in the fort, reloading, carrying powder and assisting with any that might be wounded.

All of our other companions were awarded a particular place in the impending conflict, thus prepared we retired to sleep as best we could in the cramped quarters assigned to us.

Two days went by without any sign of the French warships. The redoubt was completed and mounted with two culverins removed from the armed sloops, both lying battle damaged in the harbour. Everyone knew their place if the expected attack came, otherwise work was resumed processing salt, not without regular glances out to sea, in nervous anticipation.

A further three days passed without any alarm. We grew more relaxed as the expected attack did not materialise. Although keeping a regular watch from the fort, the remainder settled back into the normal routine of salt working and fishing. Arabella insisted the twins went up to the redoubt each day in order that they become familiar with these surroundings. Either she, Thomas or I accompanied them, sitting with them for an hour or so before returning to the fort. Elizabeth and Eloise looked forward to the adventure, becoming noisy in their demands to go if we were late. I always carried a telescope with me, allowing them to use it, spying on the people below, in which they took great delight.

It was on the following day that during my turn escorting them to the redoubt, they were occupied in their favourite game of telescope, when Elizabeth excitedly shouted:

"Do Dah, do dah, see, look, look a boat?"

"Me see, me see!" cried Eloise snatching the spyglass from her sister.

Scrambling up the bank to lie next to them, I saw, far out, a sail. It was difficult to identify at such a distance, yet through the glass another sail was evident behind the first. Turning, I shouted to the lookouts on the fort, pointing excitedly out to sea. On hearing me they followed my sign seeking the two sails slowly appearing over the horizon. Fifteen minutes passed as we all strained to make out the colours of the approaching ships, two of them in number both men-o-war, flying the *FRENCH flag*!

Good God in heaven! Instructing the twins to remain where they were, I ran down to the fort where the alarm bell was already stridently ringing. I quickly found Thomas and sent him up to the redoubt to look after the twins, then went in search of Arabella. She was already at her post, sleeves rolled up, skirts tucked into her belt Surrounded by ammunition and bandages, as she presided over both the weapons to kill and the bandages to save life; the irony of which was not lost on me.

"John, what is the news, are we in danger?"

"Yes, my love, I am afraid that we are. Two French warships are on their way toward us. They will be in range of our guns in less than an hour if the wind keeps up."

"The twins?"

"They are already at the redoubt with Thomas, how do you fare?"

"I am ready to do what I can to ensure our safety. Promise me that you will not allow me to be taken prisoner if the fort falls, promise me that?"

I hugged her close, holding tightly, kissing her neck and cheeks. She responded, our passion and love overtaking all else for the briefest of moments.

"Elizabeth, Thomas and Eloise, if anything should happen to me…?

"No, no, nothing will happen to you!" She replied passionately.

"But if it should, care for them as you have cared for me, don't let them forget me," I said.

"Never my darling, how could any of us forget you? I love you with all my heart and soul. We shall come through this, just you see."

After another embrace, we reluctantly parted, Arabella to her place and me to the battlements on the tower roof. It was crowded with spectators waiting to see what the French ships would do as they approached the island. When within range of our guns on the lower platform, the whole edifice shook as our soldiers fired a cannonade in unison. The French sheered away, surprised at the accuracy of our gunnery. Balls struck both sails and rigging, bringing down the foremast on the leading ship. A loud hurrah broke out from the observers as the sweating gunners reloaded, heaving the cannon back into the emplacements they had recoiled from. The French ships moved away, further out to sea.

"We have frightened them off," said the soldier next to me.

"No such thing," replied Major Da Silva. "They are changing tack even now, prepare yourselves to receive the reply to our shot."

The two men-o-war, turned about, completing a wide circle to bring them back opposite our position. Following in line, running parallel to the shore it was obvious, that they intended to return fire with a double broadside.

"Take cover, get out of the open," shouted Major Da Silva. "Everyone, get off the roof, now!"

The ships were barely outside the reef and moving fast. As they drew level with the fort, they opened fire, all sixty guns at once. The air became thick with flying iron, crashing against the stonework, smashing battlements and knocking cannon off of their carriages.

The noise was tremendous, I was relieved to see spurts of sand where a few random balls fell thirty yards short of the redoubt. The pole carrying the Union flag leaned drunkenly and fell through the roof into the room below. Screams and shouts from within showed it had caused some damage and injury.

Arabella! I rushed inside and in the dust and confused chaos I could see her, hard at work, calmly passing ammunition to the gunners on the platform outside. *Good!* She was unharmed. Running out to help manhandle a cannon into position to fire another salvo, I was in time to see the two

French ships preparing to run back in the opposite direction. Another broadside was clearly what they intended.

As they drew level our gunners fired with everything that they had, the very same moment that the French ships discharged their guns. For a brief moment, through the smoke, I observed our shot strike home. The leading ship slowed as it lost a mainmast over the side, rigging and sails dragging behind. At that moment the French shot arrived, beating about the walls, slicing through our defences. The exchange of fire was as disastrous for us as it was for the enemy.

The second ship had run into the wreck of the first, becoming hopelessly entangled with it, flames were visible amidships. Looking behind me, I saw great cracks in the tower, cannon balls stuck out of the stonework like currants in a bun. *What a strange thought!* I had no time to think further, for a great explosion blasted me backwards off the gun platform, onto the beach. I lay there dazed and bloody, my senses reeling.

I know not how long I lay thus. Looking up I realised that Thomas was standing over me, the twins beside him.

"Thanks be John, you are alive!"

"What happened?"

"A hot ball fell on the powder, causing a great explosion."

"Your mother, did she escape?"

"I don't truly know. I was going down to the beach with the

soldiers intending to capture the French sailors swimming ashore, when I saw you."

I tried to move, a sharp pain in my left leg caused me to fall back with a cry. Looking down it was obvious that the leg was broken.

"Help me up, come Thomas take my arm, girls you can help too, hold my hands."

Slowly, painfully we made our way back to the ruin of the fort. Less than half of the tower remained standing, the interior was a mass of wood and rubble. Bodies were scattered about, cries and groans showed where others lay in the wreck.

"Your mother was over there." I said; pointing to the place where she had been, now marked by piles of stone fallen from the shattered walls.

"Thomas, go see if she is there, I will sit here with the twins."

Finding a large baulk of timber, I sat down making myself as comfortable as possible considering the extreme pain in my leg. Elizabeth and Eloise sat on either side clasping my arms, sobbing quietly. Thomas scrambled over the ruins and finding something, he began lifting stones, pushing them aside.

"Help, help, somebody help me please!" he shouted.

A couple of convicts climbed over to his aid.

"John, she is here, she is alive!"

They all began digging with an urgency born of hope. Others joined them, soon a crowd had gathered, passing stone from one to another along a human chain. I watched, my breath, panting with fear one moment, held tightly in the next.

At last the activity ceased, a limp body was lifted, carried gently to be laid at my feet. It was Arabella, apart from soot, dirt and a little blood she appeared unhurt. Her eyes were closed, her breathing came in painful gulps. The twins let go of my arms to fall on their mother, holding her around the breast and neck. Her eyes fluttered but did not open, a soft groan escaped her lips.

Thomas sat down beside me.

"Is it serious, will she die?"

"I know not, did the surgeon survive? If so, you must seek him out, quickly now."

Unable to move, I sat, a spectator to the tragedy unfolding in front of me. Thomas returned with the news that the surgeon had died tending to the injured when the flagpole fell through the roof.

We were on our own. Instructing Thomas, I had him bandage and splint my leg. After a good long swig of brandy, with the help of the twins I was able to stand. Out to sea, the two French warships were burning fiercely, locked in a fatal embrace. The pop and crackle of small explosions sent clouds of sparks skywards. A column of dark smoke rose high into the clear sky, while ragged drifts hung over the beach in a grey pall.

"How did your mother escape the explosion?" I asked Thomas.

"I think she was protected from the upward blast but suffered injury when the masonry collapsed."

The picture of Arabella as I had last seen her was imprinted on my mind. Calm, efficient, capable and beautiful. Ready to take on whatever fate threw her way.

"Thomas, my leg must be set as soon as possible, if we can carry your mother to a ship, my leg can be mended on board."

"I will go directly to obtain a fast passage home."

Leaving me with Elizabeth and Eloise, Thomas ran off into the thickening smoke. The girls still hung on to Arabella who had not moved again, she breathed but that was all. A feeling of complete helplessness overcame me. Fighting back tears of frustration and pain, I called the girls to my side.

Thomas returned with the news that two sloops intended to make for Bermuda within the hour and were prepared to take us with them.

To my relief Major Da Silva appeared, I had feared him dead.

"John, I was on the other side of the tower and just now had news of you and your wife. Are your wounds bad?" Then catching sight of Arabella's prone body, he knelt down beside her. "She lives, there is little blood, where is she injured?"

"We think that she avoided the worst of the explosion but not the collapse of the tower."

He stood up to clasp my hand,

"My dear sir, how very sorry I am to hear such. What are your immediate plans?"

"To leave for Bermuda at once. Mayhap we will obtain treatment for her there."

"Indeed, indeed a wise decision. I will summon help to get you both to the harbour."

True to his word, he returned with a crude stretcher and willing hands to carry it. We made a sorry procession, winding our way down the beach to the harbour, Elizabeth holding my hand, Eloise hand in hand with Thomas.

Once aboard, it was necessary to ensure that Arabella was stowed comfortably as possible. When done to the satisfaction of Thomas the sloop put out to sea. Thomas wanted to have my leg set properly before we encountered rough water. He had me moved to a sheltered corner of the deck where blankets had been laid in readiness. With the assistance of two others, one plying me with brandy, I was prepared for the operation. An excruciating pain swept over me, mercifully causing me to faint away.

Consciousness returned slowly, my leg had been properly bandaged and splints of planed wood, fixed securely either side it was painful still, yet comfortingly secure in support. Thomas came to say that Arabella was awake and asking for me. Not without some difficulty, four sailors carried me to where Arabella lay, gently placing me by her side. Her hand reached for mine, interlocking fingers, holding tight. Her breath was irregular. She spoke between every gasp, sucking in air after each word.

"My… dearest… darling… husband."

A single tear rolled down her cheek to lose itself in the tangle of her hair. "I…am…so…sorry."

"Hush my love, how sorry? You have nothing to be sorry for. You are the greatest joy of my life."

She squeezed my hand; a racking cough shook her whole body making breathing more laboured.

I could not bear to see her thus, my beautiful wife, in such distress and pain. Oh, dear God!

"Love… my… son. Care… for… him."

She looked into my eyes with a fierce urgency. Falling back she closed her eyes. After a few minutes, her shallow breathing faded away.

"I love you so much, don't leave me, I cannot live without you."

I raised her hand to my lips kissing it, baptising it with my tears. Suddenly she gave a great shuddering intake of breath.

"I…love…you too …John…Rigg."

With the last, final breath leaving her body, Arabella, my dearest beautiful brave Arabella, passed to a better place.

CHAPTER
THIRTY ONE

*O*f the journey home, I remember very little, being racked with a fever. Thomas cared both for me and the twins. Our arrival in St Georges was greeted by a noisy crowd eager to hear of the events on Turk's Island. Ships had already been dispatched to bring back the French prisoners, to be incarcerated here or sent on to England.

Carrying the body of Arabella to the house attracted a throng of mourners. Keening cries of sadness rose from the household servants as the body of their mistress was carried in. I repaired to my bed, leaving Thomas once again to deal with everything, although this time he had Gideon to assist him.

Two days later, feeling somewhat recovered, Thomas, Elizabeth, Eloise and I, accompanied by Gideon, led a host of others, following Arabella's coffin to St Peter's Church, carrying me in an improvised Sedan Chair. So many had come to mourn, the church filled and overflowed.

Seated outside the Tucker family vault, little hands found mine, holding tight. The twins had cried, they knew that their mother was dead, yet somehow the emotion had been held inside until that moment. The finality struck me then, Elizabeth cried "Mamma!" without warning and with such desperation, I could not hold back my own tears. Behind me, Thomas laid his hands on my shoulders, he moved around to clasp the three of us in an urgent embrace. We shared our tears then, locked together in an unfathomable grief.

It would be foolish of me to say that I returned to my work, immersing myself in it totally. The reality was that without my wife, my lover, my friend and confidant: I was lost in a vast wave of self-recrimination. My biggest regret was that I agreed, against all that my common sense told me, to allow Arabella to accompany me to Turks Island. I knew in my heart at the time, that it was a foolhardy action. Indeed, I had told Arabella so. The desire to have her company, despite the obvious risks had overruled my reservations.

I drifted around the house, without purpose, without focus. Much of my time was spent looking backward, attempting to preserve the precious memories that even now became more difficult to recall. Even the effort required in interaction with both Thomas and the twins demanded time that I only gave reluctantly. What might the future hold for us all? Was the life ahead worth living? These and many other questions served to create in my mind the bleakest of futures. For many more months this period of darkness and foreboding hung over me, night and day.

It was finally broken by the arrival of a squadron of Royal Navy ships of the line, commanded by my friend, Captain Eli Farrington. He presented himself at the house, mid-afternoon, late October..

"My dear Sir, John! Words enough cannot express my sorrow at your loss. Arabella was the finest of women, brave and constant to the last. How are you managing without her beside you?" he asked.

"It has been the hardest test of my life, all else is nothing in comparison. The totality and finality is the most difficult to bear. I have to keep going for the sake of the children but there is a part of me that could lie down and die," I admitted.

"Knowing you as I do, I doubt that is a true wish, one born of loss and despair."

"Perhaps you are right, only time will tell," I replied thoughtfully.

"Time, yes time. I have found it can dull pain without diminishing the cause."

My heart felt gladdened at his presence: "It is good to see you Eli, at least it will help to lift my mood. Are you to stay long in Bermuda?"

"We may winter here. I have been tasked with keeping watch on traffic and trade from the American Colonies. The Government in England is concerned with what is happening there and wishes to be supplied with accurate information."

"That is good news for me," I said. "Will you agree to reside here whenever you are able?"

"Nothing will give me greater pleasure; I look forward to it."

"Thomas will want to see you, to hear your news, will you join us for dinner tonight?"

"A pleasure to accept. I must for the moment go back to my ship but will dine with you before dusk."

The talk that evening was of the attack on Turks Island, the French threat to English sea power and general news of happenings in England. Thomas asked many questions, wanting to avail himself of the Captain's knowledge of world events. It was altogether an interesting evening, serving to move my mind away from all that had occupied it over the last five months. My sleep that night was the better for it.

CHAPTER THIRTY TWO

*B*y early December my leg had mended well and I was more my old self. Regular evenings spent in the company of Eli and Gideon, often joined by Thomas, assisted to soften the absence of Arabella. Thomas was coping with the death of his mother rather better than Elizabeth and Eloise. As all children do, they played and laughed, even chattered with the servants. Yet, behind their eyes was a sadness. At least they did not resemble their mother greatly, for I would have been unable to bear seeing a daughter every day, who was the image of Arabella.

It was fortunate that they both had light brown hair, fair in places and blue eyes. However, they did have their mother's soft golden skin tone. They were undoubtedly pretty children who promised to become beautiful women. Both exhibited strong stubborn characteristics, although generous and loving also. They charmed all who met them and my love for them grew, as more time than before was spent in their company.

Both twins delighted in exchanging their clothes in order to confuse me, sometimes only answering to each other's name. At first, I found this to be most irritating but came to enjoy the game, playing along with it, soon learning to recognise each of them individually.

I had been dreading Christmas, my first without Arabella for seven years. Fate had not given us long together, even so, our bodies and souls had become so entwined that it seemed as though we had known each other for all of eternity. There was a sadness in the house during mid-December. After discussions with Thomas, Elizabeth and Eloise we decided to host a Christmas dinner for our friends. It proved to be the right decision, as each of us entered into the preparations with a desperate enthusiasm.

On Christmas morning, Thomas joined Elizabeth and Eloise in my bed chamber for the first time in many months. The twins tucked in beside me while Thomas slid under the covers at the foot. We all enjoyed the cosy family feeling and our talk, without becoming maudlin, turned to remembrances of Arabella, Colonel Tucker and Daniel.

"Do you think of mother often?" asked Thomas.

"Every day, depending on what it is I am doing, sometimes every few minutes."

"I think of her, our time together before we met you." He grinned, laughed out loud saying; "Even when I could not speak. What a sullen boy I must have been."

"Not at all, you were bright, a joy to your mother and to me once I got to know you."

"I did enjoy the fishing." He laughed again, looking at me rather sheepishly. "And it was a good time."

Suddenly, I felt sad again, too many painful memories. I looked down, my words caught in my throat. The twins, feeling the pain in my voice, cuddled tightly to me. Elizabeth staring into my eyes, saw the tears and kneeling in front of me, she brushed them away with the sweetest, most gentle touch. Eloise joined her, both of them clung to my neck. I was surprised when Thomas scrambled up the bed to join them, holding me in a close embrace. It was at that moment I realised these were *my* children, all three loved and needed me.

They let me go, Thomas sat back, looking into my face, "I have decided to call you father." He said with a positive finality that would brook no argument.

"I should like that." I replied softly.

We all hugged again. Revitalised, I jumped out of bed, shouting, "Come on, cheer up, it's Christmas!"

With happy smiles, hand in hand, we ran downstairs to enjoy the mulled wine and sweetmeats laid out for us in the dining room. The table was set for twelve, Gideon, the twins and their nurse, Thomas, Eli, Captain Harper of previous acquaintance and me. I had also invited Major Da Silva, his wife and two daughters. The others of the Royal Navy squadron were out on patrol, which was of no small relief as our party would have been too large for the room.

Major Da Silva had been a great support during the French attack on Turks Island. I had made the acquaintance of his wife the previous week but not met his daughters before. The eldest, Katherine, was tall, dark haired with her father's features. The other, Isadora, took after her mother, being fairer of hair. They both were pretty, well-mannered and intelligent, easily settling into conversation with everyone present. Mrs Da Silva, Maria, was a handsome, middle aged woman, who took an obvious pride in her place as the wife of a Major in the Kings Army. She and her daughters dressed in the recent fashion, adding much needed colour to the gathering. In all we were a happy band, to such a degree that I had to shout above the chatter, thumping the table in order to propose a toast.

"My dear friends, I ask you to stand for a moment and remember those who are not with us today. Remember the loved ones who have died. The friends, companions and loved ones we have lost."

With bowed heads we all searched in our hearts to remember. The muttered names, tears in eyes, every one of us remembered, one or many, the quiet, sober, minute of reflection ended.

"Raise your glasses in a toast to, absent friends and lovers."

We remained standing for a brief moment, many the ghosts that hung between us.

To break the mood, I said: "Come now, gentlemen remain here, while the ladies retire to the Drawing Room, where a good bottle of Amontillado awaits."

Left on our own, the conversation revolved around the American Colonies. As the room filled with tobacco smoke, the talk turned to the future, the war with France and Spain, my plans and what Thomas wanted to do with his life.

When the time came to join the ladies, I could not help but notice how Thomas made a determined attempt to sit between the Da Silva girls. They giggled at his efforts, moving aside to let him in. His attention was directed mainly towards Isadora, hampered greatly by Elizabeth wanting to sit on his knee. He bore the impediment with saintly patience until Eloise tried also to sit on his knee, causing me to go to his rescue. He shot me a glance of grateful thanks as I carried them away to sit next to me.

The evening was one of convivial pleasure, we laughed together for the first time in many weeks. Lifting our spirits to such a degree that the future no longer seemed the desolate proposition that it had before. As the party broke up, well after the midnight hour, the twins had to be carried to their beds already asleep. Thomas was absent for several minutes, no doubt whispering goodbye to the new object of his affection, Miss Isadora Da Silva. Gideon was to overnight with us at the house and after embracing me and slapping me manfully on the back, went up to his room with a glass half full of Amontillado. He was sure to have a sore head in the morning.

CHAPTER
THIRTY THREE

*T*he Year of Grace 1771 dawned fresh and fair. The occasional cold winds were interspersed with balmy days. Life returned to normal, the demands of work kept us all busy. Thomas made several visits to Isadora, where he was cordially received. I was pleased to see him thus, he was a handsome young man with a quick wit and happy demeanour. He deserved the distraction of a first love. I spoke to the Major on this matter and he expressed his delight at the obvious attachment that was forming.

The twins grew apace, they were tall for their age and caused mayhem in the kitchens and servants' quarters. Where, despite my protestations, the servants encouraged and indulged them far too easily.

"Darn't you worry, Mister John, they's no harm. We loves them both terrible much." Was the constant reply to my attempts to rein in their behaviour.

It seemed the twins were destined to be strong independent women, breaking hearts, manipulating those who loved them and causing their father an overdose of worry. I resigned myself to it with a smile, which I could not hide.

With the spring came the flowers, never in my life before coming to Bermuda had I witnessed such a proliferation and riot of colour. The trees, bushes and roadsides were ablaze, against a background of fields of Easter Lilies being grown for export to the American Colonies. Against a sea of the clearest, lightest blue the sight was uplifting and my spirit sang each time the view pressed in before me. I could have been happy, it is true, to stay here for the remainder of my days. Yet more and more I felt the call of the Lakes and Fells. Elicia came to mind often, I had done her terrible wrong. Often I thought of her situation and that of our daughter Ruenna my child, conceived by rape!

The pension I had arranged would have assisted them to enjoy a normal life. There is comfort of a sort in well-tried relationships reaching back into the past. I clung to this now, it filled the void left in my heart by the loss of Arabella. Ah, Arabella! I will never forget the wonderful years spent with you, when I finally, with your help, was able to consider myself a man of honour once more.

The spring turned to summer, becoming very hot. The high humidity sucked the energy from a body. The water cisterns below or alongside the houses dried up, creating a fresh-water crisis. Even sitting in the shade, the sweat ran down the forehead stinging eyes, God knows how uncomfortable it must be without eyebrows! Sleeping at night became difficult, well-nigh impossible. Leaving the covers off meant the sleeper became a target for clouds of mosquitos.

Around the middle of June a ship arrived carrying mail from England. A letter from Daniel was contained within the package delivered to the house. I put it aside, determining to read it at some quiet moment, that evening.

Our water cistern, though large was almost depleted and we had to ration water. The bottom of the tank was home to several Bermuda toads. As large as dinner plates, the reduction in water level left them stranded, unable to escape. Their presence made what remained in the tank unsuitable for drinking.

Eli and his Royal Naval squadron returned from a six week patrol bringing worrying news from the Bahamas. There was a move afoot to transfer sovereignty of Turks Island from Bermuda to the Bahamas as it was considerably nearer. This was of great concern to me and all of the other traders working and exporting salt. A major source of livelihood for many in Bermuda was a move that needed to be opposed.

That evening, unable to sleep, I repaired to the study to read the letter from Daniel. It was dated late in January, sealed within it was another letter, this from Elicia. I decided to read that from Daniel first. The hand was clear and precise, obviously not Daniel's writing, dated July 1770.

Moses, my dear friend,

How quickly the time has passed since my return from Bermuda. It is like a dream, almost impossible to recall the detail at times. I have found life here to be unchanged, although in Furness great discoveries of Iron ore are being made. Bringing wealth and work to many. The wad mine is still in production, a good vein of Lead, containing some silver, has been found close by. In my heart I confess to miss the nights, smuggling on the high trods. I know those times have gone but cannot help but yearn for the adventure. I miss you greatly. Life is good, Maggie and my lads are all in fine fettle. The winter weather brought snow and crisp frosty mornings, Bermuda was beautiful but my land is finer, more majestic, familiar, greener.

I do not miss Bermuda, only you, Arabella, Thomas, the twins and my other friends.

Maggie sends you her love.
Your friend as always

Daniel

I read it several times before putting it down and sitting quietly with my thoughts as the candles spluttered and flickered in the warm air flowing through the open windows. With a sigh, I reached for the letter from Elicia, noting the hand that had written Daniel's letter was hers. He had spent time in her company but not mentioned it, leaving Elicia to have her own say. It was dated the same as Daniel's:

My dearest John,

How can I tell you what you mean to me? After so long apart I am not always able to recall your face. I think Ruenna has many of your features, sometimes I perceive you in her. I am being pursued by a neighbour who is keen to become the master of my estate and of me. I admit the support of a strong capable man would be much to my advantage but I can love no other than you. I will not marry without love, never without love. Is it ever to be that you and I can be husband and wife? I need you, Ruenna needs you, please return home. Write to me, I think of none but you.

My heart is forever yours

Elicia.

She did not mention Arabella, though from our letters she was well aware of our relationship. Daniel will have related to her all that had happened here. News of the death of Arabella had not yet reached England, I knew that I had to redress this omission in my reply. I sat, deep in thought, until the sky lightened to welcome a new dawn. Retiring to my bed, I slept, well into the middle of the morning.

Before leaving the house late that morning, I read the two letters once again. In both there were passages that tugged at old memories. I felt a strong desire to return to my home across the sea, yet how was that possible, was I being unfaithful to memory of Arabella?

In the evening I wrote to Daniel and Elicia intending to place the letters on the next ship leaving for England. Captain Eli joined me in the study after supper and noting my thoughtful mood, he asked what it was that ailed me:

"John, you are not yourself, is it the news about Turks Island?"

"No, indeed not, although it is of concern to me and others. A packet of letters arrived yesterday, among them one from Daniel, also another from Elicia."

"Ah, I see!"

"They have unsettled my mood, I yearn to return home, yet I cannot."

"You have so much here, will you abandon it all and for what?" he asked incredulously.

"I would take the twins with me, possibly Thomas also. Gideon is happy here, I can rely on him to oversee my business interests," I said.

"The sea is not that safe a place to be at this time, Spaniards, French and pirates, all enemies keen to sink or take an English merchantman. You will all be taken captive or even worse, killed and tossed overboard. My command is soon to be recalled, so perhaps I can offer you safe escort to Portsmouth,"

"When is that likely to be?"

"As soon as I receive my orders, certainly before the end of September."

MY mind was made up: "Very well, I accept your offer, gladly. In the next month I will make the necessary preparations."

"Good, that is agreed." Eli rose and shook my hand. "Excellent John, we will talk further once I have definite news. When the time comes, but I will retire now."

Once he had gone I was left with a feeling of euphoria such as I had not experienced for some time. England, snow, frost and Elicia, beckoned!

The following week, I found an opportunity to tell Thomas of my intentions. He was wary at first, later asking many questions, even so I was unsure of having convinced him. Gideon understood immediately, urging me to undertake the journey. I was assured by his enthusiasm and oaths of loyalty.

Things did not happen quite as quickly as we had hoped, the arrival of a powerful hurricane in late August delayed and disrupted our plans. The first warning of the storm to come was an increase in wind bringing heavy downpours of welcome rain. The cisterns were filled to overflowing, the gutters sluiced water on every side, washing roads away, creating ponds where there had been none before. The night time was noisy with the call of excited, rejuvenated, amorous toads, gathering in large groups in every open space.

The sea beyond the reef rolled in crashing against the rocks, throwing waves fifty feet into the air. The main force battering the coast all along the north shore broke through, flooding the land, sweeping away any house not built of stone. St Georges harbour was relatively sheltered yet even so, smaller ships were driven ashore and larger vessels demasted. We took refuge in the cellar, while the storm raged outside.

Once it had passed, the ensuing silence was complete. On emerging from the cellar we were greeted by a scene of utter devastation. Very few of the coconut palms remained upright, a line of flotsam across the garden showed how far the sea had invaded the land. Anything not tied down securely had been blown around or had disappeared entirely. It was a mess, yet we were luckier than those whose lightly constructed homes had been completely destroyed.

When Eli returned from a visit to the harbour he told of the damage to his fleet of ships. It would be a least a month until they were repaired sufficiently to put to sea. Two of his sailors had been washed away, otherwise, the human cost had been fortunately light.

On the rest of the island seven people had died or were missing.

I met with Gideon regularly during the following weeks. It was important to ensure that he had a complete knowledge of our many businesses.

"Gideon, you must know how much you have become a great friend and confident to me. I wish you to understand my plans for the future. I have resolved to return to England as soon as it is possible," I explained. "Captain Eli has generously offered passage with him when his squadron is sufficiently repaired to sail. I intend to take the twins with me though Thomas I'm not so sure about, may-hap he will remain here, we are going to be away for many months, years even."

"Well John, it has been in my mind for a while that you have a need to see Elicia at some future time, it has been in your head since Arabella passed away, I saw it."

"Dear God, was it that obvious?"

"No, but I have grown to understand you very well, your curiosity is boundless, how could you not want to see your other daughter for yourself?"

"Indeed, it is true."

"I have lost all of the family that I held dear. You have lost a part; yet another remains. I would do just as you, any man would."

"What are your thoughts regarding Thomas, should he travel with us?"

"I need first to ask you this question." He paused, unsure of my reaction.

"Go ahead, ask."

He looked away for a moment, gathering his thoughts.

"Do you intend to return to Bermuda at some time in the future?"

The brutality of the question shocked me, for a moment and did not answer.

"Of course." Saying it, I tried, unsuccessfully, to look him in the eye.

"Really?"

"Yes, really." I turned away, unable to return his steady, questioning gaze.

As I lay in my bed that night, sleep evaded me while my mind returned again and again to Gideon's enquiry. I saw myself standing before him. I recognised his quizzical unconvinced expression. It was impossible to ignore the fact that in the secret, innermost places of my mind, I knew that I wanted to return to England. Bermuda held little to retain me and if my family travelled with me, there would be no need to return, ever!

Still unable to sleep, the same question constantly strayed into my mind. Telling myself to sleep did not work, thus in the end I rose and repaired to the study. Waking the next morning I was stiff and bleary eyed, having slumped forward onto the desk. I had slept eventually but dreamed strangely of weird, half seen shadows causing my mind to surface momentarily before plunging again into the chaos inside my head. For the remainder of the morning I felt detached from reality, half in my dreams, half awake.

The following day, I summoned Gideon to meet with me in the study during the latter part of the afternoon. Gesturing him to the chair opposite, he sat saying nothing, waiting for me to break the silence between us. The time had come to tell him honestly of my plans:

"You are correct in your observations, it is more than likely I shall not return to these islands once I reach England," I admitted.

Gideon said nothing, merely nodded his head thoughtfully.

"As that will be the case, all of the children will have to travel with me. Thomas knows nothing of my intentions yet and I beg you keep our discussions to yourself for the present."

"Of course John, I have never been a gossip, what is said between us, stays between us."

"Right glad am I to hear it," I said with relief. "What are your plans for the future Gideon, you can return to with us if you so wish.

"I have every intention of staying here, I have a good life, some little money and a host of good friends: I have nothing to go back to England for," he said. "The female population outnumbers the male so I have an excellent chance of finding a good woman to settle down with, perhaps even have children again."

The conversation moved on: "That is well, I wish you joy, God knows that you deserve it," I said. "This then brings me to the nub of what I need to talk of with you. The Colonel's businesses, my businesses, will remain after I have left and they will require an overseer, someone to look after my interests and the interests of Thomas after my death. I trust and respect you as a true friend, there is none other I would rather have in charge of my affairs. Some form of partnership will ensure we both profit from our association, what do you say?"

Gideon leapt up from his chair and warmly shook my hand. Smiling broadly he said:

"An offer, generous beyond anything I could have imagined. Thank you John, you will never have cause to regret your trust in me."

Crossing to the corner cupboard I took out a fine old bottle of brandy which had belonged to the Colonel. It had been saved for a special occasion and pouring two glasses, I passed one to Gideon. Raising mine with a toast, I proposed:

"To Tucker, Rigg and Redmond Enterprises, health, wealth and happiness."

Gideon repeated it after me, emptying his glass in one gulp. We poured another, settling down to thrash out the details of our future business partnership.

CHAPTER
THIRTY FOUR

"But what of Miss Isadora Da Silva?"

Was the first thing that Thomas had to say when I talked to him about my plans. The blossoming romance with his sweetheart Miss Isadora Da Silva was clearly of some importance to him. It did not surprise me, I had been aware of the developing attachment since Christmas but even so the intensity of his reaction was a shock.

"When will you come back?" he asked.

"We may not come back, who can say, with a revolution developing in the American Colonies, whether return will be possible."

"We will all go?"

"Yes, I want us to be together, I owe it to your mother. However if you decide that staying in Bermuda is all that you want, then I will not prevent it."

"Oh father!"

"Gideon is to take charge of business here and he will guide and look after you. No need to be alone."

We embraced in silence, eventually pulling free and holding both my hands in his he said:

"We are a family, you are my father, I want to be with my family."

"Miss Da Silva?"

"What I have experienced, the excitement that has been in my life, everything I have seen and done makes me thirst for more. A great adventure is more attractive than anything else."

I hugged him close again, he had grown into a remarkable human being. Arabella had been so proud of the boy, yet here was a mature young man and I loved him more than ever.

As the time for our departure approached, I felt apprehensive about everything, the voyage, our reception in England after so many years away. The changes in people I had known, even the land itself. I kept my fears to myself, neither the twins nor Thomas had any real inkling of what lay ahead.

I sent letters to Daniel and our Bank in London via a mail packet that visited St Georges some five weeks prior to our predicted sailing. Informing them of our expected arrival in Portsmouth around the end of the year, we would need to have funds available. Being a man now of not inconsiderable substance, it was important to ensure we would be properly provided for.

The same mail Packet carried news to Eli of his promotion to Commodore. His first reaction was one of irritation as he had only recently ordered a new blue dress frock coat from the tailor in St Georges. Later, obviously he was pleased, joking with me that the next step was Rear Admiral!

I arranged for Thomas, the twins and me to spend four days travelling around the Island from St Georges to Devonshire, visiting friends and acquaintances along the way. I wanted to remember all of the places and people we had known.

The weather was sunny and bright, the scenery looked pretty even at this time of the year. Nights were still warm, often with a cool wind from off the sea. Trees and bushes were noisy with the sound of cicadas. It was a memorable trip, one I hoped the twins would long remember as they grew up.

CHAPTER
THIRTY FIVE

*D*uring the last week, the whole house was holding its breath. The sense of anticipation was palpable. Elizabeth and Eloise argued and fought more often than normal, they too were aware of an imminent change. Major Da Silva and his family, accompanied by Eli and Gideon had dinner with us in the last evening .It was a happy but sad affair, I felt the separation had already begun and my impending departure carved a gulf between us, realising for the first time how it must be for every seaman when leaving home on a long voyage.

We parted at midnight, the Da Silvas' and Gideon promising to see us off in the morning. Thomas lingered outside with Miss Isadora Da Silva, I did not disturb them and did not know what time he retired. Eli stayed the night the last in a comfortable bed for some weeks.

Waking early, I washed, shaved and dressed in the clean linen laid out for me last night. Making my way to the study, I sat for a little while, soaking up the last memories of Colonel Tucker and Arabella.

Thursday the twenty seventh of October, in the year of Our Lord 1771. The sounds of a rousing household, the clatter of pots and voices of the servants caused me to stir from my seat, and go downstairs. The breakfast table was already set, Eli was sitting at one end eating from a plate of cold meats and boiled eggs. The aroma of freshly brewed coffee filled the room. With a shock, I thought, this is my *last* breakfast, *my last morning!* Suddenly the hollow feeling of loss swept over me, dampening my mood.

The nurse delivered Elizabeth and Eloise to the dining room, clean and fresh in matching dresses, they looked very sweet.

"Well my darlings, are you ready for the great adventure?"

"Yes papa." They answered in unison.

Thomas entered, rather bleary eyed and unkempt. "Good morning Thomas," we all said together. Rather startled, he looked from one to another.

"Did you get to your bed at all, last night?" I asked.

He mumbled a reply. "What was that you said?" I asked catching Eli's eye at the end of the table.

"I said I don't know when I got to my bed."

"Did you have a pleasant tete-a-tete with Miss Da Silva?"

"John, leave the lad alone," said Eli smiling at Thomas, winking at me.

"I am only doing my duty as a caring father Eli, "I said returning his smile and wink.

Thomas looked from me to Eli, then back again. Realising our teasing, he blushed deep red, bending his head to concentrate on his breakfast. Looking up briefly he flashed us a brief smile then with head down settled to eating.

As there was an hour until we were due to leave the house, I decide to walk up to the church to pay a last visit to the Tucker Vault. Taking the twins with me and just about to set off, Thomas asked where we were going. On hearing of my intention he chose to come as well. So, our little family climbed the hill hand in hand in the morning sun. We picked red Hibiscus flowers from the hedges as we passed, to lay them in a brilliant drift of scarlet on the steps of the mausoleum.

Elizabeth and Eloise knelt to pray, their little hands clasped together, eyes tight shut. Thomas and I stood behind them, each lost in our own thoughts and memories. It was a special moment in our shared grief. I said a last goodbye to the two people who had made my life in Bermuda so wonderful. We returned to the house in silent thought, even the twins were unusually quiet.

At the house we discovered that Commodore Eli Farrington had left for his command, half an hour earlier.

Friends began to gather, it was clear we were to have quite an escort to the harbour. All of our luggage had been taken on board the day before, so we had little to carry, as among the throng we made our way down into St Georges. It was a pleasant walk, the chatter and merry company in the clear light burned the image in my mind.

The Royal Naval squadron was anchored in the bay, decks alive with bustle and activity. Skiffs and small boats fussed around or dashed between them. A whaler was waiting at the jetty to ferry us across the water, crewed by eight ratings, smartly dressed, oars raised. Waving our last goodbyes, we parted the throng, stepped aboard, to be rowed swiftly to the nearest man-o-war which loomed over our approach. As our boat pulled alongside the twins were lifted up on deck by two able seamen while Thomas climbed up nimbly, needing no assistance.

The Commodore was already aboard waiting to welcome us. He was most attentive, escorting us to our cabins and seeing us comfortably settled in. The twins went to explore their new quarters while Thomas and I strolled up on the main deck to lean over the rail and wave to the crowd still gathered on the quay.

The creak of blocks and slap of sail, the chant of sailors working a capstan carried over the water from the other ships. Obviously, all was being made ready to set sail and depart. On our vessel, men swarmed into the rigging, releasing sails from the ropes that bound them. Slowly, ever so slowly, we began to move. The other four ships falling in behind, they passed in line across the front of Gates Fort, along the east coast of St Georges Island to Fort St Catherine. A loud cannonade greeted us, a salute retuned by our own gunners as we turned north east into the open ocean beyond the reef.

Thomas and I stayed on deck until the last of the islands had finally sunk out of sight below the horizon. Returning to our cabin we discovered the twins asleep on a bunk, the day's excitement having exhausted them entirely.

We were graced by a good westerly wind, the sea remaining slight. All five craft in the squadron stayed in sight of and in communication with each other for the whole of the crossing. Our journey of around three thousand nautical miles sped by at a steady four to six knots every hour.

Early on the twenty seventh day at sea, we sighted the coast of Ireland and then the Isles of Scilly on the Port quarter. The air was colder, sea mist hid the land and Eli took his fleet out further into the Channel in order to safely round the Cornish coast. Sailing past the Isle of Portland a freezing fog enfolded the ships, turning the rigging into a sparkling mass of frost crystals, delighting the twins.

Thomas had become quieter as we approached England, he complained about the cold and looked miserable.

The ships in our fleet fired a small cannon every few minutes to warn of their presence in the fog.

The eerie sound was dulled and flattened by the mist. Finding Thomas on the main deck peering into the grey fog, a blanket around his shoulders, I went to stand at his side.

"What ails you my son, are you unwell?"

He turned a grey gaunt face to me and said; "I am not ill, just……..I don't know."

"You are unhappy, why?"

"The weather, the cold, I have never known such bitter cold. I am afraid for the future, I do not like this land, already, I do not like this land!" He spoke with such vehemence, I was shocked.

"Thomas, my son, I know this is very difficult for you but all will be fine, believe me."

"I wish I had not come with you, I wish I had stayed in Bermuda!"

"Thomas."

I reached out to place my hand on his arm. Turning from me he hurried away, disappearing down the companion way, below decks. I was dumbfounded, so unlike the boy I thought I knew. He had held his feelings in check for the last week though I had noticed his change in mood, although the reason had escaped me.

In the failing light we anchored off Yarmouth to ride out the night, Eli assured me that we would be docked in Portsmouth by noon the next day. I retired to my cabin, lying awake for some time thinking of everything that awaited us.

The following morning was crisply cold but bright and clear. Shreds of fog were hanging onto the shore and obscuring the horizon. Around our flotilla, seven other large warships rode at anchor, awaiting the tide's turn. Voices and ships' bells carried across the still sea. Only a slight motion caused the boards and rigging to creak and groan. We paused, suspended in time before undertaking the last few miles ahead. The detail of the land close by, held in a clarity and sharpness of image looked much like a painting. The air smelled sharp and clean. Raising anchor together, once more in line, the five men-o-war sailed through the Solent and into Portsmouth Harbour. Many small boats busied themselves about our ships, Eli left first in order to report to his superiors, leaving us to prepare ourselves to disembark.

Thomas seemed in better heart, the bright morning had lifted his spirits and he greeted me with a wan smile.

"Father, I beg your forgiveness, I don't know what got into me yesterday, there was a darkness in my soul."

"Of course, my son, there is much to concern you but we are all together, about to start a new life. You have my word that everything will be alright, the strangeness will pass, believe me," I reassured him.

For myself, I was happy and grateful to have arrived home safely. *Home?* Yes home. England offered so many new opportunities. I was impatient to feel the land beneath my feet again.

When Eli returned on board, we took our leave, promising to send him an address once we had settled in Westmorland. Rowed across the harbour, our luggage was stacked on the quay, ready to be loaded into two carriages that Eli had arranged for the journey north. He had also engaged the services of a female nurse to look after the twins. Meeting her for the first time, they took to her immediately. Her name was Sophie, a widow aged about 35 years, pleasant of face with a jolly demeanour, dressed neatly but plainly. Over the coming journey she proved herself to be invaluable. For the rest of the week the weather remained settled with bright clear sunny days followed by crisp moonlit nights. Thomas chose to travel with the luggage. In some ways I was relieved, it was important that he came to accept his new situation. The unfamiliar country, big and so green was in complete contrast to all his previous experience.

CHAPTER
THIRTY SIX

*A*s the days passed, Thomas became more relaxed, appearing to gain much pleasure from the sights and sounds of the English towns and cities we travelled through. The twins as always sustained a constant chatter, remarking on each new scene that came into view. At almost five years of age, they were taller than most. With striking good looks they drew admiring glances whenever we halted for the night. It was their boundless enthusiasm, that and pretty smiles which carried them through every situation. Rather sheepishly I had to admit to myself that I was proud to be seen with them, proud to say they were my daughters, when asked. Would Ruenna be as pretty?

Arriving in Lancaster late on the sixth day Thomas announced that he would travel in the carriage with us tomorrow. This was good news, that he was taking an interest in his newly adopted land and his future there. The hedgerows gave way to stone walls and the thatched, wood and brick cottages, gave way to slate roofs and roughhewn stone walls. It was good to see the familiar sites of the North Country around me again.

That morning the luggage was transferred onto carts ready for the crossing of the Sands. We bid farewell to the carriages that had brought us all the way from Portsmouth. Across the wide open bay the Lakeland hills shimmered in the mist and I pointed out the old familiar fells to the children, excitement and emotion breaking in my voice. I had not, until now, dared to think of Elicia. I had suppressed my thoughts and trying to keep control of my emotions had become more and more difficult each day, as we journeyed further north. How would I find her, the woman that I had once loved above all others, yet parted from so roughly, in such shame?

Our drivers followed the stream of humanity in carts, wagons, coaches, horses, carriages, pack ponies and those that journeyed on foot with children and dogs towards Hest Bank, where the crossing of the Sands would lead us across Morcambe Bay to Cartmel.

The tide was still covering the route but it was obviously receding fast and more shining sand was revealed with each passing minute. When the depth was still over two feet, the leading horses splashed into the water, setting off across the Bay at a steady pace. When it came to our turn, the twins were especially fascinated to be in the sea, but not in a boat. They hung over the side of the wagon shouting with excitement while Sophie or Thomas had to haul them back several times else they would have fallen in. After half an hour the tide had withdrawn completely exposing the vast Sands, and It was only when crossing the many river channels flowing into the Bay that we encountered water once more. On the level sands the whole caterpillar of humanity picked up speed, moving fast towards landfall at Kents Bank.

It was a remarkable journey, Thomas in particular asked many questions of our fellow travellers, becoming quite animated. I was pleased to see him thus, a young man's natural curiosity coming to the fore. Once the column of travellers reached the shore it split into many ant like lines heading off in different directions. Our carts stayed with the largest group making its way to Cartmel. We could see the tower of the imposing Priory before the village itself came into view. A cluster of old houses and inns circled the small market square, the whole dominated by the ancient monastic church. In my previous life I had a school friend here and had known the place well.

Pulling into the inn yard, we left the carts, feeling relieved to stretch our legs, it had been a long day. The inn was full with only one room available for the five of us, however the bed was large and comfortable, so at least the children and Sophie slept soundly. I could not sleep, thoughts and memories swirled through my mind. Guilt about my treatment of Elicia became far sharper as the distance between us narrowed. I dreaded meeting her face to face. All of the self-loathing and shame I had felt nine years ago returned, to eat away at my confidence. I became nervous and excited by turns. Had I made the wrong decision, would the return to England prove to be an awful mistake?

Eventually, a restless sleep overtook me, sitting in a large wing chair. I was awoken by the children chattering to Sophie in the pale light of morning.

The weather had changed, grey clouds raced across the sky driven by a sharp northerly wind. Although our clothing was adequate, I intended to have a full set of winter clothes made for all of us once we reached Hawkshead. For the moment, shawls and blankets provided the extra protection needed. In my letter from Bermuda, I had asked Daniel to arrange accommodation for us. A reply awaited us in Lancaster, confirming that it had been done.

The final stage of our journey in an open wagon was less than pleasant. Approaching Hawkshead, a squally rain spiked with hail swept over us, stinging faces and hands. The twins began to cry and it was with grateful thanks that we clattered into the main square, pulling up outside The Red Lion. In the fading light, the luggage was unloaded while we absorbed the heat from a large peat fire, burning fiercely in the parlour.

At last, only five miles from Ambleside, across the river Brathay where Lancashire gives way to Westmorland was Elicia! I was constantly nervous and now we were here, I was filled with doubt, I knew that sleep would elude me again that night.

The landlord's wife took charge of Sophie and the twins, fussing around, serving a hot mutton stew that filled and warmed us all.

CHAPTER THIRTY SEVEN

*M*y parents had died when I was six years old. My father died first and only four days later my mother followed him to the grave. Theirs' had been a strong relationship founded on the love that brought them to be wedded in the first place. I believe that she could not face living without my father and died of a broken heart; they had been buried together in Hawkshead churchyard.

Early the next morning with the others only just stirring, I dressed, climbing the hill behind the village square to the whitewashed church and finding the headstone, my mind filled with the many things that I had to tell them. The headstone leaned out of the perpendicular, lichen filled the letters, obscuring the inscription. Using a twig I scraped it away revealing what was written there.

Here lyeth buried ye body of Isaac Rigg, gent.
Of the Old Hall, High Wray
Departed this life the 12th day of November 1742
Aged 54 years

Also here lyeth buried the body of his wife Margaret
Departed this life 15th day of November 1742
Aged 42 years
'Called by the Lord'

Bending my head in respect and noting the need to arrange for the stone to be restored to the upright, I walked back down to the Inn. Thomas, Sophie, Elizabeth and Eloise were enjoying breakfast and pulling up a chair, I joined them.

"Good morning father," The children chorused together.

"Good morning Sir," said Sophie."

I acknowledged their greeting, inquiring how everyone had slept.

Thomas asked what was planned for the day. I replied;

"I have to go into Ambleside on business, to arrange for money from the Bank, also to visit my old home. It will be easier if I can do this on my own. You can all go up to the church and seek out the grave of your grandparents."

"Grandparents?" said the twins and Thomas together.

"Yes, my mother and father are buried there, they are your grandparents. I would like it if you said a prayer for them. Sophie, would you please escort and help them with this task?"

"Yes Sir, when should we expect you back? Will you be joining us for supper?"

"Indeed, I hope to return before dark."

Hiring a hack from the stables I set out for High Wray before the clock had struck ten. The weather remained unsettled but the wild wind had abated during the night and a weak sun occasionally broke through the clouds, briefly lighting up the scene. As the road climbed steadily up the side of Claife Heights', the westward view opened towards the mountains above Coniston, lit by bursts of sunlight that lent something theatrical to the sight.

I had forgotten quite how majestic this landscape was and all the more so in contrast with the relatively flat lands of Bermuda. In a positive mood, humming tunelessly I arrived at the scatter of farms that was High Wray. Turning onto the track that ran down to meet the shore of Windermere, I arrived at the entrance to The Old Hall. The present house had been built here by my great, great grandfather, on a site once occupied by a Grange of the powerful Furness Abbey. With tall round chimneys and large modern windows, it was grand in a comfortable country way.

Not knowing what to expect, I rode into the yard, hitching my horse to an apple tree. The front door opened and an ancient man appeared on the steps armed with a shotgun, challenged me in an aggressive voice.

"What d'ye want here? Who ar'ye?"

"My name is John Rigg, this is my house!"

"Jorn Rigg? niver herd o ye!"

He advanced toward me waving the gun menacingly. I stepped back, not wishing to be accidentally shot by this old fool.

"Git yersen gorn!" he shouted loudly.

Unsure how to proceed, I turned back to my horse and began to unhitch the reins.

"Mister Merryhorn!"

A woman's voice rose above the old man's shout.

" Jeptha Merryhorn! Put that gun down, at once!"

Looking behind me I saw a grey haired woman of perhaps sixty or seventy years, coming down the steps from the front door, shaking a walking stick at the servant who continued to aim the gun at my stomach. When she drew level with him she knocked the gun barrel down with her stick.

"Now then young man, who are you and what do you want with us here?"

"My name is John Rigg, this is *MY* house!"

"John, John Rigg? We thought you far away on the other side of the world."

"I was until very recently, now I am returned home with my family. Who may I enquire, are you?"

"My dear nephew, I know we have never met, "she said, as I stood in amazement. " I am your aunt Hannah, you mothers younger sister. I see her in you now. Eight years ago, I heard of you transportation when Elicia found me. It was she who suggested I move in here to look after the house. We have been living here ever since, this scallywag is my servant Jepthah Merryhorn."

He still scowled suspiciously at me. I nodded at him as I walked past in order to take my aunt's hand.

"Aunt Hannah, my mother talked of you often, you did not come to the funeral?"

"I did not, I was travelling in Italy at the time and knew nothing of it until the following year. It was a fact of great regret to me then and has been ever since. Hence one of the reasons I decided to occupy this house for, need be, however many years," she said.

"Thank you, you have done me a great favour," I replied.

"Tush now, no need for that, come into the house for some refreshment. Your family, you say?"

"There is a great deal to relate, so I will be brief in the telling now, with more on a future occasion. For now a cup of warm grog would be most welcome."

We talked for an hour or so, seated in the great parlour, which remained much as I had left it. In relating all my adventures, I was very careful not to give too much away about Arabella. It was agreed with my Aunt that nothing was to be said yet to Elicia, leaving me to make contact first.

In the meantime, the children and our luggage would be transported from Hawkshead on the morrow. With only three hours of daylight remaining, I took my leave, riding to the Bank at Ambleside with all haste. Once there it was clear that Aunt Hannah had administered the estate very well. No debts and a healthy balance of credit gave me confidence for the future. Arranging means of allowing me to access the business profits from Bermuda would be somewhat more complex, however with sufficient funds to live on for the moment this could wait.

Once all of the business had been completed, no time remained for a visit to Elicia. I returned to the Red Lion as the last rays of the sun sank behind Coniston Old Man, casting the valley into darkness. Thomas and the girls were sitting in front of the parlour fire, chatting with Sophie. When I entered they rushed forward to tell me of all that they had done that day. Once all the talk died away, I told them of my visit to High Wray and Aunt Hannah. Everyone was excited by the prospect of finally settling in a permanent place. I answered many of their questions about the house, my parents and my previous life there.

When the twins had been taken up to bed, Sophie came down to sit by the fire with Thomas and me. Providing me with an opportunity to ask Sophie of her intentions:

"Sophie, you have been an excellent companion these last weeks, Elizabeth and Eloise love you. Is it your intention to return south now that we have come to our own home?" I asked.

"I cannot say sir."

"Well, what do you wish to do now?"

"May I speak freely?"

I reassured her that she could.

"Then, if you still need me, I should like nothing better than to remain in your employ. I have nought to go back to and your family have come to mean a great deal to me," she said.

"So be it. Remain with us as long as you want. I for one will be pleased should you decide to stay,"

I replied.

"And I." said Thomas with conviction.

CHAPTER
THIRTY EIGHT

*T*hus it was, with Thomas, the twins and Sophie the short journey to High Wray was accomplished successfully the following day. Aunt Hannah was at once adopted by the twins who chattered incessantly without pausing for breath, whilst Jepthah unloaded the luggage.

A guided tour of the house followed luncheon. Thomas had his own room at the front, overlooking the orchard, the twins shared a large room with doors leading onto the garden. Being built into a slope, the house had the advantage of a second floor on the same level as the back garden. Sophie was given two cosy adjoining rooms on the third floor. I, of course returned to my old room, next to the twins on the second floor. Aunt Hannah was occupying the master bedroom, I had no wish to move her, being more than content in the room I had slept in for all of my childhood.

The household consisted of a cook, scullery maid, coachman and groom, plus Jepthah, not large but quite adequate. The Hall farm, opposite, was let out to a tenant farmer and his family, who undertook general duties on the whole estate.

After supper the whole family gathered in the main parlour where we talked into the night, relating all the last nine years' adventures. I talked then of Arabella and Aunt Hannah listened intently, with the twins asleep either side of her, asking only occasional questions to clarify a point.

Thus it was that I returned home to what I hoped was a new beginning.

The following morning I opened the curtains to see that there had been a heavy snowfall during the night. It still fell lightly, drifting, obscuring the view beyond the garden wall. The fells had disappeared, even the lake was difficult to discern in the heavier flurries, stirred by the wind. Squeals from the twins' room next door were followed by the crash of my chamber door, thrown violently open as they entered together.

"Papa! Papa! What is it? Everything is white!"

They stared intently up at me, gripping my nightshirt, dragging me to the window.

"It is snow, beautiful is it not?"

"Papa can we go out in it, please can we, please!"

"Yes," I replied, "but first we must dress and have breakfast. Then, once you are warmly clothed we will go outside."

They rushed out, almost knocking Thomas over, who was on his way in at that moment.

"Father, this is wonderful. It must be snow! Friends in Bermuda who travelled to the Americas told me of it."

"If it keeps snowing and does not melt too quickly we can all go out to enjoy it, great fun can be had, sledging is very exciting," I promised.

"Sledging?"

"Come get dressed, have breakfast, then we will do some sledging!"

I realised that the snow must delay the anticipated visit to Elicia. After so long, I could not imagine that another day's delay would make any difference. How wrong that assumption proved to be.

Two days later with the snow and ice thawing, a horse was saddled for me and I set out for Ambleside only four miles away. The sun was shining, bringing the snow covered fells into sharp focus against a grey sky. The air smelled clean and fresh, restoring my spirits, filling my mind with happy, positive thoughts. Few other travellers were on the road, each greeted me merrily as they passed by.

In less than an hour I reached Ambleside, climbing the track up the 'Struggle' to the old lime washed house, which crouched with its back into the fell behind. As it appeared in the distance, it seemed familiar in one way, yet subtly changed. The trees about it had grown taller, a new wall built around the yard. Pausing at the gate to admire the scene, remembering the last time I had seen it, tears pricked my eyes.

No one had observed my arrival, none came out to welcome me. Tying my horse to an iron ring fixed in the porch, I rapped loudly on the stout oak door. Still no answer, until knocking with a riding crop produced movement from within. Hearing the sound of bolts being withdrawn, I pulled myself up, squaring my shoulders, straightening my cravat ready to see Elicia. The door opened to reveal a middle aged man. My disappointment must have been evident in my face and he did not speak, but continued to regard me suspiciously.

"Is Mistress Salkeld at home?"

"Who is it wants to know?"

"An old friend, wishing to pay his respects."

"Name?"

"Just say an old friend, she will know me when she sees me."

"Wait here."

Closing the door in my face I heard him move off down the passage. Some minutes elapsed before the sound of a woman's shoes echoed on the hall flags. The door opened wide to reveal Elicia who froze for a moment, then staggered backwards . Raising her hands to grasp her hair, shaking her head, in disbelief she started to scream:

"No! No! it can't be."

I was horrified. Everything that I had imagined of our first meeting, had proved wrong, very wrong. Suddenly, without warning she rushed at me, fists raised pummelling my chest in a fury.

"Why now, John Rigg, why now?"

The rumpus had attracted the servants, who were pushed aside by a tall fair haired girl who ran towards us.

"Mother what on earth is the matter?"

Elicia, fury spent, leaned forward against my shoulder and sobbing deeply, she whispered:

"John, why now?"

The young girl, Ruenna I guessed, hugged her mother from behind,

"What has happened, who is this?"

Elicia moved back, pulling her daughter to her, holding her in a tight embrace.

"This, my dear, is your father, who has chosen a time such as this, to return!"

Ruenna, for it was her, my daughter, looked at me wide eyed but still held tightly to her mother.

With tears streaming unchecked Elicia said,

"John, I thought never to see you again."

"I came as quickly as I could, the snow delayed me by a day, which is all."

"A day? One day too long for I was betrothed to Mordechai Dixon but yesterday afternoon."

"By all that is Holy, Elicia, God knows that I would have come earlier, had it not snowed," I replied in my shock and distress.

Taking my hand and laying it on her breast she said,

"Here in my heart I have held you for nine years when you did not reply to my last letter, I thought never to see you again. Mordechai has wooed me for three years past. I only accepted his suit for security and to give Ruenna a father. His farm adjoins mine, it is a most sensible solution to our situation."

Stepping forward, throwing my arms around her, with Ruenna trapped between us, I kissed Elicia full on the lips. Her body, no longer held rigidly, moulded against mine surrendering herself to me. It was Ruenna's struggles to extricate herself that forced us apart.

"We must talk, come into the back parlour where there is a fire," she said urgently.

Hand in hand walking down the passage, Elicia shooed the servants away at our approach. A fine delicate hand found my free arm I looked down to see that Ruenna had wrapped her arms around mine. In this fashion we retired to the back parlour.

Once seated comfortably, with a cup of hot tea on the table beside me, I waited for Elicia to begin.

"Ruenna my dear, I need to speak with your father on matters that will no doubt cause you distress. Will you give us half an hour alone, then you may return and hear all," she promised.

"I will go mother, please do not forget to send for me, as I shall be close by, wanting to hear what you have decided."

With that Ruenna left the room, giving me a long appraising look as she passed, closing the door quietly behind her.

"My darling, dearest John, it was such a shock to see you," Elicia said, and I felt such disappointment, anger and frustration at what happened yesterday." While she talked I studied her and saw that the years had filled her face, more woman now than girl, still handsome, beautiful even, the wild golden hair had been tamed but, her grey-blue eyes had not lost their intensity. Sitting straight backed in the chair with her composure returned, Elicia looked every inch the mature matron that she had become. The young girl I had left behind was gone. My heart stirred with love and emotion as I remembered how we had shared so much together, good and bad.

"John, I had always hoped that someday we could be together, living out our lives as man and wife. As the years went by, I heard from Daniel Bragg that you were married and thousands of miles away and unlikely to return. Early on I had Ruenna to care for but as she grew up I came to realise that she needed a father and I a companion. Mordechai has been on his own since his wife passed away four years ago. He has asked me many times to consider him as a husband. He is a good man, honest and caring, I could do far worse. Did you receive my letter written four years past? Daniel came to see me last year, bringing some news of you. I thought it hopeless

313

to cherish the idea of your return and acquiesced to the suit brought by Mordechai. Finally, yesterday I accepted his suit."

She paused, looking at me intently, wanting my understanding, my blessing. We sat looking at each other while I considered all of the options. Finally I said,

"I cannot blame you for what you have done. You needed to think of Ruenna. Do you love this man?"

"Love. What is love? He is kind, I respect him. *You* are the only man I have truly loved," she said.

"Can that ever be enough?"

"Do *you* love me John?"

"I have always loved you, since we were children I have loved you. Until my crimes were pardoned and my wife, Arabella died I was not free to return to England or to you. It was impossible and to have told you otherwise, I could not be so cruel."

"Your wife, Arabella, *DEAD*!? Did you care for her, was she beautiful?"

"I loved her, we had twin daughters together. She was killed in a great battle."

Elicia was silent, absorbing what I had said. So I continued,

"Arabella had a son from a previous marriage. He is fifteen years old. He and the twins are in my house at High Wray, this very moment."

"They are here with you? I should very much like to meet them," she said eagerly.

"What are we to do Elicia? We should be together, you must not marry Mordechai."

"I have little choice," she replied.

"We have endured so much, I am ashamed and disgusted of the way in which I treated and raped you, yet we still carry love for each other. We can have a happy life together."

"Know this John, I forgave you many years ago I have a beautiful daughter, the result of your wild passion and rape she has given me great comfort so how can I not forgive?"

"I would be very pleased to become acquainted with Ruenna, she seems to have the best of both of us."

"She does indeed, I see you in her, and she is a sweet child."

Elicia rose and going to the door called Ruenna, who appeared immediately, having been lingering nearby.

"So what have you talked about, what have you decided?"

"John, your father, now knows how I am betrothed to Mordechai. The contract is permanent and unbreakable."

"But you two love each other, I know you do. How can this be, I want my father, my real father, not Mordechai Dixon!" she protested.

Her voice was raised in the strength of her objection. I was taken aback but pleased to see that I had an ally in Ruenna. She came to stand behind my chair, hands resting on my shoulders. I felt her tears on my head.

"I will take my leave if you will forgive me Ruenna for I must get back to High Wray before dark. May I bring my family to meet with you on the morrow? It has been a difficult day."

"Your family?" Ruenna asked.

Elicia promised to tell her everything once I had left. We parted at the porch, an embrace from Ruenna, a brief kiss on the cheek from Elicia. I had much to occupy my mind on the way home.

Relating the day's events that evening, Elizabeth and Eloise were excited to hear that they had an older half-sister. Aunt Hannah expressed her support for whatever I decided to do next while Thomas was cautious. I went to bed, my mind in turmoil, trying to devise a way of approaching Mordechai Dixon.

The next day the carriage was readied for the short journey to Ambleside. Setting off in a rainstorm, the tracks were muddy and full of pot holes, as a consequence we took longer than anticipated. It was a relief when the old farmhouse came into view. Ruenna must have been waiting at the casement as she opened the front door before we had dismounted.

Hurrying indoors, away from the rain, the twins, with their usual enthusiasm, ran to Ruenna to embrace her and hold her hands. Thomas was rather reserved, but clearly smitten by this pretty creature. She charmed him immediately by greeting him as 'Brother'. Elicia did not appear until we had settled in the back parlour, Thomas behaving as a perfect gentleman of the world, was politeness itself, moving the chair back for her to sit down.

A good start for they all seemed happy with what they saw in each other. I had to admit, looking around with pride, it was a gathering of well-favoured people. The contrast between the olive gold skin of Thomas and the twins, with the ivory skin of Elicia and Ruenna was striking as was the contrast of hair colour. From the fair hair of Elicia and Ruenna to the lustrous long black locks of Thomas and the twins.

The conversation was lively and animated. Ruenna conducted Thomas and the twins on a tour of the house, leaving Elicia alone with me in the parlour.

"They are charming children, not at all what I had expected. Ruenna has found an immediate admiration," she said.

"I must speak with you about us. If there was any possibility of annulling your contract with Mordechai, with honour, will you take it?" I asked boldly.

"Yes I would John, but how?

"May be there is a way," I said, "leave it to my endeavours."

"I dare not think of us together until everything is certain and agreed."

We were interrupted by the arrival of the twins followed by Thomas and Ruenna. After a good luncheon of warm pie and cold meats we left to return to the Old Hall. The whole of the journey was filled with happy chatter about the house, Elicia and Ruenna, which was all repeated for Aunt Hannah, who listened intently to everything that was said.

   In bed that night I resolved to introduce myself to Mordechai Dixon as soon as was possible.

CHAPTER
THIRTY NINE

*I*t felt strange to be back in familiar territory, as a man of status and wealth rather than a common felon. No longer would I need to smuggle black wad, no more night time forays onto the fells, yet it was somehow disappointing to think those days were over.

A further visit to Ambleside had to be delayed until after Christmas. I wanted to visit Daniel at Wasdale Head, being keen to hear his news and catch up with his doings since we parted in Bermuda. Leaving the twins in the charge of Sophie and Aunt Hannah and taking Thomas with me, we set off on two ponies, early morning the next day. It was clear and sunny when leaving The Old Hall, the views beautiful in every direction, a dusting of snow crowning the fell tops. Taking the track up Langdale, we stopped for the night at Stool End farm. Heading out early the following day we spent our second night at a shepherd's shelter before descending via Sty Head Pass to Wasdale Head mid-morning the next day.

I showed Thomas the track that bore my name, 'Moses Trod'. It was strange to be following the route taken by our packhorses that fateful night ten years before. Thomas and I had been able to converse properly together for the first time since leaving Bermuda. Thomas had many questions, being particularly keen to hear more about Elicia and me.

Evenings in a shared bed, with the candle extinguished, made for an easy way to tackle difficult subjects. Our night in the shepherd's shelter was the most revealing.

"Father, may I ask you something?" I could sense his eyes on me in the dark.

"Of course, anything." He shifted about, unsure how to begin.

"My mother?"

"Yes?"

"Do you miss her?"

"With all my heart!"

"But you love Elicia, how can this be?"

"Elicia and I have been companions, friends and sweethearts for nigh on thirty years. Having that sort of history with another, a woman, makes for a depth of feeling impossible on a short acquaintance."

"When you loved my mother, did you still love Elicia?"

"Elicia has been a constant in my life, always there. When I was transported to Bermuda I thought never to see her again," I said.

"So you fell in love with my mother," he persisted.

"You were there, you saw what happened."

"I was young, I admired you and adored my mother."

Images from the past floated before me in the darkness. Arabella, vivid in my mind's eye. Beautiful, laughing, holding my hand.

"Arabella bewitched me from the moment that I met her. Her grace and beauty stole my heart. She intrigued me, I could not stop thinking about her. If our fates had been different I should have been content to live with her for the rest of my days. Your mother was a truly remarkable woman."

Silence lay between us, each exploring his own memories. Finally I said, "You must be so very proud of her. I know that she loved you dearly, you were everything to her."

Quietly, almost a whisper he replied, "I know."

I heard sorrow in his words, sensing tears in his eyes.

"But now you have Elicia and my mother is no more."

"There is not one day when I do not think of Arabella, should I live to be one hundred this will always be. She was the most wonderful thing that has ever, could ever, happen in my life. I have been blessed to have known her, I will never, never forget her."

The last words were spoken with the full strength of my feelings. I felt for his hand lying on the coverlet between us, squeezing it hard. He rolled onto his side towards me, placing his other hand on top of mine.

"I am glad you married my mother, I am glad you became my father. My life would not have happened in the way it has without you. I pray that you find happiness with Elicia."

Neither of us spoke as we drifted off into our own thoughts and dreams. The following morning Thomas was brighter, more content. Our frank discussion had given him back his confidence, allowing him to feel easier in my relationship with Elicia.

We reached Wasdale Head when the pale winter sun was at its highest point. Maggie came out to greet us. Wiping pastry covered hands on her apron she fell on my neck with a loud sob.

"John Rigg! The day is wondrous grand that ye are with us again. Welcome, welcome!"

The pleasure was mutual:

"Maggie, I cannot tell you how very good it is to see you and be here with you once again. This is my adopted son, Thomas. Thomas, meet Maggie, the dearest wife of our friend, Daniel. Where is he, by the way?"

"He were in the byre a while back. Like as not he knows ye are here. Have some girdle scones, fresh baked, and a pot of beer to refresh you both," she said hospitably.

She hurried off into the larder, returning with two horn cups filled with heavy, home brewed beer. We sat down in front of the fire sipping the beer until Maggie appeared again with a napkin full of girdle scones, still warm. Thomas screwed up his face every time that he sipped the beer.

"Would you prefer it warm," I asked him, "It is a cold morning, if warmed you may find it to be more palatable?"

He shook his head and took another sip from the cup. At this moment we became aware of a commotion in the yard outside and Daniel came in like a wild bull, crashing through the door, eagerly embracing us both. Saying nothing, he held on tightly to us. He smelled of the farm, of fresh mountain air and cold.

"Eh ma dear friends, ah thought ah might see ye before long."

We shook hands warmly, he held Thomas close to his breast,

"You've grown apiece, since ah saw ye last."

Thomas, pulled his shoulders back and stood back to back against Daniel, comparing their height.

"I'm almost as tall as you now Daniel, I just need to broaden out a little more, not to be quite as fat though!"

"Ye cheeky young dog!" said Daniel, laughing and taking a playful swipe at Thomas.

In this merry mood we repaired to the parlour to wait while Daniel removed his outdoor clothes. Dressed more comfortably, he joined us after only a few minutes had passed. Maggie brought in a jug of ale, setting it down in front of the fire to warm. We looked from one to another, a satisfied smile on our faces. No one spoke as the feeling of warm contentment filled the spaces between us.

Finally I said; "Bermuda seems so very far away, almost a dream but for Thomas here with us>"

"It is not such a dream to me, this is the dream! Bermuda is real and fresh in my mind." Thomas spoke with sadness.

With a flash of understanding, I could suddenly see how somewhere so homely and familiar to me should appear so alien to him.

"Tell us lad what is it that you miss most?"

"All the sights and sounds that I grew up with," he replied nostalgically. "The sea, the warmth of the sun, colourful flowers and whitewashed houses."

"Is that all? asked Daniel.

"My friends and familiar faces. This is a beautiful country, of that there is no doubt, different from Bermuda, beautiful even so. I miss my freedom most of all, being able to come and go as I please.

Having my own familiar things about me. The last three months have been a shock, I had not thought it would be so hard, but it has been." He turned to me, "Father, I am not unhappy but I do feel unsettled. It is like the time the pirates took me, I feel trapped and helpless, unsure of the future."

I was filled with compassion for this, my adopted son. He had suffered and lost a great deal in the past year, yet he was always positive and supportive of me and the twins. It had been easy to lose sight of the strain he was under in the clamour of everything else.

"Well lad, we shall have to see thee right. John, come now we must think on it, and see to it young Thomas is happy here."

"I agree Daniel," I said, "I have been too busy and not noticed what Thomas needed. All will change now, I promise."

"The Westmorland lasses are fine and bonny, set ye heart on one of them, you'll never be lonely!"

Thomas coloured, I perceived that Daniel's remark had found a response in him. But who? Surely not Ruenna? I considered this, she was indeed a bonny lass, who promised to become a great beauty in a few years. Yet she and Thomas were separated by six or so years though not too much in the great scheme of things. I decided to pay more attention when they were together, to look for clues in little gestures and glances.

We returned to High Wray two days later, the twins greeted us with noisy enthusiasm. Elicia wanted to hear all that we had done and talked of. Sitting together in the big kitchen, eating a warm goose pie and there being several vacant chairs, Ruernna chose to sit next to Thomas. She could not bring herself to look at him directly but stared down at her lap, stealing a sideways glance now and then. All the signs were clear, she and he shared an interest in each other. It was strange, I had not noticed it before. When I spoke of this matter with Elicia later that day, she surprised me by saying that she had noticed a developing regard the week previously. Women obviously possess a sensitivity denied to us poor males.

CHAPTER FORTY

*D*aniel had brought me up to date with his plan to take revenge on Rob Benson. He was often to be found either at the Citadel or Castle Goal in Carlisle. Clearly he held a position of authority but also acted as an informer, playing both sides and making a good profit out of stolen wad.

Even poor quality Wad was changing hands at seven shillings per pound in the ale houses of Keswick and Cockermouth. It was a very lucrative business for all the ruffians and rogues involved. I had heard that raids on the mine continued, ours had been far from the last. To be a guard at the mine was still a dangerous occupation. Isolated and alone at night they were vulnerable and nervous. Through his network of contacts Daniel knew that a raid was being planned and that Rob Benson was involved. One of the guards, Josh Spedding, had been advised to keep away from the mine, so the raid was imminent.

Telling Elicia that I had business to attend to in Keswick. I managed to rendezvous with Daniel, Davey Dixon and Tickle

Blencarn. Both had escaped punishment for their part in our raid ten years previously. They were arrested but had been acquitted as the case against them was unproven.

It was a jolly gathering at the George Hotel in Keswick that evening. There was laughter and tears remembering many nights out on the trod, smuggling Wad. The tale of Davey's barrels of black powder was amusing now, although it had not been so at the time. Rob Dixon's decision to bring oxen to haul the sledge appeared highly suspicious now, with the benefit of hindsight. We all agreed that his intention had been to slow us down, making it easier to capture us in the act.

We travelled up Borrowdale to Seathwaite the following morning, arriving at the mine around midday. At the guardhouse, re- built in the shelter of the hill overlooking two mine entrances, we met with Josh Spedding and four other guards. Josh had been given another friendly warning not to be on site that night and with this in mind we made our plans. As darkness settled on the landscape, the door and windows were secured with bolts and timber. Each of us, armed and ready with two pistols and a musket awaited events.

Around nine o the clock a coarse voice called on Josh to surrender, unaware that he had been reinforced. He answered with a curse, firing his musket into the darkness from one of the narrow loops cut into the shutters. The response was a fusillade of fire from those outside. We returned fire with a will and a fierce exchange ensued. Our attackers must have realised that Josh was not alone. It became deathly quiet outside, while we, choked by the smoke from the discharge of our weapons, trying not to cough, listened intently for any sound. When it came, it was the scrape of clogs on the slate roof above. Someone had managed to climb up and was now endeavouring to remove the heavy slates.

Snuffing out the candles we gathered beneath the noise from above small pieces of displaced plaster fell around us like snow. The darkness in the guard house enabled us to discern the brightness of the starlit sky through the enlarged hole in the roof. Suddenly a pistol was fired through the hole, wounding one of our men. I could not see who, but he was cursing loudly so the wound was not fatal. Every one of us discharged our weapons simultaneously, above our heads.

A grunt of pain was followed by the sound of a body tumbling off of the roof, proof that we had hit our mark. Shouts and movement outside gave way to muttered conversation, impossible to decipher; then silence. Daniel said:

"Come lads, we have to get out now, follow them, and let's find the bugger!"

"I agree", I said, "we have wounded one, he at least won't get very far."

The door was cautiously unbarred and we peered out into the night, ready for any sudden rush. None came and growing more confident we split up to search the immediate area with the aid of lanterns.

The irony of the situation was not lost on me, I was defending the very place that I had attacked ten years ago. Fallen roof slates and a heavy timber beam, leaning against the guardhouse eaves, showed where entry had been attempted. A shout from Daniel on the fellside away to my left had me stumbling in his direction with all haste. The others joined me, following the gleam from Daniel's lantern. He was standing over a figure, prone, face down on the ground.

"This here's the bugger, took our shot"

He reached down and rolled the body over. It was Rob Benson, still breathing but bleeding heavily. He had managed to stagger some seventy yards from the guardhouse, before collapsing of his wounds. From the pallor of his face and the racking gurgle of his breathing, it was obvious that he was not long for this world. I was pleased that Daniel had not caused the damage on his own, every one of us except our wounded companion had fired at the individual on the roof. Rob Benson had seriously misjudged the mood of those inside, not expecting such a fierce response to his single shot. He looked up at us wide eyed with terror, his attempt to speak was thwarted by the blood in his throat. Daniel said:

"So comes t' this Rob Benson, ye were a most wicked fellow when you betrayed me and John here. Lost, years of our lives, and for what?"

I had long wished for some revenge for his infamy, yet I could not bring myself to hate the pathetic creature lying on the ground in such distress.

"I forgive you Rob, go to meet your maker with my blessing, you have paid dear for your sins."

"Aye, like as not, ah can forgive thee too," said Daniel.

Rob Benson survived for scarce five minutes more, ere death took him.

Rob's shooting had been a regrettable incident, but it had been brought about by his own arrogance and greed. It laid the ghost that had haunted me and Daniel since our capture and transportation. We returned to our separate homes in a better spirit than that in which we had left.

Elicia greeted me with a bright smile, "Welcome back John, I have missed you," she said. Holding her in a long embrace, she asked:

"Is all well with you John, what has happened?"

Regarding me with her clear blue-grey eyes, the question hung between us.

"A long overdue debt has been paid." I replied, unwilling to give any further detail. She continued to search my face, finally kissing my lips.

"I love you John Rigg. I will ask no more questions else cause a rift between us."

"And I love you Elicia Salkeld, Will you marry me?"

Throwing her arms about my neck, her lips pressed tightly to mine, was her answer.

"I will undertake to settle the matter with Mordechai," I stated with a conviction I did not feel.

Things could no longer be allowed to drift, Elicia and I must be wedded, too much precious time had been lost already. On my way back to High Wray that afternoon I made the decision to call on Mordechai Dixon the very next day.

CHAPTER
FORTY ONE

*G*rove Farm, the home of Mordechai, lies on the flank of Wansfell ,on the east side of Stock Ghyll, where it descends from the Kirkstone Pass . Riding up from Ambleside on a blustery damp morning, my mind was busy with all the possible outcomes from my forthcoming meeting with Mordechai. The clouds hung low over the head of the valley, threatening more snow. Mordechai was in the yard, a tall figure, slightly stooped, aged perhaps in his forties. He was leading a milk cow in from the fields, her full udder swinging with her steady gait.

He stopped when he saw me and raising my hat I said, "Good morning."

He nodded but did not speak.

"I am John Rigg."

"Aye, I guessed as much."

"I have come to talk about Elicia."

"I thought you would."

The exchange was proving difficult, his response was not encouraging thus far.

"Can we get out of this wind?"

"Aye, ye best come inside."

With that he led the cow into a barn, reappearing a few moments later and headed into the house.

I dismounted, hitched my horse to an iron ring set in the wall and followed him inside. The interior was unexpectedly neat and tidy. A fine old Court Cupboard filled one wall and two oak Lambing Chairs faced the cosy peat fire. He sat, indicating for me to take the chair opposite and saying nothing he waited for me to speak. I looked around the room, taking in the polished furniture and rag rug covered flagstone floor. Composing my thoughts and words, finally I spoke, "Mordechai, I am finding this situation most difficult. You must know why I am here?"

"I do."

"What are your feelings about Elicia?"

"She is a handsome woman, no doubt and would be great help to me here," he replied.

"Do you love her and does she love you?"

"She loves *you*, 'Moses' Rigg and has done for many a year. I know she does not, cannot love me, but I care for her."

Summoning all of my courage, I continued:

"You are betrothed as of last week, I do not want to disrespect you but it is I who she desires to marry. Can you, would you give her up?"

His face saddened:

"It seems I must, for I have no wish to force her into an unhappy union with me."

I was mightily relieved to hear him say this for at least he recognised the hopelessness of his aspirations. He did indeed seem to be a decent and honourable man, the task ahead was looking somewhat easier.

"When I first came to hear of your return, I knew then that it was only a matter of time before you would come here to speak with me," he said. "The land of Mistress Salkeld and mine adjoin, it would have been good for both of us to put them together. Also, we are alone, the companionship would have proven very welcome."

He paused, staring into the fire with a sad expression on his face. I pitied him then and could feel his sadness. Looking me full in the eye, he took a deep breath,

"I release her unreservedly from any obligation, I pray that you find happiness together." He rose to shake my hand. I felt a stinging tear in my eye and stood up to take his hand in a firm grip.

"Thank you Mordechai, thank you with all my heart."

Leaving to return to Ambleside, I looked back to where Mordechai stood in the farmyard watching my progress down the track. I could not but feel immense respect for such an honest and upright man and resolved that I must see if there was some small thing that I could do for him by way of grateful thanks.

Elicia dashed out of the house as soon as she caught sight of me in the distance. She stood waiting at the gate, hands on hips, looking defiant. Smiling to reassure her as I approached, her stance softened slightly.

"Well, what news?"

Pretending to be the bearer of unhappy tidings, I said,

"Not good, there is much to be done, I am a feared."

"Oh John!" She looked about to cry and softening my heart I was unable to continue the pretence..

"Such a short time with so much to do for the wedding!"

Misunderstanding my meaning, her mouth set in a hard line and tears flowed unchecked, down her cheeks.

"Our wedding my sweet, *our wedding!*"

Her response was to fly at me in anger, pulling me from the saddle and pummel me with her fists.

"John Rigg, you are a beast!"

Laughter now, taking my arms she danced me around in circles.

"Mordechai released me? Oh joy of joys, we are to be wed!"

"Come". I said, "we must needs tell the children."

"Will it be welcome news?"

"I am certain that although they have known you for such a little time, they love you and will be pleased to call you mother."

We summoned the groom to harness a light gig, in order for Elicia and Ruenna to accompany me back to the Old Hall.

Later that evening, after supper with Aunt Hannah, Sophie, Ruenna, Thomas, Elizabeth and Eloise we gathered in the big parlour.

Elicia announced, "We have something of importance to share with you all."

"My dears, can anyone guess what it might be?" I asked, smiling around at the expectant faces.

It was Thomas who spoke first,

"You wish to get married?"

There was a surprised intake of breath from Ruenna. We had kept our secret from her, on the journey from Ambleside. The twins hugged each other in their obvious delight. Sophie looked around at all the other faces and said;

"I think that I speak for us all. It has been clear that even after so recent a reunion, your regard for each other would lead to a more permanent joining of the two families. I am surprised at the speed of events and must assume that the visit to Mordechai this morning was concluded satisfactorily?"

"You assume correctly, Sophie," I replied. "Mordechai has been most generous in accepting the situation and chooses not to press for the promised betrothal. He is a remarkable person, kind and honest. A man I would be proud to call a friend."

"I look forward to meeting such a rare human being," Sophie replied.

Thomas stood up decisively:

"A drink to celebrate this announcement is called for, Ruenna come and help me find wine and glasses."

They left the room together and we could hear their chatter and giggles as they ransacked the larder and dairy. Returning with a bottle of Port they poured it out for all, even Elizabeth and Eloise had a small glassful. Thomas had reacted very well to our announcement and he now took charge of the toast.

"We, this family, for we are soon to be one family, want you both to be happy."

The others rose to their feet and formed a circle around Elicia and me.

"To our new parents and to us," continued Thomas.

With raised glasses the toast was echoed by everyone, even Sophie. We all embraced, a glow of pleasure in every eye. Thomas had proved himself to be every inch, his mother's son.

I emptied my glass with a silent prayer to Arabella, she whom I had loved with such a fierce passion. For Elicia, my love was different, somehow more comfortable and homely even. Goodness, I must be getting old! The obvious joy and support of the children gave me confidence in the future. Truly a new beginning, I needed now look to secure my income and business interests in England. With so large a family, a dependable financial foundation was required. Plans were needed, plans for the wedding and plans for the girls' education, for they had grown beyond what Sophie could teach them.

Three months later letters and two small barrels arrived in Whitehaven sent from Gideon in Bermuda. The salt business was thriving. I was now a very wealthy man, well able to support my family. We should have to think about the possibility of building a new home for us all.

The barrels contained rum, Gideon had been trading with Barbados and become involved with the sugar plantations there. He had established a small plantation on our land in Bermuda and these barrels were the first of his own production. He suggested that we expand the sugar planting although the lack of sufficient water might be a problem. Not being a supporter of Slavery, the actual planting and harvesting would have to be undertaken by free men. Gideon had thought that forming a co-operative with interested Bermudian Quakers could be the answer.

Once delivered to The Old Hall, we opened one barrel to sample the contents. It was golden and aromatic. Elicia, who had never tasted rum before, was much taken with it. Speaking with Thomas that evening we decided to find out what demand there might be for rum if we were able to import more.

It fell to Thomas to travel to Whitehaven in the search for information. The second barrel was taken down into the cellar to be stored ready for our wedding. In my reply to Gideon, I stated my agreement to the use of our own workers in the new enterprise, urging him to plant more sugar cane while we explored potential markets in England. Here was the much needed endeavour to occupy my energy and motivate my mind. I retired to bed that night elated and excited about the possibilities that lay ahead of us.

CHAPTER
FORTY TWO

*T*he wedding plans kept Elicia busy and the date was finally set for the sixth of July. With only a few months to go, a guest list was quickly drawn up and invitations sent. We had decided on the church at Hawkshead for the service but had yet to decide exactly where the wedding breakfast should be.

Thomas managed very well in his dealings with the Customs and Excise in Whitehaven. The likelihood of us importing rum was looking good. I sent further letters to Gideon, suggesting that he investigate the possibility of importing molasses from Barbados to be processed into Rum in Bermuda. It would be a year before our cane was ready to harvest and I was keen to start producing Rum as soon as was possible. Being ignorant of the actual process of making Rum from sugar cane I also asked Gideon to send us details in his next letter.

When discussing Barbados sugar cane with Thomas, he expressed a great deal of interest in the proposal, even suggesting that he return to Bermuda in order to obtain more detailed information. I thought this a good idea but did not want him to leave before the wedding. He could however depart in August while the winds were favourable. This agreed, he became extremely excited, starting to plan and make arrangements immediately.

Elicia asked around her friends and neighbours in order to find a suitable school for the twins to attend. One in particular, Miss Dowling's Girls Boarding Academy, at 'Hill Top' above Ambleside, was highly thought of. It would mean them boarding during the week but they could be home within an hour or so. We decided to pay the establishment a visit once the wedding was over.

In the meantime I passed several fruitless days exploring the countryside around Ambleside and Grasmere in search of a suitable site on which to build our new house.

When I visited Elicia at home later that week, I was informed that she was confined to her bed, suffering from an unknown malady. Ruenna was in charge of the household. After welcoming me warmly with a kiss on each cheek, she took me up to her mother's bedchamber. Elicia was sitting up supported by bolsters drinking from a small silver posset. She smiled wanly when I entered, patting the bed beside her indicating for me to sit.

"My dear, what ails you?"

"I don't rightly know John, I feel weak and am unsteady on my feet."

"How long have you been this way?"

"Only a few days, Ruenna called the Physician, Doctor Scrambler, who says that I should rest and drink a fortified posset."

"Is that all?"

I removed my riding boots and pulled myself up against the head board, tucking a bolster under my shoulders.

"Well, I shall stay to look after you!"

"No!" she protested, "Ruenna is a caring and attentive nurse. You see to all that needs be done to prepare for our wedding day."

At that moment Ruenna entered the chamber, she giggled when she saw me cosy on the bed with her mother.

"Mother! What do you think our neighbours would say?"

"I care not for the neighbour's opinions."

Elicia turned to look at me with the greatest fondness and kissing me gently on the cheek, she said;

"This is my only love, the husband of my childhood dreams."

Ruenna threw herself across the bed, resting her head on her mother's lap, arms around my waist.

"I love you both so much, I am very pleased for you to have found each other at last. I can only hope in my life to find the happiness that you have in one another."

I reached over to stroke the mass of blonde curls cascading over her mother's lap.

"My darling daughter, I cannot express what a joy it has been for me to have found not only my first love, but a beautiful daughter as well. You both mean so very much to me."

Making my way home to High Wray as the sun faded in the west, I could not help but go over, once again, the events that had brought me to such a state of perfect contentment, despite the painful loss of Arabella. I was indeed, a very lucky man!

As the wedding day approached, throughout the month of June we were blessed with fine weather. Clear sunny days followed by balmy starlit nights. Elicia had quickly recovered from her malady and was energetically involved in final wedding preparations. We had decided that if the fine weather held we would set out tables in the paddock next to the farm opposite the Old Hall. It was a level field sheltered on all sides by drystone walls and with exceptional views towards the lake and Fairfield Mountain in the north.

With the help of Thomas the grass was cut ready for the forthcoming celebrations. Two Hawkshead carpenters laid wooden boards on the grass to make a dance floor. Lanterns were to be strung from the trees and long trestles would accommodate the many guests.

I had talked with Elicia about inviting Mordechai and she felt sufficient fondness for him and agreed that he should be asked. Deciding to deliver it myself, I rode over to visit him that afternoon. He was surprised to see me but with his gentle manner he asked me to join him in the kitchen for a bowl of hot broth.

Sitting while the maid readied the broth, cutting a hunk of freshly baked bread for each of us, I observed him again and my original opinion was reaffirmed. There was a quiet confidence about him that I greatly admired.

"Mordechai, Elicia and I are to wed in Hawkshead on the sixth of July next and we would consider it an honour if you will condescend to be our guest at the Church and the after celebrations," I ventured.

He stared at me, looking somewhat perplexed and a minute passed before he replied:

"John, I am unsure that it is appropriate for me to be there, it will cause embarrassment."

"Not at all, we both want you there, we owe you a great deal and want to show it."

"I am not sure," he said uncertainly.

"Please, I ask you as a friend although we have been acquainted for so short a time."

"As you put it like that, in all civility I can hardly refuse."

I breathed with relief, "Good! I am delighted." I leaned over the table to take his hand, "You are a fine man and I am fortunate to know you."

I rose to take my leave, we parted on the most satisfactory of terms. I pondered on all of this as I rode slowly home.

Commodore Eli Farrington had agreed to give Elicia away, so it was Daniel who I asked to be my best man. Ruenna, Elizabeth and Eloise were to be bridesmaids. All in all it promised to be a merry gathering.

The sixth of July, in the year of our Lord seventeen seventy two, dawned overcast but bright. A golden sunrise streaked the clouds with pink and purple. I and the rest of the household were up and busy by seven o clock and the sun already high in the heavens. The sounds of Elizabeth and Eloise in their rooms as they dressed carried to my chamber. I could hear the frustration in Sophie's voice as she struggled to contain them.

We were due at the church for 10-o' -the clock, Elicia, Ruenna and Eli would meet us there having made their way from Ambleside. Already the Old Hall was filling with guests and our grooms were somewhat overwhelmed with the number of horses and carriages to be tended to. The lawn at the back of the house was bright with the finery of our guests. Aunt Hannah moved amongst them, greeting each and making them welcome.

The murmur of happy voices rose to my open window, bringing urgency to my toilet. While I donned my clothing Thomas came in, to sit on a stool at my elbow, asking many questions about the day's proceedings. He was already dressed in a deep blue velvet waistcoat and breeches. He had wanted to wear clothes similar to mine so I had ordered them both together. Our coats, waistcoats and breeches were in deep blue velvet, lined in gold thread around the edges, cuffs and pockets with large buttons, also of gold. We had agreed to wear our hair brushed back to be tied at the nape with a black ribbon. Once complete we admired ourselves in a long pier glass.

"Thomas, you look quite the gentleman, we will cut a fine pair of figures and you will certainly attract the ladies. Of that I have no doubt."

It was obvious he had already thought of this possibility, as he coloured, averting his eyes from my gaze.

Wanting to change the subject, he said; "Father, I have something for you."

He proffered me a small package wrapped around with a silk kerchief. Unwrapping it revealed a Spanish gold doubloon, pierced and hung on a chain.

"I picked it up in the bottom of the pirate boat in Bermuda I put it in my pocket and forgot about it. Do you like it? I had it fitted to a chain when I was last in Whitehaven."

I beamed with pleasure: "Thomas, I will treasure this always. It will remind me of you and your mother, of Bermuda and the battles that we fought there. I will wear it always, starting right away". Fixing the chain about my neck, I fed the coin down inside my silk neckerchief. Pulling Thomas towards me we embraced silently.

"Come!" I said, "The day has begun."

Sophie and the twins were waiting for us in the garden, Elizabeth and Eloise pretty in matching pink satin gowns. The twins, Thomas and I rode in an open carriage, decorated with ribbons and flowers. The guests and well-wishers followed behind on horseback and on foot, a noisy, cheerful and colourful throng along the lanes from High Wray to Colthouse and on to Hawkshead.

Entering the village square, a crowd awaited our arrival. Daniel was by the gate and came towards us with a wide grin on his face. Linking arms we headed up the hill to the church. The twins and Sophie lingered at the gate to welcome and escort Elicia.

The old church was cool but bright with sunlight streaming through the windows. Friends and relatives filled the pews, those unable to secure a seat stood at the back or spilled outside.

Everywhere the sweet sharp scent of the floor strewn rushes filled the air. The clamour of the church bells, combined with the merry chatter of the congregation created an excited anticipation. Daniel, Thomas and I took our places at the altar rail.

As the chatter in the church stilled, turning I saw that Elicia and Eli had entered and now stood at the back. Elicia was radiant in a yellow satin gown, her hair in ringlets was woven about with strings of white dog roses. In all, she looked more beautiful than I had ever seen her before and my heart melted.

Eli was resplendent in his full dress uniform, arm in arm they began a slow progress up the aisle. Behind them Ruenna, Elizabeth and Eloise carried baskets of wild flowers. I was filled with pride as the pretty tableau approached. We smiled at each other when she reached my side, our fingers touched and entwined briefly as the priest launched into his words of welcome.

With the service over, the wedding throng made its joyful way back to High Wray in glorious sunshine. The Coniston hills on our left stood out bright and clear, the air full of birdsong and the hum of insects. Approaching Toc How Farm the vista opened to reveal Ambleside in the distance set in its vale under Fairfield and Wansfell. Further out the Langdale Pikes raised their craggy heights against a sky of the bluest blue.

It was a scene of the utmost majesty, I could not but feel the greatest delight to have been married for the second time, on such a day and in such a place as this.

Once the paddock set for the wedding breakfast came into view, we could see that many had arrived before us. The musicians had already struck up a merry tune while servants scurried back and forth, with even more food and ale for the laden tables. The view from the paddock across the fields to Blelham Tarn reflected the sky and beyond to the Langdale Pikes, their purple grey framing the horizon. Against that the paddock was alive with every possible colour as more and more wedding guests arrived.

It did not go unnoticed by Elicia that Sophie was escorted in to the lively scene by Mordechai, nor had that Thomas arrived, arm in arm with Ruenna.

Once everyone was seated, Daniel roared above the hubbub demanding silence. I stood up, instinctively feeling for the precious coin at my throat and glancing at Thomas, I saw that he had registered my action, also he had understood its meaning. We smiled at each other sharing a thought, a memory of Arabella.

"My dear friends, thank you for joining with me, my wife and our two families on this very special day. It has been ten years in coming, we have been on a long journey to get to this day."

Looking to Daniel, I continued, "One of my dearest friends accompanied me on that journey."

Daniel nodded and turned to those seated either side of him.

"I discovered another, along the way." This time I searched out Eli. "He proved to be the most constant of friends, saving my life a number of times. Without his attentive support, I would not be here today."

Everyone turned to look where Eli sat, his head now bowed in embarrassment.

"I also gained a son and two beautiful daughters to add to the other beautiful daughter who I had unknowingly left behind when I started out on my journey."

The children were all regarding me in silence, eyes wide, listening to every word.

"To say that I am proud of each one of them, would not be enough, I love them very much, they bring me joy, every moment of every day."

There was a sob from Ruenna sitting next to her mother and Elicia reached for her hands, holding them tightly on her lap.

"Elicia, my dearest Elicia." Her blue-grey eyes locked with mine, I noticed tears forming.

"We promised ourselves to each other when we were little more than babies. My love for you has always been there, deep inside, a vein of attachment running through my soul, despite myself. You have been a rock, a constant, always there, even when it appeared all hope was lost."

Her tears flowed then, although her eyes never left mine. Leaning down I kissed her on the forehead. Eli moved around the table to proffer his handkerchief for her to dry her eyes. She squeezed his hand in thanks as he returned to his seat. The gathering was silent, frozen in the moment.

Daniel leapt to his feet,

"To John and Elicia, the happy couple."

Raising his cup he drained it in one go while the other guests stood to repeat his toast.

"Right now, enough speeching, on with the party," he cried.

Taking Maggie's hand he wheeled her out onto the dance

floor. The musicians, taking this as their cue, started on a lively country jig. As one, the gathering rose to join Daniel on the dance floor. Once the first burst of energy was spent the music became more sober and stately, at which point Elicia and I joined in the dancing.

Thomas danced with Ruenna, although only ten years of age she was tall and slim, looking elegant and older than her years. It was Sophie and Mordechai who caused a stir, their eyes fixed on one another throughout the happy day. The wedding party continued as the afternoon drifted into soft twilight, the lanterns were lit. Elicia and I slipped away as the stars began to jewel the velvet sky, leaving the party to run its course without us.

Walking slowly, arms about each other's waists we made our way across to the Old Hall. As we climbed the stairs to my chamber we noticed that flowers, ribbons and candles had been arranged during my absence. Now lit, the candles cast a soft glow on the dark oak treads and red Turkey runner. The wonder of the scene was not lost on Elicia, who snuggled against me, it was a moment of blessed anticipation and intimacy.

Preparing for bed the romance of the moment continued. We undressed in silence, backs turned as we got into our night gowns, and only then did we look at each other. Elicia smiled across the bed separating us and pulling back the covers she climbed in. I could not suppress my laughter, she looked so demure, holding the covers high under her chin. Then throwing the covers down, Elicia scrambled free of the fine linen, laughing she crawled across the bed on her hands and knees.

"Come to bed, husband. Make an honest woman of me!"

Taking both my hands in hers she pulled me forwards and tumbling on top of her we rolled together laughing hysterically. Pausing, out of breath, lying side by side, I brushed the tangle of golden hair out of her eyes. Serious now, her eyes searched my face, suddenly she climbed across my body, her legs astride.

"So now you must make proper love to me, not as you left me before. I want to feel you inside me, feel your love and respect."

Rubbing herself against me, I could not stop my erection, the desire that washed over my body was warm and comforting. On entering her, it was she who moved against me, it was she who controlled the orgasm, making us moan with helpless pleasure.

Sleep overcame us as the chamber stick spluttered and went out.

The next morning I was woken by Elicia tracing the branding scar on my shoulder, with her tongue. Her velvet soft lips moved on to gently kiss my eyelids. Making a grab for her she giggled and slid away from my grasp. I rolled over to reach for her again, she eluded me by wriggling out of bed completely.

"Come here woman, you minx!"

Elicia smiled , and with her eyes sparkling with laughter she moved further away, well out of my reach.

"No John, we have the rest of our lives to enjoy each other; this morning we have guests waiting on us for breakfast."

Dressing we went down to the dining room where Aunt Hannah, Sophie, Thomas and Eli sat around the big old oak table.

"Good morning Master and Mistress Rigg, how are you feeling today?" asked Eli.

"Well, we are very well" said Elicia giving me a hug and a kiss on the cheek.

"Where are the twins?" I asked.

"Recovering." Sophie said with a smile. "They ran around until they dropped last night. We had to carry them to bed completely exhausted, as the party was ending."

"You and Mordechai..?"

Elicia tried to make the question sound innocent. Sophie did not reply immediately, she seemed rather taken aback by the question.

"He is very nice."

"Very nice? You spent the whole evening with him, you must think him more than very nice"

"Elicia, you embarrass me with all these questions." Sophie blushed and looked away.

Wishing to change the subject, Eli said: "The rum barrel is empty, they drank the lot."

I laughed: "There will plenty of sore heads this morning then."

"Yes John, I know for one that Daniel is most unwell at the moment."

He could not help a wicked smile.

Once breakfast finished we all walked out to view the scene of ruination in the paddock, for the party had long continued after we retired to bed, and much merriment had ensued. It had been a wedding celebration to remember!

CHAPTER
FORTY THREE

*A*fter all of the visitors and guests had returned to their own homes, our whole family settled into a comfortable domestic routine. Thomas prepared to travel to Bermuda while I made more of an effort to identify a suitable site for a new house. The relationship between Sophie and Mordechai developed slowly, to the delight of everyone.

Letters arrived from Gideon containing more details of the rum making process, and also a letter for Thomas from Miss Isadora Da Silva. This last came as a surprise to him and with excited anticipation he declared that he was looking forward re-establishing the acquaintance.

Elicia and I paid a visit to Hill Top in Ambleside. We were keen to find a suitable school for Elizabeth and Eloise. They were becoming wild and unruly. It was clear that they needed more effective training and discipline than Sophie could offer. Elicia thought that interaction with others of their own age would also be beneficial for them.

Miss Dowling was a kindly but competent woman of about thirty years. Her Girls Boarding Academy was efficiently run, the children polite and well mannered. More importantly, all the pupils we met were happy and relaxed. We agreed the twins would start at the beginning of the autumn term. In the meantime they would spend the summer in the fields and woods locally or down on the shore of Windermere, when one or other of us had the time to escort them.

Thomas sailed for Bermuda on the last day of July and we all rode over in carriages to see him off. The poor state of the tracks and roads made it a two day journey so we rested in Whitehaven for three nights. Ruenna was quieter than usual, the departure of Thomas had left her subdued and out of sorts.

When no more than two miles from Ambleside on our return, I noticed a pleasant spot in Rydal, under the lee of Loughrigg Fell, facing south and overlooking the river Rothay where it was crossed by ancient stepping stones. I decided to make enquiries about buying the land once we reached High Wray.

The letters from Gideon described how the sugar cane was crushed between rollers, the juice was boiled, then cooled in trays. The sugar turned into brown crystals on top of the molasses. Finally all was put into perforated barrels. These allowed the molasses to drain off, leaving the sugar behind. The molasses was then fermented and distilled into rum. It all seemed reasonably easy.

I replied to Gideon asking him to produce as much rum as was possible and to send it to me as soon as it was ready. I felt invigorated by the many interesting things to occupy my mind. Elicia and I drew closer together day by day although we, the twins and Ruenna greatly missed the company of Thomas.

Meanwhile, Thomas had returned safely to Bermuda. At the end of September we received the first letter from him. He told us of the production of rum, the condition of the house and estate and his meetings with Miss Da Silva. Ruenna ran off, slamming the doors behind her when she overheard me reading the letter aloud to the twins. I couldn't help thinking that Thomas might never return to England, but I did not share this thought with Ruenna.

Elizabeth and Eloise started school, boarding during the week, only coming home at the weekends.

Late in October the first shipment of rum arrived in Whithaven from Bermuda, fifty barrels with a value in excess of fifteen thousand pounds. A substantial investment and it was sold within days. I kept a barrel for our own use, having heard that in colonial America it was given to sick babies and used by adults to ease pain. In Cumberland taking rum was becoming a popular part of the social scene.

The Carlisle, Newcastle and Edinburgh merchants who purchased my shipment were keen to have more. The profit was tremendous and should we be successful in the production and shipping of more, there was a great deal of money to be made. I sent off more letters to both Gideon and Thomas informing them of the speedy sale and urging them to send a further shipment with all haste.

These events reminded me to seek out the owner of the land I had noticed in Rydal and upon enquiry it proved to be Sir Michael Le Fleming of Rydal Hall. I made arrangements to call on him at the earliest opportunity.

One evening, while walking in the orchard with Elicia and Ruenna, one on each arm, we heard Sophie calling for us. She came running, flustered and out of breath. Pausing to adjust her bonnet she said:

"Dear friends, I have come now in haste from Grove Farm, where Mordechai, this very afternoon has asked for my hand in marriage!" She paused looking eagerly from one to another. "Tell me, is it right, do you approve?"

Elicia was the first to speak.

"Sophie my dear, you have become an important member of our family, I love you as a sister; for myself, I am delighted you have found happiness."

"Thank you, oh thank you." She turned to me, "And you John, will you let me go, to leave your employ?"

"Sophie, it is many months since you were anything other than a sister, as Elicia has said. I believe you deserve this chance, if you so desire it."

"I do, oh I do! Mordechai is such a wonderful man, I could not be more pleased," she cried.

"Good, then our blessings go with you." We all embraced, "This calls for a drink to celebrate, come now, back to the house."

As we made our way back, through the orchard heavy with ripe fruit, Sophie said;

"John, would you consent to give me away?"

"Nothing could give me greater pleasure." I replied, honoured to have been asked.

The remainder of the autumn passed in a pleasant round of business and homely pursuits. Elizabeth and Eloise loved Miss Dowling's school, the influence of which began to have a beneficial effect on their behaviour. As Ruenna had been a pupil of Miss Dowling's she wrote in a clear round hand and I engaged her to assist me as clerk with my numerous business communications. I enjoyed her quiet company, sitting together on opposite sides of my desk, each attending to their own task. I could not help but steal a glance at her every so often. She was strikingly beautiful although totally unaware of it herself. She looked up and smiled prettily when she caught me watching her. In her I saw the Elicia that I had fallen in love with so very long ago.

I visited Sir Michael Le Fleming, one afternoon in early December to discuss the purchase of the piece of land overlooking the stepping stones at Rydal. He was very willing to sell and after agreeing the price we settled on a barrel of rum to seal the deal. This I had delivered to Rydal Hall the following week.

In the meantime a letter arrived from Eli asking to spend Christmas with us at the Old Hall. Of course we replied that it would be a pleasure to have his company for as long as he wished to stay.

I engaged an architect, Mr Robert Curwen of Kendal, to draw up the designs of the new house. He liked the chosen site when he saw it, returning to his Chambers full of ideas and enthusiasm.

We had not heard from Thomas for some time although with a worsening of bad weather at this time of the year it was not surprising.

Christmas was very special, with a heavy fall of snow on the twenty third. Luckily, Eli arrived the day before. The snow remained on the ground, freezing hard for several weeks hence, making travel hazardous.

CHAPTER
FORTY FOUR

A full year past in domestic peace and happiness and the New Year of Seventeen Seventy four, found Eli still residing with us. Chatting with him one day, sitting comfortably in front of a roaring log fire, he announced;

"John, I have decided to retire from the sea. I have a reasonable sum saved up and as a confirmed bachelor my needs will not be excessive but I do not know where to drop anchor."

"Have you not thought of places you would like to live?"

"No," he replied. "My life has been the sea since I was eleven years old, I know nothing else. You have been the only constant in my life of late."

I had a sudden thought: "Well, why not come to live here with us?"

"I cannot impose on your good will to such an extent, beside there is not enough room for everyone in this house as it is, let alone if Thomas should return."

"I seriously doubt that Thomas will ever return, also the new house is to be built this year, so you might live here to keep Aunt Hannah company in her old age."

"You make it sound most tempting. I have grown to love your family, in fact yours is the only family that I have ever really known. I can contribute to my upkeep, I have saved enough money over the years," he said thoughtfully.

I leaned forward to grip his hand.

"That's agreed then, you will come to live here."

"John, words fail me…"

Elicia came into the room with the three girls and as she took in the scene, she asked:

"What is to do here then?"

"My dear, Eli is to retire from the navy and is to come to live with us here if you will but agree."

She crossed to Eli, bending to kiss his cheek;

"How wonderful, we are all delighted."

Once the weather improved Eli left to sort out his affairs in Portsmouth, the twins returned to school and Elicia told me she was with child.

"You are with child, our child!" I responded with excitement.

"Yes my dearest, two months gone, I have waited until I was certain before telling you."

"This is wonderful news, shall we tell the children?"

"Not until it begins to show," she decided, "we will keep this as our secret for the time being."

I hugged her then hand in hand we danced around the room, until out of breath we stopped to hold each other in a tight embrace.

The month of May brought a shipment of one hundred barrels of rum, accompanied by letters from both Thomas and Gideon. The weather was fair and everything was going well with planting cane and processing molasses. There was but one cloud on the horizon as tension between the American colonies and England was worsening, which in turn caused some difficulties between Bermuda and England.

It was while in Whitehaven dealing with the delivery of rum to Carlisle, that Sir Richard Lowther invited me to sit on the Bench at Carlisle Assizes. The irony of this was not lost upon Elicia, that I should be made a Justice of the Peace, sitting in the very court where I had been doomed to transportation twelve years before. She urged me to accept out of principal if nothing else.

Eli arrived with his baggage temporarily occupying Thomas's room. He agreed to take on some responsibility for my affairs. With the Old Hall and farm, Elicia's farm and house in Ambleside, three warehouses in Whitehaven and shortly, another house in Rydal, the necessity for running all efficiently was becoming difficult. Elicia helped with these tasks although her time was limited, also her pregnancy was advancing and we had to tell the girls. Ruenna and the twins were pleased to know that another member of the family was due in July, they all wanted a baby brother!

Mordechai and Sophie wed in St Anne's Chapel in Ambleside during the second week in May. It was a quiet affair with only a small group of friends and relatives present both in the church and the Wedding feast at The Salutation Inn.

Sophie was radiant and Mordechai clearly adored her. Elicia and I were both pleased that they had found each other. On the steps of the Salutation, as we were leaving, Sophie kissed my cheek, Mordechai kissed Elicia's saying:

"Thank you both for everything that you have done for us. We are your friends for ever, come what may." He shook my hand warmly as we parted.

CHAPTER
FORTY FIVE

*T*he house in Rydal was built of stone carted from nearby White Moss Quarry. Two bay windows, one either side of the front door took advantage of the view across the river and fields towards Ambleside a mile or so distant. Raised up above the river, the bank riveted with stone, it looked very handsome indeed.

We opted to have the stone walls rendered and whitewashed, all under a roof of Coniston slates. As the site was narrow the frontage hid the degree to which the house extended in the rear. Elicia decided to call it 'Rydal Villa', very modest sounding and not too grand, neither of us cared for grand.

Our son, William John Rigg was born on the second day of July, after a happily easy birth, which up to then I had been dreading. So many women do not survive giving birth and the loss of another for whom I cared so deeply was beyond contemplation. Even though she was very tired, Elicia welcomed us all into her chamber to see the baby.

Later that evening, Eli and I drank a toast to both mother and son. Relaxed and comfortable, I remarked to Eli;

"Do you think it wise to set up a Company to secure my business interests now I have another son?"

"I do, John," he said. "I had thought it odd, that you have not already done so."

"I have been considering asking you and Daniel to become Company members with me," I ventured.

"But I have limited funds, as such I cannot bring much to finance the enterprise," he replied.

"That is of little consequence however, it is the support of loyal and honest friends that I seek."

"Well, put in that manner, I cannot but accept," he said.

"Excellent," I said, and told him I would speak with Daniel before instructing a lawyer to draw up the contract."

Daniel proved eager to be part of this new venture, so I travelled to Carlisle to instruct a lawyer recommended to me. A round faced portly, jolly man in a powdered periwig, caused me a wry smile when he said;

"This is a very exciting development Mister Rigg, for a country gentleman who has had little remarkable happen in his life until now!"

It was plain he did not know of me, nor had he been appraised of my history. When this was eventually related to him his embarrassment was deep.

"Dear Sir, I cannot but most humbly beg your indulgence for my ignorance," he said. "You are a man of much experience, excitement even. More so than I could ever imagine, please forgive my ignorance."

After such an inauspicious start, James Wilson, for that was his name, and I became good friends. He proved to be a wise and learned advisor to our fledgling Company.

The first Company meeting was held at his offices in Carlisle two months later. Elicia, Daniel, Eli and I were present, Thomas was registered as a Board member in his absence. It was plain from the first year's accounts that, should our dealings prove to be as profitable in the future, we would all become very wealthy indeed.

CHAPTER
FORTY SIX

*W*hen the new house was completed we moved out of the Old Hall leaving Aunt Hannah and Eli in residence there. In the midst of the move to 'Rydal Villa' letters arrived from Thomas in which he stated his intention to return to England before the years end. We were very surprised by this as we had assumed that the attractions of Bermuda and Miss Isadora Da Silva would keep him there. Nevertheless I was pleased he had made the decision to return.

Upon his arrival in Whitehaven that October he was met by a large party of; Ruenna, the twins, Eli, Daniel, Elicia and me. Waiting on the quay as he disembarked Elicia remarked on the degree to which he had grown. He did indeed look a well and prosperous gentleman.

He greeted us all warmly, especially Ruenna, who seemed strangely reticent in his presence. Upon mentioning this to Elicia she said that Ruenna may have lost her admiration for Thomas as a result of the several mentions of Miss Da Silva in his letters. I was bemused, I am an intelligent man of the world, yet the vagaries of the female mind, often eluded me.

Arriving in Rydal, Thomas was full of admiration for the new house. The pretty situation in particular attracted most comment from him. This was a matter of some satisfaction to me, as I valued his opinion.

After two days, the friendship between Thomas and Ruenna was still somewhat strained, Elicia challenged him on this, seeking an explanation. He admitted that he did not understand why Ruenna was so reserved towards him and Elicia advised him to speak with me, to seek my advice..

I decided to take matters into my own hands the following afternoon, Ruenna was seated across the desk from me copying out some company letters.

"Ruenna?" I said. She looked up from her work and smiled sweetly; "Yes father?"

"Ruenna, you know that I love you dearly and hate to see you unhappy?"

"I am not unhappy father, why do you ask?"

"It is you and Thomas." She looked down, avoiding my gaze. "You were so happy in each other's company, yet now there seems to be a problem."

Still looking down at her hands in her lap, in a whisper she said;

"I don't know of any problem father."

"I think that you do, tell me child, what ails you. I ask out of love, for no other reason. Tell me."

She took a deep breath and said;

"I care for Thomas, more than as a brother but he does not see me, I am just his little sister. He loves his friend, Miss Da Silva in Bermuda and will soon be going back to her."

"How do you know this, he has said nothing of returning to Bermuda, nor of any attachment to Miss Da Silva," I asked.

"I know it in my heart, he doesn't need to say it."

"Poppycock! I think you have imagined something that does not exist other than in your mind."

"Do you really think so?"

"I most certainly do! He cares for you as a sister, your mother and I both believe so."

She looked up at me with tears in her eyes and moving around the desk I took her into my arms, her body shaking with repressed emotion.

"Come now, I did not intend to distress you so, here dry your eyes," I offered her my handkerchief:

"We can think on this together, you and I, I promise."

She smiled up at me, grateful for my intervention in the matter. Coincidentally, only an hour or so later, Thomas waylaid me in the stables as I was preparing to ride over to Kendal;

"Father, may I talk with you?"

"Of course my son, what is it?"

"Ruenna, I don't understand why she is so reserved with me. We used to be such good friends."

"Ah, well! She cares for you but thinks that now you are in love with Miss Da Silva in Bermuda, and that you will soon be returning to her."

"Miss Isadora Da Silva! I think not! She is sweet and charming but nothing more than a friend. I hold only respect and fondness for her."

"Then my advice is to tell Ruenna so. You need to speak with her to resolve this jealousy it is between you two, no one else."

I left him thinking of what I had said and rode to Kendal, not returning home until twilight had enveloped the roads in deep shadow. After dinner Thomas asked to speak with me alone. We went up to the study where I poured us both a glass of Port, settling comfortably opposite each other in the large leather armchairs. He spoke immediately, rushing the words out;

"I think am in love with Ruenna."

"Slow down a moment, she is only twelve years old and you are twenty one, when was this decided?"

"This afternoon, after I talked to you I went to seek out Ruenna, we revealed what was in our hearts."

"All very well, Ruenna is still too young," I retorted, "perhaps when she is fifteen you could reconsider it. I do not know what Elicia will say and I must speak with her first."

"Will you, will you please!"

I told Thomas that I would.

The next day Elicia and I took the carriage to visit Aunt Hannah in High Wray. We wanted to benefit from the wisdom of her years regarding Thomas and Ruenna. She was, as ever, kind and understanding. Her advice was to allow Thomas and Ruenna to become betrothed but that a delay of three or four years should be imposed on any marriage. Eli joined us for mid-morning tea, he was much pleased to hear of the proposal. He was very fond of Thomas, admitting to a keen interest in all of his aspirations.

Returning to Rydal Villa Elicia accompanied me to the study, calling Thomas and Ruenna to join us. They arrived together, sitting nervously side by side waiting for us to speak.

"Ruenna, as your mother, I have every hope that should you marry, it will be to a worthy man. You are hardly more than a child, my dear, and I wish for you to learn more of the world before you are wed."

"I agree," I interjected, "we love you both, you are wonderful young people, all that we wish for you is long, happy lives. If you make each other happy and want to spend the rest of your lives together, you will have our blessing."

They exchanged glances, holding hands expectantly. "Never the less, you must wait until Ruenna is fifteen years of age at least. Three years is not so long and if you truly love each other the time will quickly pass."

They rose to embrace us, "Thank you mother, thank you father," they said together.

Elicia hugged me, then drew in Thomas and Ruenna, we remained clasped together for several minutes.

On his twenty first birthday that December, Thomas came into the inheritance that his grandfather, Colonel Tucker had left him. When examining the papers that I had been holding, we discovered an unopened letter, addressed to him which unfortunately was undated.

My dear grandson,

It has been in my mind of late, that I should ensure a future for you. It is my intention that you follow me as head of the many business ventures that I am party to. I will work with you to help in finding your feet, this will be a great adventure that I relish embarking on.

If however I do not survive long enough to be your mentor then I shall appoint John Rigg to be in charge of your education. You must know the feelings I have for you and the special place you hold in my heart.

I wish you an extraordinary life. As you are now reading this letter you must know that I will not be there to share it with you.

With the greatest respect and affection
Your loving Grandfather

We both read it in silence, Thomas looked up smiling, it was infectious, and my own smile brought the Colonel back sharply to mind. His kindness and generosity would never be forgotten by myself and so many others. For the remainder of that week contentment enfolded me in a warm bubble. Elicia even remarked on it after finding me in the garden, humming to myself while gazing at the nearby Fells.

CHAPTER
FORTY SEVEN

*A*s the years passed, all of our business interests with the Company and the various properties gave much to occupy everyone. William and the twins thrived. I considered myself, John Rigg, sometime known as 'Moses', smuggler of Wad ,convicted felon, blessed to have had such good fortune amidst both family and friends. A level of contentment filled my soul, the trials of the past faded to such a degree that they might have been a dream but for the scars I carried on my body. Arabella remained a constant companion in my heart, seeing her image in Thomas brought her often to my mind.

Sitting on the Bench in Carlisle as a Justice, I took every opportunity to intercede on the behalf of some poor wretch whenever possible, as they stood before me in the very spot where once I had stood.

Early March, in the year of our Lord 1777, Daniel arrived in haste from Keswick, bearing news of an auction due to take place in five days' time for the mineral and mining rights of the Goldscope mine, in the Newlands valley, near Keswick.

He was convinced that it offered a great opportunity for our Company to invest in a promising local venture. I had concurred with his assessment and called a meeting at short notice to discuss the proposal. Daniel, Elicia, Eli, Thomas and I travelled to Carlisle on the morning of the auction. We met with our Lawyer, James Wilson, at his Chambers in Paternoster Street. James was the first to speak;

"I have made some enquiries regarding the present condition of the mine in question. It is standing in ore. Yet there are no records of the quality nor amounts of ore raised, dressed and sold. This is quite irregular. Accordingly I have written to Sir Richard Lowther's Land Agent requesting further details. Without a reply as yet, I would counsel caution."

"The sales starts in one hour," I added with urgency, "If we wish to purchase this mine we will have to make a decision here and now." I said looking around the table at the others.

"Ah say, buy it," volunteered Daniel.

"Eli and Elicia. What is your thinking on this?"

They exchanged glances but remained silent.

"Thomas, do you have anything to add?"

"I do father, it is a chance for this Company to branch out into another venture. One that does not rely on rum brought many miles across the ocean".

"Well said Thomas! The rise in rum smuggling and the government excise tax are all making it more difficult for us to expand that business further."

Eli rose to his feet, thumping the table.

"I say, let us attempt to purchase this mine, if we do not succeed we can seek another opportunity elsewhere." He raised his right hand. "Come, who is with me?"

One by one the whole gathering stood, hands raised to show agreement. The Board had voted unanimously to bid for the lease, despite James Wilson's reservations. Daniel was commissioned to bid on the Board's behalf.

So it was that we obtained the rights to extract lead and copper ores from the mine situated just over the mountain from the wad mine in Seathwaite. We had come full circle from the events of that fateful night nearly thirteen years before. So much had happened, so many sad deaths and far too many tears.

After advertising locally, an experienced and skilled force of eighty miners, smiths, carters and surface workers was assembled. Much had to be done to clean, repair and extend the ore treatment mill before any mineral could be raised or sold. In fact many frustrating months passed rebuilding the surface machinery. Once completed, the men turned their attention to the conditions underground. We had employed a well recommended miner, lately of the Alston Lead Mines as Mine Manager. known to all as 'Jago' . He was a stocky, solid individual not above thirty or so years of age. A quiet, thoughtful man, competent in his work yet uncommunicative, even surly. Daniel did not take well to him but I was impressed with his experience and ability, and pushed the others to agree to take him on.

It was not until late December in the back end of the year that the mine and mill were ready to begin production. Goldscope was an ancient mine, none we knew could say with any certainty quite how ancient. It had been worked by men from the kingdom of Prussia and the Mines Royal in the days of Good Queen Bess.

Working by the light of tallow candles, cutting with pick axes through solid rock, a few inches a day; they were hardy and determined men.

We, on the other hand, had the advantage of Black Powder to blast the rock apart. Jago informed James Wilson that he was ready to start driving forward underground, and I showed the note with the news to Thomas, Elicia and Eli who happened to be visiting at the time.

"James Wilson tells us that Jago is wishing to commence exploration and expanding the main tunnel from the wheel chamber," I announced.

"That is good news," said Eli, "Surely we will soon see if this is the rich mine we hoped it to be."

Elicia asked, "The wheel chamber, I have heard talk of it, would a visit be possible?"

"You wish to see the wheel?"

"I certainly do," interjected Thomas.

"Yes, and why not, although being the only woman in this Company, I am as interested as any man might be."

"Elicia my dear, it is quite dangerous, are you sure?" I warned her anxiously.

"I would suggest early in the New Year, weather permitting." said Eli.

"So be it. I will write to Daniel, as he may wish to join with us on such an expedition."

For the next two months the fells were under a thick coat of snow. The lakes and streams froze solid. It was not until a thaw began in mid-February that the proposed mine visit could be arranged. Daniel wanted to be in the party and came over from Wasdale to spend the night at Rydal Villa.

The journey by carriage to Keswick took longer than anticipated, forcing us to seek lodgings at a farm in Little Town. We spent a merry evening sat at a long rectangular table. The farmer sat with us at the head, his wife and one other of his children waited upon us the remainder sat by the fire teasing and spinning wool.

Little Town lies at the foot of the valley a little over one mile from the mine. An early start was planned for the next morning but we had not allowed for the wonderful dinner that was provided for us. Mutton-ham, eggs, boiled fowl, roast pike, cabbage, peas and potatoes, wheat bread, butter and cheese. All followed by preserved gooseberries and cream! Needless to say we went to our beds overfull and slept to past nine in the morning. Although offered breakfast, not one of us could consider eating anything more. We paid the ten pennies each, as requested for bed and board, departing for the mine at ten of the clock.

The day was overcast, the sun low. The west side of the valley was already in shadow. Grey waste tips from the mine were difficult to pick out on the flanks of the fell already sunk into shadow. The head of the valley was obscured by mist rising from the sodden grass. A less inviting view was difficult to imagine, we all grew silent as the carriage rumbled along the track past Low Snab farm and into the mine yard. Above the buildings, banks of waste stone and rock rose up to a gigantic gash in the fell side, almost as though a huge axe had cleft the mountain asunder.

Elicia looked up fearfully, "Oh John, I never thought to see such as this. It is like a scene from Hell."

Jago came forward to meet us as we gathered at the foot of a wooden stairway leading upward, face as sullen as ever. He regarded us with something akin to resentment. Silently, I berated myself for having employed such a man.

"I expected ye yesterday and wondered if ye would even come yet today."

"The journey was more difficult than anticipated, we had to overnight in Little Town."

He nodded, not bothering to discuss the explanation further.

"Come then, ye need be readied to venture underground."

Elicia was unsure about proceeding any further, peering into the tunnel entrance without enthusiasm. I was surprised, her normally confident demeanour had gone and she was looking more vulnerable than I had ever seen her before. It was Daniel who made an attempt to reassure her.

"Eh lass, you're braver than most men ah know. Ah knows very well thee can do this."

Eli and Thomas added their voices, trying to persuade Elicia to enter the mine.

"Oh very well, I will do it," she said with determination.

Hitching up her skirts, tucking them into a waist belt, she stepped forward to be issued with a leather hat, a tallow candle fixed to the brim by a lump of clay We had all taken the precaution of donning suitably heavy footwear and were pleased we had done so, as a steady stream of water issued from the tunnel mouth. After lighting each candle Jago led us inside.

The passageway twisted and turned, the walls scored with a myriad pick marks by the old miners. As the roof dipped low in places I was glad of the protection the leather hat offered. Elicia seemed to have regained her confidence, walking between Eli and Daniel, occasionally remarking on some feature that we passed.

The tunnel echoed and boomed with our voices and footsteps but another sound grew louder as we moved forward. Rushing water, loud creaks and groans as of some imprisoned giant made further conversation impossible. Eventually our party emerged into a large chamber, the roof of which disappeared into the gloom. In the centre of the space a monstrous machine clattered, turned by a river of water, spray hung in the air, damp and cold. A wooden waterwheel, greater than any I had seen before, had been built into a slot carved out of the solid rock, water to drive it sluiced down out of the darkness above.

Raising my voice to be heard above the racket I said;

"My God, the power, you can feel the power, it is terrifying!"

The turning wheel created a strong draft of air making the candles flutter, casting weird shadows upon the whole scene. Truly hellish, I looked to where Elicia was standing but was unable to see her for the others standing between us. I saw her pale, frightened face in my mind, regretting that she had been made to come against her will.

We stood mesmerised by the awesome sight. A couple of young boys about nine or ten years of age tended to the monster, greasing axels, brushing away twigs and leaves tossed out of the overflowing buckets by the speed of the wheel's revolution. A worker sat to the side regulating, with the aid of a long chain, the sluice delivering water to the top of the whole apparatus. Jago stepped back allowing us a clear view of the whole operation.

Suddenly Elicia pitched forward towards the edge of the wheel pit. Reacting swiftly, Thomas managed to grab the back of her cape, preventing her from falling head first into the mechanism. Even so he was not strong enough to stop her sliding, feet first, downwards. Her flailing feet were only inches away from disaster, when both Daniel and Eli went to his aid. Between them they succeeded in dragging Elicia back to safety. Her screams raised above the noise of the wheel and tears coursed down her cheeks.

"Sweet Jesus!" said Eli, wiping her face with his neckerchief.

I had been slightly to the side and had not witnessed the drama as it first unfolded. The noise of the machine had drowned out the sounds of the struggle, although I noticed that now it was abating. Gathering around her, the general hubbub was full of questions and concern.

Kneeling by her side taking her hand in mine, I asked;

"My love, thanks be you are safe, what happened in God's name?"

Between sobs, still fighting for breath she replied; "I was pushed, pushed from behind!"

"Pushed, are you certain? You could not have just slipped?"

"No I was pushed, knocked violently forward from behind," cried Elicia choking in her distress.

This answer only served to increase the expressions of concern and the many questions that it gave rise to. Looking up I nodded to Daniel who, on glancing around the chamber, noticed Jago hurrying towards the exit tunnel. With a roar of rage Daniel set off after him followed immediately by Thomas.

Eli helped me to raise Elicia to her feet. The operator had closed the sluice in an attempt to abort the unfolding tragedy. Even so, the water wheel continued to revolve slowly, steadily losing momentum. Speech was now fully possible as the noise of the machine subsided.

"John, my dear friend, what would possess a man to do such a thing?"

"I know not Eli, I feel horrified and confused by such a pass. Who is Jago, what is he?"

"Jago, you think to accuse Jago?" asked Elicia.

"Who else among us would have wanted you injured or even killed? It can only have been Jago, there was none other nearby."

We set off slowly, supporting Elicia between us, pausing for her to catch her breath and rest every now and again. During the journey back to the surface my anger and frustration increased as I sought for an explanation to the frightful events of the past hour. Elicia ceased to tremble and sob but remained unwilling to talk further about the awful fate that Thomas's quick wits had averted.

Once we finally reached daylight Elicia sat down, pale and drawn, deeply shaken by the dreadful experience she had suffered. The tips of her boots were torn and shredded, the great wheel had come so close.

After ensuring she was agreed, I left her in the care of Eli and descended quickly to the mine yard, urged on by the angry shouts that rose up from below. In the yard a scene of chaos and confusion greeted me. Jago was in the centre of a large group of workers being jostled and dragged hither and thither. Blows were striking him from many fists, his face was bloodied and bruised. Daniel shouted above the noise and commotion seeking to gain control of the mob, while holding Jago tightly around the neck.

As I approached, Daniel's efforts to quieten the general uproar began to have an effect. It was then that I noticed Thomas in the crowd gathered round the captive. He cleared a path for me to reach Jago, pulling men out of the melee. An expectant hush settled over everyone as I came face to face with the would -be murderer. He defiantly regarded me, one eye closed completely from a blow, the other full of malice.

"Jago, why?" I demanded, trying to control my anger.

Daniel loosened his grip on Jago's throat.

"Speak you stinking worm, else I'll crack your scrawny neck!"

"What have I done to you that would cause you to injure me or those I love?" I demanded.

He opened his mouth to speak. Blood dripped from his chin as he spat out several broken teeth, yet he made no other sound.

"I gave you my trust, offered you a job against the advice of others, why repay me thus?"

"Ye do not know who I am?"

"You are Jago ,I do believe, is that not so?" I asked attempting to control my anger.

"Jago?" I turned to find Elicia behind me, supported on Eli's arm. She asked again, more firmly;

"Jago, do I know you?"

"No but I know ye, the whore of the man who murdered my father!"

"Ah should surely kill thee now, you snivelling pig," said Daniel through gritted teeth, tightening his grip and lifting Jago at the same time, until his feet were off of the ground. Elicia approached Jago, her face close to his.

"I am no man's whore," she whispered fiercely, "Even if I were, there is nought I have done to you that can justify your attempt on my life."

"An eye for an eye." Was his response, voice hoarse, feet struggling to stand on tip-toe.

Pushing in next to Elicia I demanded. "What was the name of your father?"

"You knew him well, 'twas Benson, Rob Benson."

Daniel released his hold, throwing Jago to the ground with some force;

"Ye son of a swine!" he said kicking him in the ribs.

"I, we, did not kill your father, it was an accident, a return of fire. He had betrayed us and not for the first time, but it was another who fired the fatal shot."

Jago looked up at us, pure hatred in his eyes.

"We suffered much as a result of your father's treachery."

As further discussion was pointless and the light fading,; he was tightly bound, bundled onto a cart for transport, under escort, to Keswick lock up. The crowd of bystanders dispersed leaving me alone with Elicia. We stood silently regarding each other, silenced and horrified by the dreadful turn of events. With a short sob, she fell into my arms. We remained holding on together, almost too tightly, for some moments.

"John, what almost happened is too awful to contemplate," she spoke at last.

"Elicia, how could I have lived without you? I love you with every particle of my being. You are my life, my love, my, everything!"

"John, my dearest, this is a reminder of how brief our time together can be. How easily all that we have may be taken away in an instant."

"Never, never will I leave you again," I said softly, kissing her neck.

"We will always be more than husband, wife, lovers and friends even. You, my darling husband are my dearest friend, I love you with all of my heart."

Our party followed in the carriage, not reaching Keswick and the Packhorse Inn until midnight. Daniel volunteered to see the horses safely stabled, also checking with the Parish Constable that the prisoner was securely confined.

By the time he returned to the Inn, Elicia, Thomas and Eli had gone to their beds. I had felt unable to retire and had taken a seat by the fire. My thoughts wandered over the first attack on the Wad mine, transportation to Bermuda and all that had happened there. Colonel Tucker, Arabella, Elicia and everything since. I yearned for all that had been lost and thought with fear of all that had been near lost that afternoon. It was while in this mood that Daniel found me. Without a word, he drew up a chair and sat staring into the fire, he said:

"In the name of God John, ye were seconds from disaster today, ah reckon."

"I know, thanks be for Thomas. I cannot bear the thought of life without Elicia. Too many of those I loved have gone, slipped through my fingers."

"Well, ye were lucky for certain, now I'm away to ma bed."

Daniel stood, resting his hand on my shoulder for a moment before leaving the room. I could hear his heavy tread on the stairs. The floorboards and beams creaked as he went to his bedchamber.

As the fire died, the Inn fell silent. Suddenly I felt cold and lonely, the silence became oppressive. It was with a heavy heart that I made my way up to our chamber. Elicia was asleep, curled tightly under the coverlet. She moaned, moving onto her side to face me as I climbed into bed beside her. Her hand reached for mine under the covers. Thus sleep overcame me but not without a procession of strangely disturbing dreams.

CHAPTER
FORTY EIGHT

*R*eturning home, Daniel left for Wasdale Head, Eli to High Wray and Elicia and I to Rydal after collecting William, Elizabeth and Eloise from Aunt Hannah. We related to Ruenna the events at the mine but kept the more distressing parts to ourselves. Her reaction was one of horror and concern for her mother. Elicia recovered to such an extent that she chose to accompany me to Carlisle the following week. Jago Benson had been transferred to Carlisle to be examined at the Assizes and we were both eager to attend.

"What will be his fate?" Elicia asked me while on the journey north.

"Difficult to say. The Murder Act of 1752 may make a hanging inevitable."

"Attempted murder, is not that a lesser crime?"

"Only lesser because his plan was foiled, my love. I could have lost you, the children would have been left without a mother. I for one cannot forgive him."

"I do not forgive him, yet is there no other alternative to the gibbet?"

"Transportation perhaps. How strange it is for me to have to say that."

Elicia snuggled up to me, laying her head on my shoulder.

"I do not wish to have his death on either of our consciences. Will you do what you can?"

"You are too good." Kissing her cheek I continued, "I will speak to James Wilson, also perhaps to Sir Richard Lowther. We will see what can be done, I promise."

The three days spent in the city were not wasted. After several consultations with James Wilson he advised us that, as the injured party, we could influence the fate handed down to Jago. The overwhelming evidence against him would seal his fate and he was handed over to the Sheriff for transportation without delay. By appealing to Sir Richard and using my influence made certain that the destination would be Bermuda.

Before departing Carlisle, I wrote a letter to Gideon, telling him of all that had happened. Requesting that he prepare for the day when Jago would arrive in Bermuda.

1778 proved to be a year of changes. The mine expanded, with exploration discovering a new vein of good Copper ore. Early in June, Thomas and Ruenna wed in Hawkshead Church. The twins looking so pretty in their new dresses.

It was a chance to look back with contentment, two young people setting up home at 'The Stepping Stones', next door to us in 'Rydal Villa', starting a newChapter in the story of 'Moses' Rigg.

That same month a letter arrived from Gideon.

The Tucker House
St George's
Bermuda
April 21st 1778

My dear friend John,

To say that I was horrified by the contents of your last letter, would be an understatement. I thank the Lord that the worst outcome was not to be. I trust that now both you and Elicia have recovered from such tribulation and have been able to put it all behind you.

Business here is good, we continue to make rum at a profit. The war with the American Colonies following the battle of Saratoga on the Hudson River has affected us greatly although Bermuda is keen to remain uncommitted to either side. We hear many rumours, it is difficult to make sense of it all and I wonder at what effect it will have on us next year. I am asked every day, who Bermuda would side with if we are forced to choose.

The French are very troublesome but the forts have been able to prevent a landing on the coast. I regret to have to inform you that

Turks island is soon to be made part of the Bahama colony. The loss of income from salt production might be compensated for by extending trade in other areas. We must think on this for the future.

I wish you were able to see all that has been accomplished on the Estate. My family are well, as am I.

Your enemy 'Jago' Benson, arrived with a shipment of convicts last month. I succeeded in having him placed in my custody and have set him to hard labour in the quarries for the next five years. I have to say, he is the most unpleasant fellow, I will make it my responsibility to ensure that he is given no easy treatment.

I shall write once more before the year's end after seeking out other trading opportunities. Please pass on my sincere greetings to Daniel, Eli and Thomas.

Sealed and sent in friendship
Gideon Redmond Davey

Partner /Manager
Tucker, Rigg and Redmond enterprises, Bermuda.

Lightning Source UK Ltd.
Milton Keynes UK
UKHW040619100722
405600UK00002B/295